DECONSTRUCTING DELILAH

ALISON RHYMES

To request permission, contact: alison@alisonrhymes.com

Editors: Zainab M. at Heart Full of Reads Editing Services and Virginia Tesi Carey

Cover Design: Kris Hack Designs

Interior formatting: Diana TC, www.dianatc.com

A NOTE FROM ALISON RHYMES

Any trigger or content warnings for Deconstructing Delilah, or any of my other titles, can be found on my website alisonrhymes.com

To those still on their journey.

PART I

CHAPTER ONE

I t's the black dove I see first, not the man attached to it. One feathered wing sprawls up a strong neck while its dark and hollow eye follows me through the room. I'm not moving a muscle as I cower in my corner, uncomfortable with all the people and the reason they are gathered.

A wedding.

Not like any I've witnessed before, and there have been many.

New Orleans has been my home for a few months now. Before that, it was Virginia City, Nevada. An oasis in the middle of the desert and as far away from Utah I could get at the time. Yet, the decadence of life—normal life—is something I'm still quite unused to.

Lorelai is more beautiful today than I've ever seen her. She's always pretty, but today, she's marrying the man that she loves, and it shows like sunshine on her skin. The man, Noah, loves her back in a way I never dreamed existed. It's not the sort of love I grew up with. It's not the sort of love I was told God blessed.

She's not subservient to him. Instead of quieting when he's around, she becomes more alive. Noah lets her move freely through the day. Lorelai has her own life and does what she wants. She works, she drives, she watches the most horrific movies, and dances when she thinks there is nobody watching.

Lorelai is free, and I've never been more envious. I'm ashamed of myself for that. The book of James says jealousy and ambition lead to every other sin, but it's hard not to want what she has.

Carlotta, the woman I stayed with in Virginia City, told me it was like this outside of the ranch I grew up on. I saw evidence of that in her own life, but Carlotta doesn't have a man in her house. Only women, or girls, seeking a safe space. She says she's a survivor of abuse, too.

Abuse.

A word I still struggle with. Was I abused? It comes down to perspective, I guess. I was punished, yes. Carlotta and Lorelai say it was more than that. They say I didn't deserve the things that happened to me. They say God didn't want me punished like that.

I'm not so sure.

Noah doesn't think God exists at all. But I don't speak much to Noah. He's rather frightening. Not because he's mean; he's kind and gentle with Olivia, Lorelai's toddler sister, and me. He's a presence though, large and powerful, and I don't know how to be around such things yet. He gives me my space and I'm appreciative of that.

The day I turned eighteen, Lorelai was in Virginia City to pack me up and move me here. It's what I wanted as soon as I took my first step off the ranch. But I wasn't legal then and Nevada has laws that allowed me to stay there safely. Now, my family has no legal claim on me. Lorelai brought me to her and Noah's home and gave me a small guest apartment. A place where I can learn my independence while still feeling secure.

They have given me a lot. What they can't give me is my childhood back, or an instant knowledge of the world I now inhabit. Which is far, far different than all I've ever known.

Lorelai says to give everything time and respect the process.

I'm trying, I really am. I'm scared of so much, though. Cars, noise, people.

Men.

Noah's presence makes me uncomfortable, while other men terrify me.

Except *him.* The one with the onyx dove painted on his neck. Pope, they called him, but I wonder if that's even his real name. He's here to officiate the wedding. Lorelai told me Noah's been friends with him for years and that the first time she met Pope, she was very taken aback by him. She's come to like him but warns that he spews scripture at random times. Lorelai doesn't like the scriptures. They remind her of her father and her childhood.

She grew up on the ranch, too. Only she escaped at the age of twelve. It took me five years longer. Lorelai's mother, Martha, is to thank for that. She bundled me off the night before I was to marry my sixty-seven-year-old uncle. I'd have been his thirteenth wife, not including the three that had died over the years. David had not been granted a new wife in several years, so he was very excited to be given me.

My father was very happy to be promised one of David's daughters in return.

I, however, was not happy. I don't believe Jillian, my cousin, was thrilled at the prospect of betrothal to my father, either. Jillian is only eleven. As messed up as my family is, they don't marry us off that early. Martha promised to try to get Jillian out before marriage as well. I pray she can deliver on that promise, and more.

Though, praying is beginning to mean something different to me now. I question my beliefs and my faith every day. Lorelai says that's normal, too. So does the therapist I've been talking to. Dr. Price says it's only natural to doubt the things that were forced onto me in my childhood, and that many adults question what they were taught when young.

I no longer have a family. My home is temporary. If I lose my faith, what am I left with?

The book of Matthews says, *'And whatever you ask in prayer, you will receive, if you have faith.'* If I don't keep faith, there is no hope that my prayers will be answered. There is so much I pray for, mostly for those I left behind. But some prayers are for me, too.

Martha stars in my prayers nightly. As do Lorelai and Noah, for all they've done for me. I know Noah was the one that paid my way to Nevada and donated generously to both the charity house in Utah that helped facilitate my escape and Carlotta's home. I could never repay them for that. But there's been more. They hired a tutor to work with me to get me through the general education development tests, which now allows me to get higher education. Noah's paying for that, too. On top of free room and board for as long as I need.

Education at the ranch for girls was limited, at best. We were taught to read because they wanted us able to read scripture, rules, and recipes. I read well, even if my critical thinking and comprehension sometimes lacks. I learned rudimentary mathematics, but getting my GED proved that I have more skill there. I understand numbers. Math is black and white, true or false. Evaluation rather than judgment. I'm more confident when I don't have to make calls based on acumen or gut reaction. Because I was never allowed to have my own thoughts about things.

Dr. Price encourages me to look at things from every angle now.

Right now, my vision is tunneled on the one they call Pope.

People mill around the backyard that's been set up for the wedding, each taking their time to find their seats. They greet one another, chat, speak about the mature foliage that surrounds the space with a sweet jasmine scent. It's a small affair. Lorelai says she doesn't have many people to call her own. But her family is growing right along with the baby she carries in her belly. She includes me in that count. We are technically cousins, but I think she means it differently.

I take in each of the guests one by one. I've met all of Noah's family—his father, brother, and mother, Grace. She's been especially kind to me, wanting to be a mother figure for me as she's been to Lorelai. They're all here dressed just as impeccably as Noah always is.

A few of Noah's co-workers are here. A couple of Lorelai's, too.

I move closer to the couple I've yet to meet, though I know who they are. The McKennas. She's Noah's best friend; he's something from Lorelai's past that doesn't get discussed but I know is important. They're both quiet. I like the quiet since my head is loud enough all on its own.

Soft music starts as the harpist begins to play. A sign to take our seats if I had to guess by all the people beginning to move. The dove man moves down the aisle to stand at the end under a large magnolia tree that is alive with fresh blooms. Noah said it was still early in the season and it's a sign that they opened, as if the flowers wanted to be present for their special day. It's a pretty sentiment. One that made me smile, which isn't something I do on wedding days. But this isn't like the other weddings I've experienced.

Grace sends me a smile, an invitation to sit by them if I'd like. But I choose one of the chairs in the back, opposite the aisle to the quiet couple. Easy enough to escape it if I need, easy enough to hide behind other heads while I watch Pope.

He's a tall man. Broad, too. I know he works in finance; Lorelai says he helps very wealthy people stay very wealthy people. Looking at him, you'd think he does much more dangerous things. We didn't have men that look like him on the ranch. Tattoos were a sin, for one. The men mostly wore their hair shorn short, while Pope's inky black locks fall below his chin. Though, today, they're pulled back neatly at his nape. Probably to look more proper in his perfect black three-piece suit.

Even in the suit, nothing about him seems proper. He looks dangerous, dark, and diabolical. He looks like the devil himself.

Except the words that come out of his mouth are soft, tender, and hopeful. Words of love and support, rather than obedience and possession. Noah isn't looking for ownership of Lorelai; he's instead promising her a partnership.

By the end of the ceremony, I'm more confused and envious than I was at the start.

Many of the women cry, including the McKenna woman. She tries hard to hide it, but I see. I see a lot as a pale shadow hiding in the corners. I don't think her tears are one thing or another, not just happy or only sad. But she's smiling at her husband by the end, before they sprint out the same door I do. Them toward whatever their destination is, me to my favorite part of the Lorelai's home. The library.

Shortly after I arrived here, I watched a movie with Oliva. *Beauty and the Beast*. A story of a monstrous-looking beast and a beautiful, young, empathetic woman. The beast gifted her a library, and I cried.

Where I come from, books aren't given. There is only one book really, but multiple versions of it. And only one way for it to be interpreted. What the Cleric said the Bible meant, is what the Bible meant. We were not allowed to question.

I love books now. I read as many as I can, often finishing a book a day. Lorelai helps me pick out the titles, worried that I'll throw myself into the deep end too quickly. She's careful not to censor information from me but also not to overwhelm me with it.

Currently, I'm reading a young adult science fiction title. At times, it makes me feel childish. Not only because I'm reading books that were likely written for readers younger than me, but also because the characters are much more worldly than I am. They have an understanding of life that I don't. I'd never been inside a grocery store until I lived in Nevada. The only time I'd ever been in a vehicle was one of the rare times I was transported from one end of the ranch to the other for an odd chore. I didn't know televisions existed, or public transportation, or technology at all for the most part. We didn't even have items like microwave ovens or laptop computers. The only women I ever saw wore their hair long past their waists and dresses past their wrists and ankles. It was a shock to get on a bus from Utah to Nevada with women and girls dressed in vibrant colors that showed an array of body parts.

It was a shock that the men in their lives let them.

The story I'm reading now has some of the same power dynamic I'm used to. A government in so much control over its people that every aspect of the citizens' lives is determined by the powers that be. There is a familiarity there that's almost comforting. Though I know it shouldn't be.

My newfound freedom is a prize. One that some days feels like it will swallow me up, body and soul.

So entrenched into the fictional world I am that I don't hear the doorknob turn. It's the shaft of brighter light entering the room that has me peeling my eyes off the page and on to the man that has occupied my thoughts too often today.

Pope enters the room, cell phone to his ear and confidence in stride. He says something down the line about moving figures from one account to another.

"Do it immediately and email me the confirmation," he says before ending the call and pocketing his phone.

He hasn't noticed me yet; I've become somewhat adept at becoming part of the wallpaper. He also doesn't leave. Instead, he slowly peruses the shelves as if looking for something.

"Are you lost?" Boldness I shouldn't possess forces the words out, and I realize they're the first ones I've uttered in what must be hours now. My voice is small and raspy, but loud enough for him to hear and turn on his well-polished heel. A graceful move on such a hard-looking figure.

"Are you trying to be found?" Pope answers in a deep voice after eyeing me for a moment without discernable emotion on his face.

"Do those who want to be found often hide behind closed doors?"

"In my experience, they are the ones that want to be found the most."

He's right in some regards, not so much in others. For there are many ways I'd love to be found, and many who I hope never to find me. While I mull over the words, I remember what Lorelai said about Pope and scripture, and I put it to the test.

"I was found by those who did not seek me."

"Isaiah 65:1," he says after making a low humming sound. "What do you believe that verse means?"

He gives me time to formulate an answer by casually making his way to the chair opposite me. He makes no sudden movements and breaks eye contact with me. Maybe so that I don't feel like prey to a predator. Inexplicably, I don't view him as such.

Perhaps that alone will be my downfall.

"God desired the people of Israel to find him, but many rebelled and worshiped false gods. Yet they claimed holiness while persecuting other nations. He was instead found by the Gentiles."

"His desire superseded the human's own desire."

"Of course."

"Why of course?" he asks me thoughtfully.

"Because he is God. The Almighty," I say without hesitation.

"And his desire is the only desire that matters? Does he not claim holiness while persecuting others?"

"Are you not a Christian?"

"Born and raised," he says with a smile, holding his hands up as if in praise. "And then I began thinking for myself."

I nearly gasp at his audacity and pierce him with a glare. Except, he's not entirely wrong. At least about me. I wasn't offered much opportunity to think for myself. Questioning what the Cleric or the elder men on the ranch said was prohibited entirely. Besides, anger, like wrath, is a sin and I must not succumb.

"That's not something I've had much experience with."

"Do not tamp down your rage with me, Lamb. If I say something that offends you, tell me and I'll happily discuss it with you." He crosses one leg over the other knee, his suit pants stretching to contain the muscled thigh sheathed inside as he folds his hands on his lap.

It's not a threatening posture, but it makes me feel... something. Things I ought not, things God would not want me to feel.

"My name is Delilah. I'm not anyone's sheep." *Not anymore.*

"You are though. You're still part of God's flock." He pauses, and I nod. "A deity that would have left you to be wedded against your will. Raped. Bred. Enslaved. Is that the god you pray to at night?"

"Yes. He gave us free will; some use it to sin."

"They do," he agrees. "And your god would let you, and those like you, suffer for the sins of others. For sins that he created. For sins, that if he is all good, all knowing, and all powerful, he could prevent."

"Spoken like a true sinner." I raise my chin and lower my book into my lap.

"Some sins are delicious and delightful, Delilah. I don't murder, or rape, or abuse. Should I suffer eternal damnation because I don't blindly follow an old book?"

"I'm certain you've had sinful thoughts, at the least." I'm sure he has. Only I'm no longer certain of the punishments for such things.

"Of course I have. As I'm sure you have. But if we are damned because we have a thought in which we never act on, then can we really claim free will?"

Skipping over his point, I focus on his idea that I have sinned with thoughts alone.

"I have not."

"What? Free will or sinful thoughts?"

About to blurt sinful thoughts, I pause. If I think about it, I've had neither. Not really. The one and only time I disobeyed what I was told to think or do was the time Martha found me sobbing in the cold storage basement beneath my father's house. I was terrified that she'd tattle on me, but I could no longer contain my fear. Once David had been told of our betrothal, he began paying me more and more attention. I hated it; my skin crawled each time he looked my way. I took a chance that Martha may understand. That small act of defiant bravery was what saved me.

Had I stayed quiet and obedient like I'd done my whole life, I'd have been a child bride. And I'd likely be impregnated by now with my uncle's child.

Weakness got me nowhere.

"Sinful thoughts," I answer, because I do have free will now and I don't plan on ever giving it back.

"Never?"

"No."

"Not even toward the men who pulled your strings?"

"No. I wished for a way out, but I never wished harm on anyone."

He studies me as if committing me to memory. I take the opportunity to do the same. Taking this man in that by all measures should make me uneasy but doesn't. It's the longest conversation I've had with a man, and the first one where I feel like my words matter. Like I'm heard, even if not fully believed.

"Your wish for an escape could be construed as a sin though. Exodus says disobeying your parents is as good as disobeying your lord, does it not? Regardless, it would be all right had you wished for it."

"Harm?"

"Yes, Delilah. It is natural to wish harm to those who harm the helpless. It's also okay to have other sinful thoughts."

I can't say for certain what Pope means, but my mind recalls the moment ago when he crossed his legs. The urge to drop my eyes back to his lap is strong, but I force them to stay on his face. So, I see it... the spark in his eyes, the twitch of his lips. I don't know how he could know where my thoughts drifted, but I'm sure he does, and heat flushes my cheeks.

Growing up on a polygamist compound, sex was a big part of life. It was not discussed openly in regular conversation, of course. The youngest children lived blind to it all. But I remember my first day of 'Family Instruction' and each course after that.

Because I've only ever feared it, I've never experienced desire. There is something that stirs in me with Pope nearby. My stomach tightens, and my fingers tremble. Maybe that's desire, maybe it's something else I've never had the knowledge of.

"Is Pope the name you were given at birth?" I try to veer the conversation in another direction. Off me, preferably.

"You know they say never give a fairy your real name? It gives them power over you."

"I've never heard that," I say, embarrassment making me cast my head down. If not for watching movies with Olivia, I wouldn't know what a fairy even is. "Besides, I'm not a fairy, and you already know my name. It seems only fair."

Pope throws me a wide smile full of perfectly aligned white teeth as he stands from the chair and takes a step closer to me.

"Oh, my dear Delilah," he says, reaching out to tip my chin up toward him. "I never said I play fair."

A shiver runs down my spine, and Pope removes his fingers as if touching me caused him pain. Then, he stalks off toward the door, and I let my dark hair fall to curtain my face. I don't want him to see how much I like watching him, how much I want to trace every inch of his painted skin with my eyes and hands.

"If you ever need to speak to someone regarding questions about your faith," he says while standing in the open doorway, "I'll make myself available. I was once on a similar path. It's hard to travel it alone."

CHAPTER TWO

It's been a month since I started classes at the community college, and it hasn't gotten any easier being around the other students.

When I was living in Nevada, I wasn't ready to cut my hair or wear clothes much different than the modest ones I'd always grown up with. When I got here to New Orleans, though, I felt more comfortable. Probably because Lorelai and Olivia are at ease with their shorter hair and regular clothes. Now I wear my hair in soft curls to about the middle of my back, and my clothing is more modern, even if it's still modest compared to my peers.

I don't stand out, at least. Well, not because of the way I look, anyway. My shyness sticks out like a sore thumb, but that can't really be helped. It isn't like I have a lot in common with the other students. We don't share the same similar life experiences to reminisce on. Popular culture is still something I'm trying to immerse myself in. But eighteen years of music, books, and movies, is a lot to catch up on.

Everyday I'm on campus, I make a point of eating lunch in the small cafeteria. In some ways, it feels like home, the communal feel of so many breaking bread together. In other ways, it's a whole new world. But I get to sit and eavesdrop on the conversations around me. It's a class all on its own, one where I can independently study human behavior. I'm taking classes for business and finance.

Finance makes sense to me. Numbers come easy. Business, not so much, but budgeting resources was something I learned growing up and it's not so different from the basics of business so I'm catching on quickly.

I've always been a fast learner, a sponge for information. The girl to quietly sit in the corner and observe everything. It helped me be able to perfect the things I tried. Perfection garnered less punishment from my father and my uncles.

Laughter from the table catches my attention. A group of four women giggle while discussing a date one of them went on last night. The man went home with her, and the others are peppering her with questions about it.

"I'd guess about seven inches, but the circumference was ahhhmazzzing," she says, dragging out the word for emphasis. Experience isn't needed to know the size is pleasing to them all. Their sighs and smiles confirm it for me. "The best part was that he called me his good girl. I never knew I'd like that but damn, it was hot."

"I'm not into that daddy kink shit," one of the others says.

"Right? I'm not calling any guy who's dicking me daddy."

I huff out a breath and pick at my salad, wishing I understood more of their conversation.

"It's okay, you know?" a bright voice says. A young woman, about my same age, with wide-set eyes, takes a seat next to me.

"What's okay?"

"That you're a virgin," she says in a hushed voice. "You're not the only one here."

"What?" I ask, amazed that she can tell that just by looking at me.

"See that table over there?" She nods across the room to where two guys sit with two girls. "The blonde girl and the redhead dude? Both virgins."

"How could you possibly know that?"

"It's a gift," she says, shrugging one shoulder.

"How do you know I am?"

"The flustered look all over your face." She shines a crooked smile at me that makes her look even more friendly than she already did with her hair twirled up in dark buns above her ears. "My name's Cookie."

"It is not," I protest with a smile of my own.

"Swear it. My mom is one of those free-spirit types that doesn't believe in conventional names. My brother's name is Fig, no lie."

"I kind of love it. I'm Delilah."

"Oh, that's a pretty name."

"Thank you." My name isn't something I've always liked. In the Bible, Delilah was a harlot that betrayed her lover, Samson. Father often told me I was too pretty for my own good and would wind up like my namesake if I wasn't careful.

"I guess I should admit that I've seen you around. I watch you while you watch the others." She grimaces as she says it.

"You're sly. I've noticed you, but never you watching me."

"It's a bad habit, but since you seem to have it too, I guess it's not a big deal." Cookie takes a bite of her turkey and cheddar sandwich. "So, we should be friends."

I've never had one of those. Sisters and cousins, I've had many, but that's not the same.

"I lack the experience, but I'll give it a shot," I say, shyly.

"Figured as much. You never talk to anyone. Not that I can blame you there, most of these people are idiots or douchebags. Or both."

"What's a douchebag?"

"How old are you, Delilah?" Cookie asks in awe.

"Eighteen."

"Did you grow up in a bunker or something?" She laughs. When I grow still and return to picking at my salad, she stops. "Oh shit, really?"

"Not a bunker. A compound." It's weird telling a stranger this. Cookie puts me at ease, though. Maybe because she sees more and that means I'll have to tell her less.

"You don't have to tell me. I'm nosy but not pushy, I swear."

"What are you studying here?" I ask after giving her a weak smile. I'm grateful she won't pry and take the cue to change the subject.

"I'm on the nursing track. What about you?"

"Business. I want to go into finance, I think."

The day after Lorelai and Noah's wedding, a package was delivered for me. Inside were three books, all fantastical tales of fairies. Along with them was a black business card with gold embossed letters spelling out Pope Blackwell—CEO of Blackwell Financial Group. There was no phone number, but there was an email that I haven't yet mustered the courage to write to.

At the very least, I should thank him for the books which I devoured immediately while imagining myself as Belle and Pope the beast. A fanciful and ridiculous daydream, of course. Truth be told, those books are the most precious gift I've ever been given. The only one that feels like there weren't strings attached.

I did take the time to research Blackwell Financial Group. Seemingly, Pope's company specializes in financial planning for the wealthy. It kindled something in me. Or maybe it only fueled my obsession with the man. Either way, I want to do what he does.

Lorelai was surprised when I told her. She expected me to want to help people in need, I think. She has a physical therapy business, but she does a lot to help women outside of that. Women like us and girls that grew up like us.

I'm not excluding that from my future by any means. Of course, I'd like to give back what was given to me—a chance at a life of my own. I'm just taking a different path than her. Playing to my strength, which isn't altruism as much as it is figures and calculations.

Instinct tells me I'm doing the right thing, and Lorelai is

supportive, of course. But my guilt still creeps in regularly to tell me that God doesn't want me concerned with such a worldly thing as wealth. It tells me I should be rich in good deeds, instead.

For once, I'm focusing on what's good for me right here and right now. I want this degree, and the life that I hope it helps me get.

"That's cool, I'm awful at money. Constantly on the verge of over drafting my checking account."

"I could help you. I mean, if you wanted," I say.

"Really?" Cookie asks, her face hopeful.

"Sure." I shrug. "It would be good practice for me and helps you out at the same time."

"Like something a friend would do."

A friend.

"I've never really had one of those. I may not be very good at it," I admit. The prospect of friendship is appealing, though. I often feel alone. Lorelai and Noah have been more than welcoming, and Olivia is great, but it doesn't yet feel like home or family to me.

"You'll be fine at it. I have good sense for these things."

Her conviction is nice, but I'm not convinced. Regardless, we finish lunch without discussing anything too weighty. After trading cell phone numbers and class schedules, we part ways, and for the first time in my life, I believe I do have a friend.

"How was your day?" Lorelai asks as we all sit down for dinner. She and Noah try to have this family time every night. Olivia is always entertaining while she chatters about her day, and typically the conversation is always light. I'm not obligated to eat dinner with them, my guesthouse has its own small kitchen. Though growing up with communal eating makes it weird to eat by myself. It's slowly getting easier, but I also like spending time with my new family.

"Good. I think I made a friend."

"Oh, that's great," Lorelai says, her eyes sparkling with emotion. She told me that she struggled to make friends after leaving the ranch. She didn't know how to relate to other kids and instead stayed busy with her studies, much like I do.

"A best friend?" Olivia asks around a mouthful of carrots. "Like Charlie? He's my bestest friend."

"Yeah, yeah, we know," Noah mumbles. He always pretends to be jealous of the poor boy; it makes Olivia laugh and I think Noah lives for the smiles of the girls in his life.

"I guess she's my best friend. She's my only one, anyhow."

"You'll make lots and lots of friends," Olivia responds. "What's her name?"

"Cookie."

"Oh, I love cookies! Snickernoodles are my favorite."

"Snickerdoodles," Lorelai corrects her. "That's kind of a great name, really."

"It's fun," I say. Most names on the ranch were biblical. Lorelai was Abigail at birth, but it changed when she was able to run away. She once asked if I wanted to change my name, but honestly, I wouldn't even know what to pick.

"I was wondering something," Lorelai hedges. "You haven't been to a church since you left the ranch. Is that something you'd like to do?"

The thought had crossed my mind a time or two. Back home, we had services two nights a week and then sermon on Sunday. Only, that's something else I wouldn't know how to pick. Noah's library has a handful of books on different religions. I have not read them all cover to cover, but I have skimmed them all. None are like what I was brought up in.

"I wouldn't know what denomination to go to."

"You could try some different ones," she suggests. "Or none. It's up to you. I don't want to sway you either way."

"Right," Noah agrees. "Your faith is your decision, and we'll support you through any healthy choice you make."

Healthy. The ranch and their perverted version of Mormonism wasn't healthy for anyone. I know that much.

"Maybe I could just talk to someone? Without having to go to church services."

"That's a fair idea. We could help you find someone," Lorelai says with a kind smile. I think she'd like it if I left religion behind completely, like she did. But I don't think she'd ever say that.

"I might know someone. But I'll let you know if it doesn't work out."

If they know I mean Pope, they don't let that show. Instead, they nod and let Olivia take over the conversation. Truth is, I've been looking for an excuse to talk to him further. More than just a thank you, anyway. Lorelai just handed me that. He did say he'd 'make himself available' after all. The short conversation we had on the day of the wedding comes to mind often. It's been weeks, but I can't get it out of my head.

Or him, for that matter.

He's made me ask myself questions that I never dreamed I would. And now, I want to ask them to Pope.

We finish dinner, and like every night, I offer to clean up. Lorelai always cooks, so it's only fair. Plus, she's pregnant and doesn't often slow down. It makes me feel like I'm paying her back in some small way by letting her curl up with Noah and watch a movie with Olivia.

And, truthfully, I like the quiet without being alone. Laughter from the trio still finds its way to me in the kitchen. It's soft and doesn't disturb my wind down after an eventful day.

I have a friend, I have a plan, and I have the determination to not fear either of them.

My cell phone dings on the counter next to me, startling me since the only people that call or message me are in the house with me. My curiosity gets the best of me, so I stop mid-pan wash to check it.

COOKIE

Do you want to hang out tomorrow night?

Tomorrow is Saturday, a typical night for people my age to go out. Only, I've never done such a thing.

ME

What is your plan?

A safe question to ask. Whatever her answer is, I can discuss it with Lorelai, so I know what's expected of me.

COOKIE

Shopping. Dinner. Then we'll see?

The first two sound safe enough, anyway.

ME

That sounds fun.

Before I go find Lorelai for advice, I finish my task. She's exactly where I expect her to be; on the couch with Noah rubbing her shoulders and Olivia passed out next to them.

"What do you suppose this means?" I ask, handing my phone to her.

"How old is Cookie?"

"Nineteen."

"Then she doesn't mean a bar. It probably means hanging out at her place, or yours," she says, turning her face up to me and handing back my phone. "Would you be comfortable with that? If not, you can always come home straight after dinner. You aren't obligated to do anything."

"I'm not sure. She doesn't know about—" I start, but stop. They know I mean my childhood which consisted of little else than molding me to be an obedient wife.

It's not that I want people to know about me. At least until I've come to terms with it all myself. That's a long road, I fear.

"That isn't something you have to tell her about until you're ready. Trust is earned, not given. Don't force the process," Noah says.

"When did you know about Lorelai?" The two went to college

21

together, but they haven't always been together.

"Not until I earned it, and trust me, she made me work for it. She told me only after she was sure I wouldn't use that information to hurt her."

"It's not our fault, Delilah," Lorelai says. "It's not our shame to carry. We are survivors, not victims."

"Okay," I agree, though I don't fully feel that. I am ashamed of so much. Dr. Price said that takes time. I hope it doesn't take too much. "I'm going to head out to the guesthouse."

"Your house," Noah corrects, as he always does. I give a weak smile of gratitude before leaving.

The path from the main house to my house is bordered with foliage and perfectly placed dim globes of light. It reminds me very much of the fairy world in one of the books Pope sent me. I half expect a mischievous sprite to pop out behind a bush each night.

I've thought a lot about the power names have, even though I know Pope didn't mean the fairy reference literally. Lorelai not only changed her first name, but her surname as well. She had reason. Hiding from her father, who was the Cleric at the time, was crucial. My father won't be coming for me; at least I don't believe he will.

However, I don't like being a Simms. Or the association to my father and his family. They're not unknown, by any means. When I learned how to look for things on a computer, I searched and found plenty. Plus, the government is building a case against them. I've already spoken to agents a handful of times to give them any information I can.

Which means it's only a matter of time before there is a raid and it's splashed all over the news. Then my last name will become infamous.

It's a strong reason to change it. But that's a decision I don't need to make just now, and it's not the most pressing thing on my mind. An email to Pope is.

So, I sit at the desk with the computer and pull up the email application. In most aspects of my life, words don't come easily. Often, I'm shy, confused, overwhelmed with the situation I'm in because it's new. This isn't any different.

> *Dear Mr. Blackwell,*
>
> *Thank you for the books. Not only do I appreciate the gesture of the gift, but I enjoyed each story as well. Especially the one that bounced between the fae and human worlds. I feel as if I do the same, ping-pong between my reality and everyone else's. Still so unsure of my place in this world.*
>
> *The idea that giving someone your true name gives them great power over you resonates with me. I know you know some of my past, I'm sure Noah has spoken to you about it. So, you must know what my family is.*
>
> *My question is this… Do I change my name so that only those who know the truth have the power of that association over me? Or does keeping my birthname give me power over it?*
>
> *Maybe you didn't mean anything more than that you didn't want to give me your name. Whatever the reason, I'm focused on it now.*
>
> *Along with other things. Faith based things. Lorelai suggested I speak to someone. She meant clergy, but I'm asking you instead. You offered, after all.*
>
> *I'm taking classes full time at the community college, but I'm hoping we can meet for coffee. I've attached my contact information.*
> *Sincerely,*
> *Delilah*

I read it over three times before I send it. And once it's gone, sent out through the wires and waves that will deliver it to wherever he is, I begin to shake with the heaviness of it. Or maybe it's desire that causes my spine to shutter. A bone-deep wanting to see him again, face to face.

But what would I know about that? What would I know about much of anything?

CHAPTER THREE

"They have great oysters here, if you like those," Cookie says as we look over the menu at a restaurant not far from the shopping mall she wants to go to. We decided to eat first, since we were so hungry.

"I don't know. I've never had them."

"Girlfriend, where the hell did you grow up?" she says, surprised.

"Utah."

"That explains it. I always say not to eat seafood in landlocked states." She shivers, and I laugh.

"What do they taste like?"

"Sand wrapped in snot."

"What?" I ask, snorting with more laughter. "Why would I eat that?"

"Because they're good! Some people say they're an aphrodisiac, too. But that's never been the case with me."

"A what?"

"Aphrodisiac. It means they make you horny. Want sex, whatever."

"Oh."

"I have so much to teach you, my young padawan," she says, then smiles deviously.

"Start with that," I tell her, trying to not let the embarrassment show.

"Oh, my stars! You've never seen *Star Wars*?"

"I've heard of it, but no."

"After we shop, we'll start the marathon watch. But shopping is a must. I have a few things I want to pick up."

"But first, sandy snot."

"Yes!"

We order six, I eat three. I hate them all, but I enjoy it for what it is. It's one of many new experiences for me, and I try to take none of them for granted. We also order etouffee, something I know I already love, thanks to it being a favorite of Noah's.

Cookie keeps the conversation moving with her bubbly personality and genuine curiosity. But she doesn't pry or ask me anything too personal about my past. She did ask if I lived at home with my parents. I explained that I live in my cousin's guesthouse and that was enough for her. Thankfully. Though I felt her eyes on me while I offered up a small prayer before eating, she gave no opinion or commentary.

I'm more and more comfortable with her by the minute because of it. Not so much that I'm willing to spill my life story, but I'm more trusting of her by the time we order dessert. Cookie, she readily admits, has a huge sweet tooth. I, on the other hand, am still getting used to so much sugar readily available in life.

Just as her cobbler and my turtle pie are placed on the table, my cell phone dings with a notification. It's an email. I don't get many of them, and my hand trembles as I press on the icon to open it, anticipating that it is an answer from Pope.

Tomorrow. The Country Club. 3PM.
Do not be late.
Pope

"What is the Country Club?" I ask Cookie.

"The place that does Drag Brunch in Bywater? I've never been there, but I've heard good things. They have a swimming pool you can buy a day pass for. Why?"

"Oh, umm. A friend wants me to meet him there tomorrow." Friend isn't right, of course, but I'm not sure what to call him. An obsession? A frustration? The only man I feel even a little comfortable around even though I probably shouldn't.

"For a date?" Cookie's mouth tips in a wide grin.

"No, nothing like that. Pope is a friend of my cousin; he's just helping me out with something."

"Pope? As in Pope Blackwell?"

"You know him?"

"Mostly by reputation, but I've met him once or twice. My parents and he travel in the same social circle." Her eyes dart down to her dessert, and I realize that Cookie has family secrets too.

"You don't have to tell me anything you don't want to. I won't pry, like you haven't pried with me."

"It isn't as if it's a secret, really. But my parents have a lifestyle that's... I don't know, awkward to speak of." She shrugs as if it's not a big thing, but the bashfulness is easily read.

"Mine too, so I can relate."

"Somehow, I think mine and yours are a lot different." She smiles; it's friendly and some of that discomfort leaves her. I want to keep her smiling, but I also want to get to know her. She's the only friend I've ever had, that's not something I want to lose. I also know that I will if I'm not willing to open up to and trust her.

"My family is part of a religious cult. Polygamist, to be more direct. I left it just before I turned eighteen because I was set to be married off." I leave out the part about my betrothed being my uncle. What I've just told her is heavy enough.

"Fuck, Delilah. I guessed something religious, but not that. They let you leave?"

"No, one of the other mothers helped me escape. I had to hide for a couple of months before my birthday. Then I moved here to be with Lorelai."

"How long ago was that?"

"About six months. Two in Nevada, four here." I take a bite of the decadent dessert. Cookie takes another dainty bite of her cobbler. She's something of a contradiction with her boisterous personality, fun look, and classy manners. Tonight, she's wearing pink pants that hug her form and a bright yellow t-shirt covered by a blue and purple striped cardigan.

I wish I had the kind of confidence that would allow me to put myself out there like that. Instead, I'm dressed in nondescript clothing, plain denim jeans and a long sleeve gray tee. It occurs to me that I'll be meeting Pope in public, looking like a boring little mouse next to his bold, dark looks.

"Will you help me pick out something I can wear tomorrow? I want to fit in at whatever this place is."

"Girl, yes! I got you."

She patiently helps me pick out an outfit befitting a meeting with Pope's big presence, all while still allowing me my modesty. In subtle ways, she encourages me to try items outside of my comfort zone but doesn't push.

When we're done, we head to her tiny apartment uptown to watch *Star Wars*. It's the most normal I've ever felt and though my nerves have been firing on all cylinders this evening, I can admit that I've had a better time than I have at any other point in my life.

And I might be a little in love with Han Solo.

Yesterday's anxiety is nothing compared to today's as I step off the streetcar and walk the few blocks to my destination. The hottest part of the day has the sunshine beating down on my head, sweat beads on my brow. Luckily, I'm perpetually early to everything so I don't feel rushed and will have a few minutes to cool down and compose myself once I get to the Country Club. Which is a yellow, French Colonial bungalow, if I properly recall the information Noah has been giving me on the regular family walks we take around the Garden District. He likes to educate us all on the architecture of the city. I don't mind, I'm something of a sponge for all new things.

In the two months since Noah and Lorelai's wedding, I've become more at ease with my cousin's husband. He's blunt and stubborn, but also a deeply caring man and I know how much I owe him for the financial help he's already given and what else he's offered. The fact that he does that simply because of the love he holds for my cousin who didn't even know me since she left the ranch when I wasn't quite two, is not something I take for granted.

Cookie took me to a store called Anthropologie to pick out the dress I'm wearing. It's called a maxi dress, she said, and it buttons from my neck to my hem. The periwinkle color plays off my gray eyes, making them a shade close to the long-sleeved ensemble I'm wearing. The dress is soft and wraps around my legs as I walk up the steps to the entry.

A young woman, not much older than I am, if I had to guess, opens the door from inside before I have a chance to.

"Miss Simms, welcome. Follow me, please," she says pleasantly before beginning the journey down the hall past several rooms and small crowds of guests. She leads me into a bar, and I feel the room close in on me.

Not only am I underage but alcohol around makes me jittery and unsure as well. Atop it all she leads me to Pope who sits in a corner under a painting of statue showing his... appendage. It's not crude, and I know it's some famous sculpture, but that doesn't ease the discomfort I feel. Or stop the welling water in the corner of my eyes.

"Your guest, Mr. Blackwell." The hostess pulls out a chair for me before leaving, Pope gives her nothing more than a sharp nod. His gaze scans my face while I try to get comfortable.

"What?" he snaps, and my spine straightens under the command.

"Nothing," I say, forcing eye contact. "I'm fine."

"Do not lie to me, Delilah, or this ends before it begins."

"I'm overwhelmed," I admit after a deep breath. "This room, it's a lot."

Pope doesn't miss my eyes darting to the frame on the wall.

"Naked I came from my mother's womb, and naked I shall return there."

"Job," I confirm the scripture. There's a comfort in the words, yet it doesn't seep into my bones. It doesn't take away the darkness or the fear that lives there. "It feels like I can't look anywhere else, as if everyone here is focused on this spot."

"Come with me," Pope says, standing. He waits for me to stand back up before his palm grips my elbow and he leads me deeper into the bar, I wear the heat of his hand like a badge. We stop at a corner table surrounded by walls painted with butterflies and moths. No nudes.

Instantly, I am more at ease.

"Better?"

"Yes, thank you."

The waitress who followed us to our new corner asks to take my order, and I pick black coffee. She asks Pope if he wants his usual and he gives that same nod to her.

"Thank you for meeting with me," I begin.

"Wait for our drinks," he stops me. We say nothing for the several minutes it takes. My head turns down and I pick at the baby pink polish on my thumbnail. Olivia picked the color, wanting us to have matching fingertips. Eventually, the server returns with my coffee and a thick glass with a small amount of amber liquor in it for Pope. "How is school?"

"Different, but good," I answer, assuming Noah has told him I've been attending.

"What are your goals there?"

"Finance. I'm quite good at numbers. I don't yet understand business but I'm a quick study."

"Interesting," he says as if he doesn't find it interesting at all. He drains his drink before he continues, "And have you been going to church?"

I shake my head, matching the fingers that grip the warm mug.

"What does your god think of that?" His tone turns almost sinister, making me flinch.

"The same as He has always thought, I imagine. I've never stepped foot into a church. That's not what we had at the ranch."

"What did you have?"

The blood drains from my face, and my trembling intensifies. So much so that the coffee nearly sloshes out of the mug.

"The Offering Room."

Pope doesn't take his eyes off me as he holds up his now empty glass, as if he knows without doubt the waitress is watching. Sure enough, she appears quickly to replace his drink.

"And what did you put up on offer in that room?"

"Whatever was asked of us." My voice breaks but the tears don't fall.

"You know it wasn't a deity that asked anything of you in that room. It was a man. *Men.* Corrupt, selfish, and evil men. Correct?"

"The Bible says those who are generous will prosper. I had little else to give but my obedience." The message was taught to us early and often. Not only by the men but the mothers as well. I wasn't allowed to say no, I had no autonomy on the ranch. My place was to submit to my betters.

"Fucking hell," Pope laughs, throaty and deep. I watch his Adam's apple bob with it, and I feel the same tightness in my belly as I did with him the day of the wedding. Unfamiliar. Uncomfortable. But not unpleasant. "*Give not reluctantly or under compulsion.* Corinthians says that, but I imagine your men didn't preach that part. Or made it clear that by giving these men whatever they desired, you were giving to *them*, and not to your lord."

"Not *mine*," I say. "He is the Lord of us all."

"Do you honestly believe that, Delilah? That every other religion is invalid? Or that atheists have it entirely wrong?"

"What's an atheist?"

"A person who does not believe that there is any proof of a god. It's a term most widely used for those who do not believe in the existence of any god, but that is an antitheist. It's a minute but profound difference. One says I don't believe there is proof of its existence, the other says I believe it does not exist. One perhaps still a question, one is definitive."

"Oh. I never dreamed those people existed. Even after I made it to Nevada, I figured the non-religious and sinners did it to spite God."

"Some do. Others just live their lives without the cloud of Hell hanging over their heads."

The Cleric didn't always use Hell or purgatory as a tool. But we were always taught that sinning would cause God not to love us. The Lord's love was, above all, the most important life goal, the only way to gain entry to the Kingdom of Heaven. I'm not so naïve that I don't understand that the things demanded of us girls were because the men on the ranch were evil. I know that. It's why I wanted to leave. Distance has given me even more clarity on the subject. But that doesn't mean that the Bible is wrong or that God doesn't exist.

Only that men manipulate faith for their own reason and desire.

"Which are you?"

"Both." Long fingers land under my chin, tipping it up so he can see my face. "I don't care if there is a god, or multiple gods, or no god at all. I care about what people do here, now. If I do something out of spite, it is to spite a person that is horrible to another person in the name of their god. Not to any god themselves. Do you understand?"

I shake my head. "If someone does something because God directed them to, how can you be mad at them for it?"

"Had Abraham murdered his son because his lord commanded him to, it would still be murder. A deity sending their son to Earth knowing mortals will kill him, is still filicide. A horrible act to prove your love to someone else is still a horrible act. I cannot abide by that any more than I can live with the idea that I must believe and love in a heavenly figure or I'll spend eternity in a burning world."

Never has anyone challenged my belief so bluntly.

"It's more than belief and love. You must live a life without sin, as well."

"Must I? If a god exists and he created all things, then he created sin. Why? To test us? Are we nothing more than a game for him? Entertainment? Or is sin just a tool to punish us with? Or is it nothing more than a man-made construct? What is sin? Rape and murder, surely. Though there are plenty of scriptures that would contradict that. Sex? If sex is a sin, then why would he make it a pleasurable act, or the first source of creating new life?"

"I don't know." Anger taints every word I snap out, frustration I'm unable to hide. Pope's hand immediately returns to my face, pinching my lips together between his fingers. Not forcefully, the touch is feathery light, but I get the point.

"Do not speak to me in that tone, Delilah. It's uncalled for. We're having a healthy debate is all. These are not questions you need answers for right now. Rather, they're questions for you to mull over, let them steep, then make your own conclusions."

Except I can do no such thing. Not while my mind hyper focuses on the fingers at my lips. Every touch from every man before had me shying away or flinching in fear. Pope elicits some other kind of feeling in me. My lips part, and his eyes dart to them as we both still.

I am an innocent woman, but not entirely naïve. On the ranch, they kept us uneducated on sexual things, until they didn't. Until they began to prepare us for marriage and what would be expected of us. That happened way too early. While I understand the parts and the mechanics of it, desire and want are new territories completely.

But I can admit to myself at least that I want Pope in some kind of way.

He doesn't pull his fingers away from me, instead he softly traces the corner of my bottom lip. Studying it as if he's looking for an answer to an unasked question. That same boldness I felt after the wedding rushes through me, and I push my tongue out to taste his finger.

His hand rears back as if I bit him, but the intensity on his face says he didn't hate it. It's embarrassing all the same.

"I'm sorry," I stammer, rising from my seat. "I need the restroom." Pope points in the direction I need to go, and I hurry away without looking at his face.

Shame cloaks me on my short journey down the vibrant paper covered walls. That man does things to me, he elicits feelings that never occurred to me before.

I think I'd do anything he asked of me. And more. *What a terrifying thought.*

Pushing the door to the restroom open, I quickly tuck myself into the first stall. I don't need to use the toilet; I just needed a minute to escape whatever power Pope held over me. It was unbecoming and unclean, carnal even, for me to act the way I did.

I can't believe I tasted him.

And I want to do it again. I want more.

"She's awfully frumpy." The voice comes from further in the restroom.

"I wouldn't call her frumpy," another voice says. "Plain, maybe. But she looks young."

"Definitely not Mr. Blackwell's type. The last time I was at Lupus et Agnes, he was fucking four gorgeous blonde women at once. This girl must be just a friend."

"Maybe, but he wasn't looking at her like she's just a friend."

"God, I know! I've tried for a year to catch that man's eye. What does she have that I don't?"

"You practically drip with desperation." The other woman laughs. "It's a turn off. You need to chill."

"Whatever," she pouts, and they leave the restroom.

Four at once?

It's not as if I don't understand how far out of my league Pope is, but it's still shocking to hear of his behavior at whatever Lupus et Agnes is. Maybe he's not so different from the men in my family after all. Religious beliefs aside.

Though, to my knowledge, the men slept with the mothers one at a time. If that was happening at the ranch, it certainly wasn't spoken about. Except, I'm aware there were things that happened to the girls before they were of age and that wasn't spoken about either. Anywhere but in the whispering corners where we were not supposed to hear.

None of it matters. Pope is nothing more than a religious counselor of sorts for me. Any information outside of that is useless to me. Regardless of what emotion he sparks in me, I'm sure he sees me as nothing but a damaged child.

When I finally return to the table, both our drinks have been refreshed and Pope has pushed his chair further from the table. While I should be comforted by the small distance gained, I'm not. Only more confused and embarrassed. I want to apologize again, but he doesn't give me the opportunity.

"Have you decided if you'll change your name?"

"I think I'll keep it, for now. It's one of the few things I can truly call mine, after all."

Pope doesn't respond to that; instead, he twirls his glass atop the table as if contemplating. What? I have no idea. I take the moment of silence to study him the way he does his glass.

There is a scar that runs along the outside of his wrist and up his forearm, disappearing under the shirt sleeve he has rolled up. He looks like he works with his hands, they're big and rough as opposed to the well-manicured ones I'd expect from a businessman. There is a history in them that doesn't align with what little I know about the man. It only makes him more intriguing.

"If you are serious about a finance degree, you should be enrolled at Tulane. Not the community college. It would give you more credibility in the industry later."

"I'm aware," I sigh. "However, because I didn't have much of an education… before Nevada, I don't have the transcripts or test scores to get me into a university. The community college was challenging enough to get in to."

"Fair point," Pope concedes. "How are you finding living with Noah and Lorelai?"

"I like it. It feels safe, even though it's quieter than I'm used to."

"Even with a toddler running underfoot?"

"Even then," I say with a nod. "I grew up with a hoard of children at any given time."

"What was it like? Growing up the way you did?" His face turns from the strange dark frustration he's been wearing to more inquisitive.

"When I was very young, it wasn't so bad. I don't remember a day that we didn't have a long list of chores, but there wasn't much more expected of us at that age. The older I got, the more it changed. The more I saw that the girls were treated vastly different from the boys. When I was old enough to understand—" I pause to arrange my thoughts. Looking to the wallpaper… to the moths that look so beautiful but are so deceiving. "When I was old enough to understand what was happening, I became nothing more than an old garment slowly being eaten away by the moths that ran our ranch. The men. The cancer that slowly took away anything that was me in order to replace it with what they wanted."

The hand holding his glass tightens, his fingertips turning white with the effort.

"Lorelai said it was strict," he grunts.

"I think you know it was more than strict. It was manipulative and abusive."

"And yet you don't have hate toward those men," he states as if he's certain I have not changed my mind since our first conversation.

"No. I pray for them."

"Love your enemies, right? My father argued that Luke 6 meant not to endorse the evil in those who hate you, but to seek out the good. I wonder if there is any good in your father, or your uncles, or any of the other men that prey at that ranch. I wonder more what purpose it serves you to fight to find it in them."

Honestly, I have no answer to that. Again, I feel foolish for so easily reverting to the teachings of my youth. I pray for them because that's what they taught me to do. In hindsight, it's rather ridiculous since they are the ones that tortured me in countless ways since the day signs of puberty showed on my body.

I should have the same curiosity that he does. Instead, my mind wanders to other worries. I wonder if there is any good in a man like Pope and what it would feel like to burn alongside him.

CHAPTER FOUR

POPE

"I s it done?"

"The email was sent this morning," Lucinda answers. She's the most efficient executive assistant I've ever had, I'd go as far as saying she's the best this city has to offer. I pay her handsomely for it. At five foot eleven and with curves that bring men to their knees, her talents were often underappreciated by other companies.

I may be a man, but I'm far from stupid when it comes to my money. Her capabilities didn't go unnoticed by me. So, I stole her from a competing firm four years ago. Neither of us have ever looked back. She knows what's expected of her and in return I know what she requires from me as her employer—ample pay, generous benefits, and a safe work environment.

Lucinda is the only woman in my world that looks the way she does, sexy as hell, who I haven't fucked.

Except for one.

Delilah Simms.

Only I'm not sure a woman is what I should be calling that lovely creature. Her age aside, she's like a newborn chick taking her first steps out of the shell. Naïve to the core. Even if I wasn't nearly twice her age, which I am, she isn't someone anyone should be taking to bed. No matter how much I'd like to when she stares up at me with those damned silvery blue eyes as if I'm some kind of fucking god.

I'm nothing of the sort. I'm nobody's savior. Rather, I corrupt, I ruin. Like the men she ran from, I'm rust. Just another moth ready to eat away at her in order to fulfill my own needs.

For weeks now, we've been meeting regularly to have conversations about her ever-present faith. Not that it's her Christian beliefs that are the problem, it's more the way she all too easily accepts the things she's been taught about them. I no longer believe in any god, but that isn't something I'm trying to convince her of. Only that she looks more critically at the preaching of the Bible, particularly the incredibly bastardized teachings of her cultish family.

Delilah used to be more cryptic about the small tidbits of information she'd given me in regard to how she was brought up. This past week, she opened up more. A sign she's trusting me, I guess. Regardless of how misguided that may be.

She told me how young she was when her father started 'shopping' for her future husband. Eight years old and forced to dress up in white frills while she was paraded in front of grown men who touched, prodded, and leered. The tale made my blood boil. Thinking of any child being sexualized in such a way angers me, but picturing a young Delilah suffering through it elicits something more than anger in me.

Noah told me Lorelai has been working with the FBI for years as they try to come up with a case to take down the ranch. Delilah has spoken with them, as well. She's given information in great and grotesque details. So far, it's not enough. Delilah's father, the cleric or whatever fucked up moniker he goes by, is careful. He's also wealthy, which has more to do with it than anything.

I don't yet know how much wealth he has, but I will soon enough. As well as where it's coming from. He's paid to keep his sins safe. I'll pay to expose it. We may both dwell in the underbellies of this world, but his and mine are not the same. It won't be simple or easy, but I'm determined to find a way to set all the young Delilahs free.

There may be similarities between the man and I, but the differences are much larger. It's those differences that I will use to bury the man and his loyal followers.

One day, when Delilah looks at me as if I walk on water, there may be an infinitesimal shred of truth behind it.

"Natalie is here. Would you like me to send her in now?"

"Yes," I say, blinking away the thoughts that had overtaken my focus for a moment.

A moment after Lucinda departs, Natalie arrives, closing and locking my office door. She is another statuesque and curvaceous woman. She's also another handsomely paid one. My schedule has been such that I have not been able to hit up Lupus et Agnes for more days than I care to count. Lucinda arranged a house call, if you will, for me.

As I said, she's the best.

Natalie knows the routine, and as such, disrobes slowly and completely before striding to me and kneeling at my feet.

"Good afternoon, Mr. Blackwell," she purrs, resting her cheek on my thigh as she peers up at me through long, dark lashes.

"Good afternoon, Natalie. Make yourself wet," I tell her, running my hand over the side of her head and down her cheek. Her hair is cut in a shoulder-length style, honey blonde and straight as a board. My usual preference is blonde. Today, it's all wrong as I picture sable waves halfway down a stiff back.

The image enrages me, and I forcefully shove my thumb between lips that aren't heart-shaped and naturally berry-stained.

"Suck it."

Natalie complies in both ways, busying her mouth at the same time her fingers find her cunt. The phone on my desk rings, and I see the disappointment in Natalie, but I ignore her and pick it up.

"Yes?"

"Your five o'clock is cancelled."

"Thank you, Lucinda. You're free to leave for the day, if you'd like."

"I will."

"Have a good night," I say before hanging up and turning to the woman mewling at my feet. "Are you dripping, Natalie?"

She hums around my thumb.

"Get on the desk and prove it." Pushing my chair away, I give her the space to perch her round ass on the edge in front of me. Each of her heels come to rest on the arms of my chair, allowing her knees to part further apart. When she spreads her folds with her fingers, I have a perfect view of her glistening pussy. "Have you already come today?"

"No, Mr. Blackwell. As instructed."

"Good girl. Taste yourself."

She dips two fingers inside herself, working them around for a generous length of time. Her nipples harden as she does, and my dick follows suit. So much of this woman is artificial, but her breasts are not. They're exactly as I prefer, natural, large enough to suffocate on, but not so much that they overpower the rest of her body.

Leaning forward, I bury my face in her scent. Not close enough to taste her myself, but close enough to drive her closer to crazy. I inhale deeply before moving up to bite at a nipple, inciting a throaty moan from her, the sound deeper than the one I wish to be hearing.

Delilah's voice doesn't have the sultry, whiskey rasp that Natalie's does, and I imagine the sounds she'd make while I fuck her would be lighter, breathier.

Fuck. If I believed in a god, I'd be cursing them for placing that lamb in my world. She's forbidden fruit and I want to suck out every drop of her sweet juices.

While it's not Natalie's fault that I'm in the mood I am, she's taking the brunt of my frustration as I close my mouth more and tug my head back. With her breast still taut, I smack the underside. Her eyes wince at the sting, but her hips rise at the same time. Natalie enjoys her punishment, no matter if she was the one to offend or not.

"Were you bad since last I saw you?" Her eyes narrow on me as I ask the question. I always ask this question, so I already know from her reaction that the answer is yes. However, she doesn't say the word. *"Whoever conceals their sins does not prosper."*

"You aren't my confessor," she says with a pout, but I see the excitement written all over her face. *Brat.*

I stand abruptly, causing my chair to push away and her feet to fall, but I brace her with a tight grip on her arms before pulling her to the other side of the desk. We'll need more room for what comes next.

"Hands on the desk, Natalie. Stretch out as far as you can and stick that ass up high so you can receive what you deserve for that little remark."

A tremble shudders through her body as she takes her position. I've never met a woman that likes spankings as much as she does. But I don't give it to her right away, instead opting to undress at the slowest pace possible. It only makes her more anxious and needy. The buildup is half the fun. Natalie tunes in completely to my actions, knowing when I'm finally as naked as her, she rises onto her toes with anticipation.

It's a fucking beautiful thing, her unmarred ass ready to take my palm. There's no warning when I give it the first slap, and though it's a natural reaction to flinch away from it, Natalie quickly rights herself. She's ready for more, she *wants* more. Who am I to deny the woman?

"One," Natalie says with what sounds an awfully lot like glee. I'd laugh if I was a different man in a different mood.

By the time we get to ten, she's gripping the desk forcefully by her fingertips, and her ass is the prettiest fuchsia color.

"I'll ask again. Were you bad since last I saw you?"

"Yes, Mr. Blackwell. I tried to seduce a married man. Twice."

"Twice with the same man, or two different married men?"

This is Natalie's modus operandi. Married men are her vice. We've been trying to correct that, but she's stubborn as hell.

"Two different men," she says with a heavy huff.

"Fucking hell." This woman is a menace to every husband in this city. Mostly, I couldn't give two fucks who she shares herself with. Except, I know she's set her eyes on Noah Anders. He'd never partake, but he's a friend, of which I have few. I protect my own. "Ten for each, keep counting."

When we get past the next twenty, she's so wet I can see it trail down her thighs and I'm harder than I've been in weeks. I'm about to put us both out of our misery when a knock sounds on my office door.

"Go away," I yell, but that knock only gets harder. Lucinda and I were the only ones still left in the office, since she went home the place should be a graveyard. "We're closed."

"Open the door, Pope!"

Precum drips from my dick, and I hate that it's because of the voice on the other side of the door rather than the nude, ready body in front of me.

"Go home, Delilah. I'll call you tomorrow," I say without kindness. It can't be found right now.

"No, open the door. I'm not leaving until you explain yourself!"

What the fuck is she talking about?

Spinning, I rush to the door and throw it open.

"I don't explain myself to anyone, little girl," I snarl.

"How..." she starts but stops as the blood drains from her face and her eyes dart from my face to my chest, then lower.

Fuck!

"Wait right there. Do not fucking move a muscle, Delilah," I say before slamming the door shut. Grabbing my pants from where I left them, I pull them on quickly but forgo anything else. Delilah is skittish enough. If I give her any amount of time to run, she likely will. "You don't move either, Natalie."

"Yes, Mr. Blackwell."

Delilah is hastily swiping at tears when I find her. She isn't where I left her, instead she's moved to the furthest corner. Getting as far away from me as she could without actually leaving my place of business.

"What is this about?"

"You got me into Tulane," she says around a hiccup.

"I did."

"You paid for it, too."

"Yes. Are you here to confirm what we both already know?" I snap, and she flinches.

"I'm here to decline." Her spine stiffens, and she glares at me with more empowerment than I've ever seen her show. *Good, Delilah.*

"You'll do no such thing." I laugh.

"That's not up to you. None of this is up to you."

"It's a fucking gift, Delilah. One you've earned. Take it and rejoice in all things and give thanks in all circumstances." It's a low blow, using her precious Bible to get her to accept, but I've never claimed to be a good man.

"I've done nothing to earn this."

"You endured what no girl should, that's earned you some good things in life. This is one. It's done, take it and use it to create a better life. You can't give it back, so use it or it goes to waste."

We stare each other down for a few moments. Me waiting her out, her trying to calculate something; thinking so hard I can practically see the synapses.

"I'll pay you back," she says, looking up at me like I hold up the fucking moon. I don't know her well enough to make too many assumptions, and maybe it's my mind playing tricks on me... but the way hearts practically pop out of her eyes, it seems like I could ask her for anything, and she'll comply.

Readily.

My body screams at me to take her, but my brain takes charge. I should tell her that whatever our relationship is, it's not transactional. That no relationship she enters should ever be transactional. But that's not how I live my life. I don't think any relationship I have whether it be a woman I fuck, a friend, a client, is free of tit for tat. It's not who I am. I get something from Delilah, even if that something is only a maddening depraved desire. She's a craving I can't quench.

As a man who is so used to getting everything he wants in life, this woman before me has become the bane of my existence in an instant. When a minute ago, all I wanted to do was sink so deep inside her she'd never lose the feeling, now… now I just want her gone.

"I don't fuck lambs, Delilah," I bark at her. Turning back to my office, I make sure she sees the naked woman inside before she leaves.

CHAPTER FIVE

Three months later and I still fall asleep each night to the sight of a naked, pissed off Pope Blackwell. We have not seen each other since that day. Nor have we spoken. I finished the semester at the community college and have recently started at Tulane. Lorelai and Noah convinced me to take the gift from Pope. It unsettles me still.

Not as much as the image my head conjures every night. Or the shame from the audacity I had to go to his office and confront him at all. It's why I haven't spoken to him since. He's texted to set up more coffee talks, but I've ignored them all.

How can I face him after what I saw? Or after what he seems to have assumed I was offering? Of course, he'd reject such an idea. I'm nothing more than a naïve child. It wasn't as if I'd even thought about such a thing, and I can't help that I don't have much in life to offer.

The first currency that comes to mind being the only one I own. *Me.*

I've played out that evening so many times in my head. How it could have gone differently, and how he ended up spending it after I left. Every time, I find my way to the same ending; me and Pope together.

My desires are few in life, really. I want security, I want to rescue more girls from the ranch, and I want Pope. Seeing him, bare as he was, didn't frighten me. My reaction was wholly different than even that first meeting at the Country Club. Fear wasn't what stirred inside me.

I'm not scared of sex with Pope. Maybe that's me being entirely stupid. It probably is exactly that, but that doesn't change the fact of while every other man has me running scared, I want to run *toward* Pope.

After that day in his office, I was so distraught I began praying for long periods of time. Much like I had done when I first left the ranch. Lorelai worried, but I worked through it with Dr. Price who helped me see that I shouldn't feel badly about any of it. It's natural for me to have fantasies, even lustful ones about men in my life. Sex has always played a very significant part in my life. It's different now, of course, but it's still a consuming factor for me.

And as far as God is concerned, if He punishes us for thinking about sex outside of wedlock, then He's got bigger fish to fry. I've come a long way since life on the ranch, and though it's still a struggle, I do try to be more critical of my faith, and what I was told to believe.

I'm a good person. That should be significant enough to count for something. That's been a hard lesson to learn, but I'm getting there.

Tonight, Pope will be here at my home. Or Noah's, rather. He and Lorelai are hosting some fundraiser dinner to benefit something to do with a high school football team. I offered to babysit Olivia and Piper, the newborn baby. I love being with the girls, so it isn't a hardship, plus it gives me reason to hide out here in my guesthouse with them in the hopes of avoiding Pope altogether.

"Let it go! Let it goooooo!" Olivia sings along, off key, to the movie she insisted we watch. It's her new favorite and she watches it every day. If her pattern continues, she'll find a new one in about two weeks. I don't mind though, she's carefree and I love that about her. I'm thankful for it, and the fact that Martha was able to get her out so young. She won't know the horrors that I did, she won't even remember anything about the ranch. When she's old enough to understand, I'll make sure she knows her mother helped me as best she could.

If only my own mother had. But Beth never would, she's as devout as they come. My whole life, I never heard her question any teachings or directive from any of the men. Even if one asked something of her that went against the teachings of the cleric, she'd comply, saying that women need to obey their husbands. On the ranch, every married woman is a wife, and every married man is a husband. She often refused to see the distinction between all husbands and *her* husband. The men's decisions outweighed women's in her mind. The one time I brought up a Corinthians verse that says women came from man, but so also are men born from women, she told my father, and I was punished with the rod.

I was seven and I never questioned it again. Pain and fear are strong motivators.

My childhood wasn't filled with love, support, or even nurturing. So, loving these babies is easy for me because I want them to have all the things I never did. Noah and I have grown closer because I see that he wants that, too. He no longer terrifies me, and I'd go as far as to say we've become family.

Cookie and I have talked about moving in together when I'm able to pay my own way, but the truth of it is I like it here. The security Noah provides makes me feel safe in a way I never have before. Dr. Price cautions me to not rely on a man for that, but we both know that's something else that's going to take me time.

It's hard not to place a lot of faith and devotion into the few people in my life that have been good to me. I imagine Pope's voice asking me how far my faith and devotion got me before I left the ranch. His voice is often in my head these days, still challenging me even when he's not around.

I miss our talks. I miss his presence. I miss the sight of his strong, muscled chest that tightened with annoyance when he told me I was too young and naïve for him to have sex with.

Lamb.

It's what I am, but it's not what I want to be. Little by little, I find my own strength, and someday, I'll be as fierce as him.

"Am I a princess?"

"No, Olivia. Remember we talked about this?"

"Right. I'm strong and impendent," she says, putting her fists on her hips.

"*Independent*, yes. You don't need to wait around for anyone to save you." A couple of months ago, Olivia began reenacting different scenes from the movies she'd been watching. But they were always the ones where the princess was waiting for the white knight to come rescue her. None of us particularly liked it, even if it was harmless. Maybe it's our pasts that make us so critical, but we're trying to reinforce her own strength.

Just like I'm trying with myself.

"But I still get all the pretty dresses!"

"You sure do, Livi."

Piper purses her lips and squirms in my arms. She's been passed out for about twenty minutes, but I haven't yet settled her in the bassinet. I've swaddled a lot of babies in my short life and it's comforting for me now. The funny faces she makes, and the smell that is so unique to babies makes my heart smile.

Before too long, Olivia's energy wavers and she too climbs up to snuggle with me and Piper. It's only minutes until I hear her soft snore. Slowly, I stand with care not to wake either child, first depositing Piper in her crib, then Livi in my bed.

I'm heading back to my sofa to find something to watch, preferably without singing, when there is a soft knock on my door. There's no question to me of who it is. Honestly, I half expected him to seek me out.

Maybe I'm half excited about it, too. The other half is wary as can be.

I steel my nerves as best I can, then open the door.

"Delilah," Pope says, and it might be my imagination, but he says it like seeing me is a relief. That can't be right though.

"What can I do for you, Mr. Blackwell?"

"You can stop with the formality," he says with flared nostrils.

"It's polite, not formal."

"Don't give me that shit, you never called me that before."

"I never called you much of anything, if I recall," I say. I remember how he said my name with perfect clarity, but I don't know if I've ever said his name aloud to him. "What can I do for you, *Pope*?"

"You'll stop avoiding me now. It's childish. I can understand that it would be jarring and embarrassing seeing a man naked for the first time, but it's no reason to ghost me for months," he says as if placating a child.

"It wasn't the first time," I blurt out, not meaning to.

"It wasn't the first time you saw a man naked?" Pope asks darkly while stepping so close to me that I retreat back until I'm against the wall. He looms over me, glaring down at my face with unhinged rage in his eyes.

"N…no," I stammer.

"Explain." He snaps the word out harshly.

Panicked, heat rushes through me. It's how it starts every time I retell one of the more horrible memories of my life before. Within seconds, I start to shake, and I blink quickly to stave off the darkness around my vision.

"Delilah." He calls my name, but it sounds like it's at the far end of a tunnel. A palm, softer than I'd expect, lands on my cheek, and I blink more. "Delilah, breathe."

"They made us watch," I gasp. "When we started menstruation, they made us watch. Said it was to teach us. I was ten, an early bloomer they said, and I had to watch my father have sex with his new wife. I had to learn."

"Fucking hell," he curses, pulling me into his chest and wrapping his arms around me. It's suffocating, but I finally feel like I can take a full breath of air. Wrapping my tiny frame around his long arms is like sinking into a warm bath after a long day. The tension ebbs as he twirls the ends of my hair in his fingers. Pope keeps me there for several minutes while I calm. "Was it only the one time?"

"No. It was a regular thing. It was my father only that first time."

"Is that why you've been ignoring me? Did it trigger something?"

"No," I laugh, and it sounds hysterical. I *am* hysterical, but at least my shaking has subsided. "You don't scare me."

"I very fucking well should," Pope says, pulling away at arm's length.

"Well, you don't. You're the only man who hasn't. I avoided you because I was ashamed of myself, Pope. I didn't mean to imply what I did, it was an uncontrolled reaction. And I don't know how to handle that."

"Come sit down," he commands, leading me by the elbow to my sofa. I take my place at one end, and he takes his at the opposite. "There isn't anything to be ashamed of. You interrupted a moment not meant for your eyes, is all."

Right. Because it's not that I suggested using me the way he used her. That would be too laughable for him to acknowledge at all. I'm more insignificant to this man than I thought.

"You've started school recently, yes?"

"Yes," I say and even I hear the vacancy in my voice.

"Good girl," he croons, and my heart swells. But my body is an idiot, a betrayer. "And how is the deconstruction?"

"What?" I blink up at him.

"Deconstruction, Delilah. It's what we call it when people unravel the faith that was forced upon them."

"Oh. I still believe in God. But I don't believe everything I was told," I say with a shrug.

"*I did this so that your faith might not depend on the wisdom of people but on the power of God.*" Another scripture, one I recognize but can't place. It's his way of reminding me that he doesn't think every one of God's quotes in the Bible is real, or true, or interpreted correctly. And that he thinks the Bible was written to control and not to be questioned.

"I do depend on the people I trust," I say with a furrowed brow, because I have been listening to those around me who are more critical of my faith. The struggle is still there, but I'm more open-minded to other opinions than I was just a few months back.

"Even the ones who tell you there is no god? Or that if there is, he's awful for making a child like you suffer?"

"I suffered at the hands of *men*."

"In the name of God. And your god stood by."

"I'm not yet knowledgeable enough to have this debate with you. But that doesn't mean you're right."

"Good girl. That's the strongest thing I've ever heard you say."

"Are you here to get a rise out of me?" Between further questioning my faith and praising me as good, my head is beginning a dull throb at the temples.

"No," Pope says, standing. "I'm here to check up on you, which I'll continue to do. Do not ignore my calls again."

He leaves abruptly, not waiting for any response from me. The man makes my head spin. Part of me wants to comply. Part of me wants to be as obstinate as ever, and to fight like hell.

All I know is that he's as confusing to me as he always has been.

CHAPTER SIX

POPE

"Thank you, William," I tell the man placed very high up in the university's administration as I check my phone to ensure the email he just sent has arrived. Even though I pay her tuition, on top of the exorbitant amount I handed over to get her accepted, I'm not due her schedule.

However, I've witnessed this man taking a strap-on by his wife while he sucked his Dom's cock. I couldn't care less what kinks William is in to. However, he doesn't want the world to know. I'd never tell, but he doesn't exactly trust that. It affords me special privilege. Who am I to turn it down?

Delilah refuses to follow instructions. It's been three weeks since I've seen her, and she has yet to answer a call, text, or email.

She's left me little choice.

If she were mine, I'd punish her in the most delectable ways. Delilah isn't mine to punish though; she's mine to protect. Even if no one has asked that of me. It's a gut feeling, instinct, or maybe compulsion. Whatever the reason, she consumes too much of my head space. And it's why I now make my way across the campus to where her current course is about to be complete.

I catch sight of her as she exits the building, her wavy mass of dark hair hard to miss even in the crowd. She doesn't see me because her attention is caught by a boy rushing up beside her. His hand grips her forearm, causing her to stop, and I don't miss how she stiffens and pulls loose of his grip.

His attention is unwanted.

The boy's brow dips low, and his mouth purses before it spits what I imagine is to be an insult, and Delilah rushes off in the other direction. I don't follow her. She was my prey a moment ago, now it's this pencil dick fuckhead who just made the biggest mistake of his life.

Following him between buildings, I analyze his stature… tall, but not as tall as me. Wide shoulders, but not as wide as mine. There's a wallet in his back left pocket. He walks on the outside of his feet and shows no concern for his surroundings. He thinks he's safe, that nothing can touch him. I'd guess he grew up a pampered little rich kid whose Daddy never blamed him for anything, and Mommy still does his laundry.

When we reach a parking lot, a quick glance lets me know there are a few others around, but nobody nearby. As he reaches to open the door of his shiny sedan, I lunge forward, trapping him between me and his car.

"You don't touch her again," I say while I move one arm to push against his back, and with my other hand, I pull the wallet out of his pocket, flipping it open to see his license. "Aaron Probst. I know where you live now, you piece of shit. If you even look at Delilah, I'll visit you in your sleep and start removing the parts you love most one by one. You lay another finger on her and I'll straight up fucking kill you. Understand?"

"Get the fuck off me, man," he yells as he struggles to get out of my grip.

"Do you fucking understand me, Aaron?" I purr in his ear, pushing him harder into the side of his car and tossing his wallet on the ground.

"Yes, fuck! Yes!"

"Good boy, don't fuck up now."

Taking a few steps back, I let the shithead get in his car and drive off, his puffed-up face glaring at me. I smile and wave, then I immediately send an email to William for a copy of Aaron Probst's class schedule. After that, I send one to Lucinda to dig up everything there is to know about Aaron and his family. By the end of today, I'll know exactly how to ruin him.

If it comes to that.

Because of this douchebag diverting me, I've lost Delilah. She doesn't have another class for an hour. Pulling up the interactive campus map, I locate the building for that class and see a coffee shop next to it. That's where I head and luck strikes because she's there, sitting with another young woman, smiles on both their faces. The café is set up with a slatwall partition, separating the space which allows me to come in undetected and sit near enough to hear the conversation.

It's borderline stalkerish. Luckily, I have no qualms about that. She brought this on herself.

"Has he asked you out yet?"

"He did this morning," Delilah answers. I don't have to see her to know she's blushing.

"Yes! Way to go, Joey."

Joey. What kind of adult man goes by Joey?

"It's just coffee. I don't know why it makes me so nervous."

"Because it's your first date. It's okay to have nerves about it. You've never spent time with a guy like that. Well, except for he who shall not be named." The other woman laughs.

"You can say his name. Pope isn't Voldemort."

"You don't know that. Also, bonus points for the pop culture reference. You've come a long way, my padawan."

"Whatever," Delilah says with a laugh of her own. "I should be an old pro by now. You've been schooling me for months."

"You had a lot to catch up on. Besides, I adore spending time with you."

"Maybe I don't say it enough, but I adore you, too. You're the only peer that has never made me feel like the oddball I am."

"You aren't odd, Delilah. You had an odd childhood is all, and that's hardly your fault. You're unique."

She's special, a diamond that hasn't yet been shined to brilliance.

"Too unique for Joey to have sex with me?"

My body turns rigid at her question.

"What the hell, Delilah," her friend whisper-shouts. "You barely know him, and you already want to have sex?"

Yes, Delilah, what the hell?

"It's not that I want to have sex with him, specifically. It's more that I want my virginity out of the way."

"Why?"

"Where I grew up, it was used as a commodity, something of more value than anything else about me. If it's off the table, I'll have a better idea if a man is interested in me and not just it."

"Damn, Delilah. I sort of get that, but also... I'm not sure it's the healthiest reason to have sex. Have you talked to Dr. Price about it?"

Good question. I like this friend of hers.

"As long as I'm responsible and honest with myself, she understands my reasons. She doesn't condone it, but she also says it's healthy for a woman my age to be exploring her sexuality."

"Fucking hell," I groan, not able to keep the frustration of this conversation in. I stand and walk around the partition. *"Let marriage be held in honor among all, and let the marriage bed be undefiled, for God will judge the sexually immoral and adulterous."*

"Hebrews," Delilah says, defiantly lifting her chin. "If the Bible makes the rules, then I guess it wouldn't have been wrong for me to be married off to a man who already had multiple."

"According to the book of Isaiah, Chronicles, Judges... to name but a few. Are you admitting the good book is full of shit?"

"I'm admitting that some of God's messages have been manipulated to mean something they were never meant to be."

"Because your god is all good, but not all powerful enough to make sure his intentions are clear?"

"Why are you here?" she asks, diverting away from the questions that always end with a deep crease between her brows. I understand how it works now. We can have our back and forth for only so long before it becomes too much for her. But she's clearly made progress.

"You've been ignoring me again."

"They're called boundaries, my dude," her friend says. I angle toward her; she looks vaguely familiar, but I can't place her.

"Pope Blackwell," I say, reaching my hand for her to shake.

"Cookie Parnell." She raises a brow and shakes my large hand with her delicate one.

Parnell. Cookie is the daughter of Jasmine and Bradley Parnell. Clients, members of Lupus et Agnes, one-time fuck buddies of mine. I've never had sexual intercourse with either, but that's barely a technicality. Jasmine is probably the most renowned dominatrix in New Orleans. Bradley is a very accomplished sub, and neither mind sharing one another. You don't exist in the lifestyle without knowing the two of them. Suddenly, I'm no longer sure I like her as a friend for Delilah. The Parnell family exists too close to my world and I'm already finding it difficult to not blur lines where the little lamb is involved.

She looks up at me with her black eyes in a way that says she knows exactly who, or what, I am.

"I'll respect Delilah's boundaries, when she shows me the same respect." *Lies.*

"Does she owe you that respect?"

"She owes me nothing. But it would be considerate to not make me worry about her," I direct the statement to Delilah.

"Is she yours to protect?"

"You ask a lot of questions, Ms. Parnell. I'll allow it because I see how protective you are of our friend."

"Oh, you'll allow it?" she asks sarcastically.

"I will allow it," I say, deeply and slowly. The same way her mother would speak to an obstinate brat. Cookie slumps under the force of it.

Good girl.

"Be nice, Pope."

"I'm nothing if not cordial, Miss Delilah," I say to her rolling eyes. "I'd like a moment to speak to you. Alone."

"That's fine," Cookie sighs. "I have to head back to my own campus anyway. I'll call you later, Delilah."

I watch her leave, so much dark skin on display. She's beautiful, like her mother, but I'd guess she's much more like her father.

"How long have you been friends with Ms. Parnell?" I ask, taking the seat she just vacated.

"A while," Delilah says, shrugging a shoulder. "We met when I was still at the community college."

"She attends the community college?" The Parnell's have the money to send their daughter to any school in the world.

"Yes. Don't look down your nose at it, she wants to pay her own way through school."

"Admirable," I say, but I mean idiotic. Why these young adults won't take help when offered is beyond me. I fought hard to get where I am. I'd have appreciated any assistance. "What's this nonsense about Joey?"

"It's not your business." She tries to school her features, as opposed to her usual angelic face. It doesn't work, but I'll credit her an A for the effort.

"Under no circumstances will you be losing your virginity to a boy named *Joey.*"

"Unless you're offering to take it yourself, it's not your business." She states it with direct, piercing eye contact, and I feel it in my cock. It's convinced that it's the only dick qualified to accomplish the task. The look on her face tells me Delilah agrees.

"I don't fuck with lambs," I remind her. Though I've never wanted to more, her reasoning for wanting both sex and me is highly concerning.

Delilah is everything I've dreamed of. She's gorgeous with her near black hair, her light, shining eyes. But it's her personality that draws me to her most. She's stronger than she thinks. Most women, experienced women, don't stand up to me the way she does. And the way she's willing to criticize her faith but not give up on it completely, tells me more about how she'd be in a relationship than anything else.

But she's still eighteen. Much too young, even if she didn't have the background she does.

"I can't be anything but a lamb until I'm no longer a virgin though, right? So, Joey it is." Delilah is so nonchalant about it, as if it's a given this boy will fuck her. As if it's not a big deal at all to lose her goddamned virginity.

"Even if you fuck this man-child, I wouldn't be an option for you, Delilah. I'm thirty-four, I could practically be your father." She rolls her eyes again, but they glisten with wetness this time. "I'm telling you to take your time. Find someone you care about for your first experience; someone you can trust to take care of you through it. Do you even understand the basics of it?"

"Of course I understand the fucking basics," she angrily whispers at me. I've never heard her curse before. It's hot as sin. "I've been witness to the basics for years. Do you even know how many virgins I saw married off and raped by their husbands who wore expressions of pure glee? I don't have the number; it was too many to keep count of. It's not a fate I want for myself."

"Shh." I reach up to swipe a stray tear with my thumb. "I wasn't trying to upset you. I'm only pressing the importance of this decision."

"Then you do it, Pope, as the only man I trust. It weighs on me like a burden and I want it gone."

And lead us not into temptation.

Delilah may appear angel, but the words she speaks are pure fucking evil. Never have I been so drawn, so obsessed by any creature as her. My grip on the edge of the table is so strong, I fear the wood will splinter, but it's all I can do to not leap across it and take her right here on the floor of this café. Like an animal, all my instincts scream to breed her. Here. Now.

She's mine, she's mine.

But I can't have her. I'm not the right man, but taking Delilah is too wrong, even for me. I can't subject her to another sort of ownership when she's only just fled that life. And it would be that with me. Rules, expectations, I have so many. She'd drown in them when she needs to be free.

Damn, what a gorgeous concubine she'd be if circumstances were different.

"I won't do that, Delilah."

"Then leave me alone, Pope."

I won't do that, either.

CHAPTER SEVEN

"Wait, really?" Joey asks after I've just told him I grew up on a religious compound. This is our second 'date'. The first was a short visit at a campus coffee shop and I wasn't yet comfortable enough to tell him too many details of my life.

Now we're on round two. We're keeping it very casual at an ice cream parlor, but I thought I should attempt to deepen the conversation. Dr. Price stresses the importance of not being ashamed of my childhood but instead being proud that I found a way to survive it.

I shouldn't be scared to discuss it with people, especially those that I want to have a meaningful relationship with. Maybe that isn't exactly what I want with Joey, but I do want something from him, and I need to give in return.

For three nights after the last time I saw Pope, I cried myself to sleep. It wasn't entirely true what I told Cookie about my conversation with Dr. Price regarding my virginity. She does encourage me to explore my sexuality; she also worries that I put so much importance on it.

Virginity hangs over me like a raincloud and I have no protection to keep me dry. Despite every argument Dr. Price, Cookie, or even Pope has against it... I want it over with. It's a heaviness that I can't carry any longer. I am more than that one fact about me, yet I feel as if it's the only thing people see. As if I can't be whoever I am supposed to be until it's behind me.

Perhaps that isn't a healthy way to look at it, but I already know I'm not mentally stable. Not yet anyhow. I get a little stronger each day, a little more open to possibilities and what my life can be. Noah tells me it's a journey, not a race. He tries to talk to me more now that I'm not so terrified of him. Now that I trust that he's a good man, a fierce protector with a huge heart.

It's the same qualities that attract me to Pope. Even if he tries to hide them behind stern words and hard expressions.

"Is your family like a bunch of super religious freaks?"

"They're all religious. I wouldn't say they are all *freaks*," I say, my hackles raised by his humorous tone. People in my life have challenged how I believe, but not one of them has laughed at the fact that I'm a woman of faith. While I fully understand the criticism of my father and the men like him, the ranch is full of girls like Olivia and women like me. It wasn't a choice to be born into it or brainwashed to believe such horrific things.

"So, you still believe that shit?"

"I," I start, then pause to collect my thoughts without getting overly defensive. It's not Joey's fault that he doesn't understand. "I believe in God and the scripture. What I've learned to not believe in is the abusive, polygamist life that was pushed upon me."

I'm distracted by a figure awkwardly exiting a car that has just parked outside the window Joey and I are seated at. Aaron Probst, the annoying guy that, for weeks has pestered me to try and go out with him. He's been pushy, overbearing, and scary in how relentless he is. At least now I know I can outrun him, because he's on crutches with what looks like a broken leg. A man, I assume his dad, helps him hobble to an office next door.

I shouldn't revel in his misfortune; it isn't virtuous of me. Maybe it was God's will to make him as uncomfortable as he has made me. Though a broken leg hardly measures up to sexually harassing me.

"You really think there is some magical being in the sky that created us all and is answering prayers of everyone on the planet?" Joey gestures around the ice cream shop with his hand, the smirk on his face becoming more prominent.

"I do believe in God, in creation. I don't think He's a magical fairy or anything."

"But what about evolution and the science behind it? You don't believe it?" Joey takes another lick of his ice cream. He ordered a cone, one scoop of birthday cake flavor, another of something called cookie monster that is an unnatural shade of blue. He laughed when I didn't know what birthday cake tasted like, as I've never had one. I ordered simple strawberry, in a dish. The look he gave me says he thinks my choice was boring.

"I don't honestly know enough about it to have an informed opinion." It's the truth, I feel stupid admitting it, but I'm not a liar either.

"If you did learn about it and saw that the science backs up evolution and basically disproves that we humans were not created in god's image, or whatever, would you stop being religious then?"

Joey asks me a question I'd expect from Pope. Except that the way Joey asks it doesn't come across as wanting to challenge me to think more critically. Instead, I think Joey's intent is to make me feel dumb for my beliefs. He's condescending and snide, making me feel small.

His hit lands. But I am not feeling stupid about my faith, I'm feeling stupid for agreeing to this date at all. Maybe I'm not ready for Joey, or maybe he's not ready for me. All I know is that every day I struggle to be in my own head and sort through my own thoughts. A difficult task on its own, I don't need anyone else in there with me. At least, not without knowing they have good intentions of being there.

"I can't say for certain," I say, quietly, no longer interested in this conversation. Or any conversation with Joey. Which is a feat all on its own. A year ago, I would have succumbed to this type of pressure from a man. "I wouldn't want to guess at the outcome."

"Isn't that all religion is? A bunch of guessing shit a bunch of old dudes wrote a long time ago?"

"No, it's belief in, and a love of something greater than us. It's a moral compass that helps us make the best decisions for our own humanity."

"How'd that work out for you in your cult?" He laughs.

Cult. I looked up the word once. People having religious beliefs or practices regarded by others as strange or sinister, the definition read. Since I am not sinister, it labels me strange. I feel it every day, a difference about me, an awkwardness that not even the most awkward people I meet possess.

Then I remind myself that Lorelai isn't strange from coming from the same beginnings. She's made a life for herself, she's strong, she's self-aware, kind and loving. She's my greatest role model. Lorelai is what I strive every day to become. Not the same, but alike.

Lorelai wouldn't abide this mocking.

"I think I should go," I tell Joey.

"You don't have to go, Delilah," he says, finally seeing the full effect of his words. "I can lay off; we can be friends."

"Thank you, Joey," I say with a weak smile. "I'll see you in class."

"Delilah, wait," he calls, but I ignore it, dumping my half-eaten treat in the trash on my way out.

I wander the Garden District some, lost in my thoughts as much as my steps. It's not a very large place, all things considered. It feels smaller still with how often I see familiar faces. The same mother walking with her two toddler boys from her house to the nearby park. The elderly man that sits out front at the deli every day eating his lunch. So many faces with set habits, folks that have found what makes them happy, where they feel most comfortable.

Envy washes through me, followed closely by the guilt of feeling a sin. This happens often, it's not new, the feeling that my thoughts are sinful. I've felt guilt my entire life, no matter how hard I've tried to be good, clean, virtuous in the eyes of the Lord. Envy is new, however. I hadn't had that before leaving the ranch. Now it is as if I spend much time each day holding its hand.

Envy isn't the only sin I indulge in these days. Lust weighs heavy on my shoulders. Not a day goes by that I don't picture Pope in his office that day. Nude, rigid with muscles decorated in inked art, his hard manhood prominent for that short moment before he realized what he'd done. I remember with vivid detail the way the dove on his neck fluttered when he swallowed, the way the broken cross that sits over his chest shimmered with his perspiration.

There isn't anything I've wanted more than Pope. Not even wanting to escape the ranch. It terrifies me to admit it, but it's the truth. I risked everything to escape my father. What would I risk in order to gain Pope?

Something tells me the answer is anything. I suppose it's good I have so little. Nothing much more than myself, which I've offered to no avail. Perhaps, someday, the rejection will sting less. There's nothing I can offer him, of course. I remember what the strangers said in the restroom, how he likes multiple women. Why would he choose a lonely, inexperienced girl?

As I often do when I take these walks, I end up at the gold door. His house is surrounded by a tall stone wall, ivy covering it from bottom to top, except the gilded iron door. Both ominous and regal, it invites you to the decadence or debauchery taking place inside. This is where Pope lives. I know because I saw the thank you card Lorelai addressed to him; the address easy enough to remember here in the Irish Channel just off the river.

It's a large house, the second story just visible over the wall and through the mature trees, a tall, Victorian home painted a gothic gray. Of all the times I've passed by, I've never seen anyone coming or going, never heard any noise from the other side of the wall. Today, a faint thump can be heard. Music... he must be home.

"Shit, girl, we're late. He hates that," a woman says from behind me. The blonde punches a code into the keypad on the door and it clicks open. She gives me a wink and a laugh and rushes through the door. "I hope you like punishment as much as I do."

I follow at a much slower pace, though my blood pumps as fast as her feet move. I feel like I'm committing a crime being here.

Between the wall and the house is a mature garden, a trail lit by small shimmering lights hung in the trees. Like the fairylands in the books Pope gave me. The other woman left the front door ajar, a shaft of light inviting me in, even though I know I should stay out.

The glimpse inside his world is too big a prize to ignore.

The foyer walls are painted deep blue, almost the color of midnight against the dark wood floors and trim. They're decorated in vibrant modern art though, giving the old space fresh life. As I creep further in, I see a dining room to the right, dark again but this time green. To the left is a living space draped in deep teal and filled with furnishings in both mustard yellow and a near magenta pink. Masculine and feminine both, and not what I'd expect of Pope's bachelor pad. Honestly, I don't know him well enough to have assumptions, only fantasies. Those I have plenty of.

The music grows louder, the tempo coming from upstairs. I climb them faster than I should. Fear should have me slowing, not running toward whatever is happening, whatever punishment is about to occur. But it's Pope, and around him, I don't feel like the dress being eaten away by destructive insects. With Pope, I'm the moth and he is my flame.

It's wrong, so wrong. I know it, he especially knows it. There isn't an explanation for why he feels like my safe space, it just is, and I'll risk a lot to be near him. *Obviously.*

"You're late, Lacey," I hear Pope say when I'm halfway to the top.

"Sorry, Sir," Lacey responds, but she doesn't sound apologetic. She sounds excited.

"Palm or paddle?"

"Flogger?"

"The paddle it is, you fucking brat," he bites back. "How many minutes were you late?"

"Eleven, Sir."

"Count," Pope commands, and there is laughter from at least two other people.

I don't move past the top step. Another foot and I'd be able to see into the room they're in. The visual isn't needed; I can hear each swat and Lacey clearly calling out the number that belongs to it. Spankings were a very integral part of my childhood. They happened regularly when anyone acted out of line, but also occasionally as a preemptive measure to ward away sinful thoughts. Or so we were told. Now I know they were part of the abuse, a way to control us or a way for the man delivering them to 'get off'.

I'm not so messed up that I don't understand what's happening in the next room with Pope and Lacey is different. Lorelai and I have spoken in great length about consent and age-appropriate sexual behavior. I *am* still messed up enough to have flashes of memories bombard me with the first few slaps of the paddle on Lacey's behind. There was a time in my life when spankings happened with more regularity. After I was too young and before I was too old. Maybe I should count myself lucky, I didn't have it as bad as some of the other girls, but nothing in my life had much to do with luck. Except Martha helping me escape it.

"You don't get my cock tonight, Lacey. That's the bigger part of your punishment," Pope says after they get to eleven.

"Please, Sir," she whines.

"No. I'm giving you to Mr. James."

"Yes, Sir." There is dejection in her voice this time.

On the ranch, my father, and the Cleric before him, preached that marriage was sacred between a husband and his wives. But I know that wasn't always the case. Sometimes, wives were shared with other men. Mostly it was the wives that didn't protest it, like my mother. I once heard her tell a sister wife that it didn't matter who fathered or gave birth to a child, if children were plentiful. I know now it was her way of excusing her own sexual deviancies, and maybe a way, too, to get a taste of that power the men had.

It's not lost on me that whatever small amount of power she had, she used it for self-gratification instead of helping her children.

The sound of movement and murmuring brings me back from the sour thoughts of my parents. Neither gave me much thought outside of what value they could trade me for, I don't owe them space in my thoughts.

Finally, I move the tiniest bit closer to those in the other room. Far enough that I can see part way into the room. It's as dark as all the others, this one with a wine-red baroque wall covering. It's beautiful but not as much as Pope standing just inside the doorway, as naked as he was that night that is singed in my memory.

Another woman, not Lacey, crawls to his feet and positions herself primly with her head cast downward. Pope grasps his penis, working his hand from base to tip while he watches something farther inside the room. I can't see what from my position of hiding at the top of the stairs. He must enjoy whatever it is because the rise and fall of his chest grows faster and his penis longer. Pope drags the tip of himself down the woman's nose to her lips.

"Open."

Nothing but her mouth moves as she obeys. Pope rims her lips with his fingers before he pushes himself in. His hands go to either side of her head, holding her steady as he has sex with her mouth. Still, she doesn't move. She's nothing but the vessel for his pleasure.

Giving honor unto the wife as unto the weaker vessel.

This verse of the book of Peter was discussed when I was old enough to begin to understand the meaning. Rather, what the men ruling the congregation wanted me to understand. Men are stronger in nature, their parts stronger and giving. Whereas women are fragile and made only to receive. *To obey.*

Suddenly, I'm no longer present here in Pope's home. I'm back at the ranch, small and shaking in my skin. Skittish, sad, and too naïve as my father lays down the rules for the day. How I have to behave, be polite, smile. Never stop smiling for the men coming to meet us, formally. Some from our own ranch, some from sister properties in other parts of the state. Those scare me the most, because at least if I'm home, I know what to expect.

"Smile, Delilah. If I see you frown, it will be the rod for you tonight."

"Don't move. Good girl."

"Be Daddy's good girl, Delilah. You'll catch us a good prize if you're good."

"Just like that."

"Just like that, good girl."

Fingers pushing my smile in place. Fingers tangled in the woman's hair.

I can't keep up, can't keep track.

A cry escapes. Hers. Mine. Maybe both.

Then there's a rush of air and a hand at my throat. All delusions wash away to be replaced by the black eyes staring hard into my very soul.

"What the fuck are you doing, Delilah?" Pope's words lash me like a whip, hard and angry.

"I… I don't," I try to speak but can't. Between his grip on my neck and the trauma I haven't yet swallowed down, I can't. "I…"

"Who's this?" a man asks, appearing over Pope's shoulder.

"Back away, James. She's a goddamned child."

I've never felt more like one in my life.

"I'll leave," I gasp. "I will. Please let me leave." Tears stream now as my body shudders with shame and the need to flee.

"You're done here, Delilah," he says the words so quietly, but they sting so deep as he whispers them at my ear. Before he releases my throat, he leans in and licks one long trail of my tears. "Run home. Now."

Kind enough words delivered with nothing but pure hate. Except it's his tongue on my skin that I focus on, the searing rush that it sends through me. New, frightening, above all... pleasant.

I run, stumbling and tripping my way down the stairs and out his front door. I run all the way back to Noah's home, despite the thunderstorm that's rolled into the city while I played voyeur to Pope's life. The rain doesn't matter, not when my head and my pride hurt so much. Block after block, I make my way home as quickly as I can. Each strike of thunder reminding me of the words Pope rained down on me.

Child.

Done.

Run.

I pushed too hard, took too much. Assumed I could make him want me like so many men did before him. By the time I'm home, I'm sobbing and soaked through.

"Delilah," Lorelai exclaims as I run past her in the backyard to my guesthouse. She follows me. I hear the worry in her voice as she asks what's happened. I hate it. I don't want to be worrisome to anyone. I don't want to be a burden.

I don't want to be seen.

Except by Pope. I'd be the weight chained to his ankle if I could.

"What have I done, Lorelai? What's wrong with me?"

"Nothing is wrong with you, Delilah. What's happening?" she asks, pulling me into her arms as soon as we're inside the house.

I cry through the whole sordid story, starting weeks back. I don't leave much out.

"Oh, honey. I knew you liked talking to him about religion. I didn't know it went deeper." She smooths my wet hair back from my face and leads me to the sofa where she grabs me a blanket. "What is it about him?"

"I've always felt safe with him. From the first time I met him at your wedding. I thought that meant something," I tell her weakly, snuggling down into the blanket. I should change out of my wet clothes but that takes effort I can't seem to summon just now.

"Of course, that means something, sweet girl. But maybe it doesn't mean more than friendship. He's much older than you, experienced, with a life that you know so little about. But I understand, you know? That's how I became infatuated with Noah when I first met him. I recognized something in him that matched me. And I, too, pushed it too hard and too fast. To the point where he was my whole existence until it all fell apart."

"But you found your way back."

"Sure, after a lot of years, and even more mistakes," she says. "I had to learn what I wanted from life, and how to stand on my own. You need to take the time to do that, too. You had eighteen years living one way and have had less than one living another. Give it time, give yourself some space to learn. Some grace to make mistakes. It's not a race."

"It's a journey," I finish for her. "Do you think I'm sinful? I wanted to see him that way, is that wrong?"

"No, Delilah. It's not wrong to explore, it's not wrong to desire. It's wrong to take it when it isn't offered. That was your only mistake tonight, okay?"

Lorelai is being too kind to me, I'm sure of it. I let her stay long enough for her to be sure I'm okay before I shower to wash away the day. And then I kneel at my bedside to pray for forgiveness, for guidance, for the grace to accept my mistakes and learn from them.

The Lord may punish me for my indiscretions, but surely, He will forgive if I repent. So many voices enter my thoughts even though I attempt to focus on penance, growth, redemption. I hear Lorelai telling me there isn't anything wrong with me, Noah questioning the existence of God. Loudest of all is Pope asking me what I did that was so bad it warrants such response from me or a punishment from God.

Panic overtakes me as questions fly at me at once. It's too much and I succumb to it in a sobbing ball on the floor next to a bed that's too soft, in a room that is too lavish and comforting. I'm undeserving of any of it.

I'm undeserving of it all.

PART II

CHAPTER EIGHT

"I'm proud of you. We're proud of you." Noah emphasizes the plural and nods in the direction of Lorelai who's straightening the decorative pillows for the eleventh time. She's having a hard time today as she and Noah help move me into my own apartment. Well, mine and Cookie's.

Being a constant figure at her home for nearly six years, today is a big milestone for us all. But it's time.

"I wouldn't be here if not for you two. I'm your babysitter for life, you know?" Olivia is ten now. Before long, she won't need anyone to watch her. Piper is about to start school; Beckett is two and exactly what you'd expect from a toddler boy. Rowdy and wild.

The addition of Beck to the family isn't the only thing that's changed. I graduated Tulane and interned with Cookie's mom at one of her three companies. Tomorrow, I will start at another one of them. Anxiety and excitement over the position weigh in equal measure.

Plus, Martha kept her promise to me, and Jillian is safely away from the ranch and hiding in the same Nevada safe house that I did. She's several months from turning eighteen, but Noah has sworn to me that she's safe and will be moving in with him and

Lorelai as soon as possible. And she isn't alone. Two others came with her.

One of them is fourteen and was married off the week before she escaped. My father is taking chances with his congregation that Lorelai's father never did. My heart breaks for the girl, Hannah. If there could be a silver lining in the situation, it would be that her rape has escalated the federal investigation which had become stagnant. Jillian says something has happened over the past couple of years and it's made my father more erratic, much more unpredictable.

Power changes people. Perhaps becoming leader is all it took to send him over the edge from borderline illegal to full on. I can't be sure. All I know is that I'm happy to have three more girls safe. Jillian said Martha could have gotten more out, but most are still entirely too afraid of the outside world or to disobey my father's preaching.

Lorelai's father was awful, my father is worse. He's taken to claiming any atrocity in the world or any natural disaster, as his doing. All in the war against the sinners. It brings new fears to his flock. But the federal agent working on the case thinks they are closer to being able to charge my father than ever before. I hope that's true, but I also know that there are men there that would gladly take his place.

"If we keep up this pace, we may need you for life." Noah laughs. They aren't deciding on a number when it comes to children. They'll stop when they're ready, Lorelai says, whatever number that lands on. They are amazing parents, and I don't see that ever changing. Gentleness, humor, freedom, and most of all, love are the tools they use. So entirely different from the world Lorelai and I were born into.

I've learned we aren't doomed to the future our parents press on to us as children. I'm not destined to be anything or anyone. I can make mistakes, I can learn, and I can grow as a person. That's what I strive for each day, to gain more knowledge, more self-awareness, and better critical thinking. All things denied me for so many years.

"I'm only a call away if you need some… alone time," I tease.

"I don't know what you mean, Delilah." He winks. "If you need help, or advice, *I'm* only a call away."

"Thanks, Noah. For everything."

He pats my shoulder, then moves to haul Lorelai closer to the door. She's said goodbye already, more than a few times, tears in her eyes.

"I guess you two are all set, then," Lorelai says.

"Yep, all good. I'm going to put a couple more things away, then go read this anti-gravity book I've been reading. I can't put it down," I say.

"Oh, good grief." Lorelai laughs. "That was a bad one, even for you." I've become an expert at dumb dad jokes, tending to let one loose whenever emotions run a little high around me. It's a coping mechanism, I know, but at least it's not a harmful one.

"I'll be fine, Lore. Cookie has my back," I say.

"I'm your ride or die," my friend confirms.

"I know, I know. Maybe I just don't like change," Lorelai muses.

Maybe she's pregnant again.

"It's a good change," Noah says. "Remember how far you've come."

"Remember who you are," Lorelai says, a reminder she often gives me, so that I don't fall to societal pressures. She frames my face with her warm hands for the next part. "You can handle whatever comes your way. No matter what."

"No matter what," I confirm, letting her know I understand.

"I love you, sweet girl."

"I love you, too, Lorelai." I smile warmly and hug her tightly before they leave.

"Wine?" Cookie asks.

"Yes, please. Let's celebrate our new place before I call it a night."

"You're going to do fine at the new job. My mom wouldn't have hired you if she didn't have faith in you."

Jasmine initially hired me to intern at the talent agency she owns. It was a paid position, and since I had no bills of my own, I invested my paychecks. My returns were sizeable. Jasmine was so impressed with both my skills in the office and with my portfolio that she got her friend who owns a brokerage firm to sponsor my securities testing and series 7 and 65 exams. After that, she offered me a position at a club she now co-owns. Technically, I won't be just a financial advisor for the club, I'll be more of an office manager with plans to eventually be the CFO.

She wants to expand to other cities and states. She'd like to offer more services to her clientele. All of which takes capital. Jasmine would prefer not to keep increasing membership fees. That's where I come in. Maximize investments and capital.

For a twenty-three-year-old woman, it's an insane ask. Jasmine assures me I'm up to it. Succeed or fail, it's a great opportunity for me straight out of college and with a past like mine.

"I'd rather hire a young, tenacious woman than a crusty old asshole who thinks he knows everything," Jasmine had said when I expressed my concern.

I agreed to a trial contract, giving her an out if I mess everything up. It's not that I'm not confident in my skills at investing. I am. These past several years I've done little else but throw myself into learning everything I can about the business of making money. I'm very good, if I allow myself a little bit of vanity.

Noah thinks that not having a lifetime of preconceived notions about business helps me see things from a fresh perspective. I'm not tied to the norms and traditions. Maybe that's true, or maybe it's a sole focus to never be reliant on a man to provide me with my basic needs again.

My anxiety about this new position isn't due to so much to my lack of experience in business, though. I can learn anything I need to on that end. The environment, the people I will be working with and around – that's what has me most nervous.

I'm still rather awkward around people, the years away from the ranch haven't fully remedied that. Dating has helped force me out of my shell, even if I'm not very active with all of that. I did have a boyfriend for several months though. Andrew, he was a sweet guy, pious and understanding about my past. We got on well until he was ready for more. He proposed one Saturday night along the river, under the stars. It was romantic, but it didn't feel right. I asked for time to consider it. Though he said that was fine, and I could take all the time I needed, two days later, he took it all back. He hasn't spoken to me since. I reached out for weeks and got nothing in return. It's hard to understand what went wrong.

Losing a friend made me sad, losing Andrew as a boyfriend did not. So, I guess no would have been my answer regardless. Besides, we'd only been dating for a few months, it was too fast.

"I'm proud of you, too," Cookie says, handing me a glass of red and taking a seat next to me.

"What for?"

"You've come a long way since that day I forced you to be my friend," she says, and I laugh because that's not exactly how I remember it. "You're confident in yourself and your abilities. You don't shy away from any sort of challenge. I've never known anyone to push themselves as hard as you do to learn something or accomplish whatever you've put your mind to. Plus, you're kind of fun to be around."

"You only say that because I'll watch all the movies with you that other people think are cheesy."

"*Bring it On* and *Step Up* are not cheesy." She frowns.

"We cheer and we lead.

We act like we're on speed!

Hate us 'cause we're beautiful. Well, we don't like you either!

We're cheerleaders!

We are cheerleaders," I yell as I do my best to move my arms in the right positions without spilling my wine all over our carpet.

"Yeah, okay," Cookie laughs. "It's a little cheesy. But you love it!"

I didn't get the jokes the first time we watched it, but I'm much less sheltered these days. Cookie always takes the time to clarify things for me. We've only grown closer these past years. She's my confidant in all things, and I am hers.

She has told me how much pressure she felt growing up with such a strong and ambitious mother figure, how embarrassing it was when some high-school classmates figured out who her parents are and what they're like in their private lives. Cookie doesn't have a dominant bone in her. Fig, her brother, takes after their mother more than she does. Cookie is much more like her father, Bradley. Quiet, observant, and caring.

She felt unremarkable in her mother's shadow. Though that was a self-induced pressure and she's worked her way through it. Her parents are fantastic, as far as I'm concerned. Nothing about them says they would ever want either of their children to be anything they aren't. And they'd be loved regardless.

It wasn't easy for me to understand how she worried about such things coming from a family like she has. But the more we talked, the more I realized not all wounds are delivered with direct blows. And Cookie and I are not so different when you break it all down.

We're both much stronger women than we were when we first met.

"I'm proud of you too, you know? You're the best person I know, and I love you."

"I know," she says with a laugh. It's how we always answer each other when we express our love; with a nod to Han Solo and the first movies we watched together. She still calls me her padawan, but I don't mind. I do still have much to learn.

The following day, I arrive at Lupus et Agnus earlier than needed. Anxiousness has gotten the better of me. I'm excited to work, to learn a new business even if the butterflies in my stomach are screaming that this place is a den of sin.

I've learned not to judge others for their lifestyle choices, though. If it causes no harm to anyone, it's not for me to look down upon. Lorelai and I spoke in detail about what I witnessed that evening at Pope's house, a lot about different sexual preferences and kinks.

Talking about them and witnessing them are two completely different things, though.

Now here I am, about to enter the belly of the beast.

The club is housed in an old three-story building at the edge of the French Quarter. It's rather nondescript from the outside, painted a rainy-day gray with black iron balcony railings. The only thing that stands out is the dark plum door with an ornate L on it.

Not knowing the protocol, I push the button to ring the doorbell and wait, once more checking over myself; smoothing wrinkles that don't exist. This world I'm about to step into is about as far from the world I grew up in as I can imagine.

Well, except for it centering on sex.

Years of therapy have helped me see more of my upbringing for what it was. A sex trafficking ring under the guise of religion. It's changed my relationship with my faith. I still believe in God. I don't so much believe in religion any longer.

Jasmine answers the door before I have the chance to fall too far deep into that rabbit hole.

"You're early, dear," she greets. "Wanting to get the lay of the land?"

"Am I that obvious?"

"No, not obvious. But I like to think I know you well enough now to understand you," she says, holding the door open for me. "Come in, I'll introduce you to my partner in crime."

The foyer is dimly lit, Edison bulb fixtures dance light across the charcoal walls of the small space. There is a door to the left, and straight ahead, another one is flanked by a hostess stand.

"This is where members check in before heading inside the club." She points to the door in front of us. "We have them check in and out, for added security. The offices are this way."

She types a code into a keypad, and I follow her through the door on the left where a staircase takes us up two floors. The walls here are all void of color, just as below. Maybe I shouldn't have expected anything less of a sex club, but it's going to be an adjustment for sure. At least the office area has a few front facing windows allowing natural light in.

"This is my office," she says, pointing to the first office. "Yours is next, feel free to do with it what you'd like. The previous owner told me he liked the gothic atmosphere, wanted everyone to imagine a vampire was watching them from the shadows, or some nonsense." She waves her hands at the walls as she rolls her eyes. At the last door, Jasmine knocks.

"Come in," a faintly accented voice calls from the other side.

"Fabienne, this is Delilah. Delilah, meet Fabienne Basquiat."

"It's nice to meet you, Ms. Basquiat," I say to the statuesque woman. She's rather breathtaking with white hair, terra-cotta skin, and draped in a long dress that plunges down deep below her cleavage. Fabienne isn't as young as Jasmine, I'd guess at her being in her mid-sixties. Yet she's still exquisitely handsome.

"Fabienne, and Fabienne only, my dear," she says with a wide smile. "Jasmine tells me you are something of a savant with money."

"I wouldn't go that far." I laugh. "I'm good with figures and a fast learner, is all."

"Well, Miss Fast Learner, how would you like to start?"

"With a tour, if you don't mind. I need an understanding of what happens here, how it all works. Honestly, I'm rather naïve to the lifestyle."

"We all were at one time," Fabienne says. "You just happen to have the two best teachers around, though."

"We're teaching her the business, Fab, nothing else," Jasmine says with a sternness that her eyes betray. She's told me several times that whatever questions I may have about all things sexual, she's happy to answer. Jasmine believes in empowering women in any way she can. That's likely why she took me under her wing when Cookie and I filled her in on my past. Like me, she doesn't want me beholden to anyone.

"Oh, of course. But if that ever changes," Fabienne lets her words drop off. "We're still closed for another two weeks while we finish up the changes we're making to the place. The contractor will be back tomorrow. If you'd like your office painted, pick a color from the samples on my desk and I'll have him take care of it. Oscar believed everyone could live happily in the dark all the time, ridiculous man that he was."

"I'll do that, thank you," I reply as I follow the pair back down the stairs to the small lobby.

"Every member must check in. For security, we like to know who is here at any given time. But also, so that they can't walk a guest in who hasn't gone through the proper vetting," Fabienne states.

"What's the vetting process?"

"Lupus et Agnus is very exclusive with a high caliber list of clientele. Because of that, not just anyone can be brought in. We run a background check on any potential guest. If they pass that, they go through a thorough orientation. You'll need to go through that as well."

"Of course," I agree.

"The first thing you should know is that Lupus et Agnus is a community, a family. We don't exist for the sole purpose of letting people come in and work out their kinks. We hold regular events aimed to educate on different aspects of the lifestyle, from aftercare to proper caning techniques, we even have a shibari expert who comes by a few times a year."

"Shibari. That's the Japanese ropes, yes?"

"Yes. People outside of the lifestyle seem to think clubs like ours are nothing more than BDSM dungeons. We are a little bit that, but we're also so much more," Fabienne says.

Jasmine opens the second door, holding it for me to enter. An infinitesimal shutter runs through me, but I swallow it down and enter the sex club. The first room is a bar which Fabienne calls the salon, I imagine members gathering here. Relaxing and waiting for the right person, or persons, to appear. It's still rather dark with deep blue subtly printed wallpaper, rather than the black of every other space I've been. Jasmine explains that they'll be making little improvement here, as members prefer the warm and inviting space while they shed the bright, loud outer world.

Fabienne schools me on the bar and its strict three-drink limit. Again, a security measure to ensure there is no question regarding consent. The bartenders have full power to cut off any member before that third drink, if they see fit, and guards are always present to back up any of the staff. The rules, and measures in place, ease my nerves some.

From the bar, we take another door leading to a long, wide hallway lined with windows on both sides, plush armchairs set here and there.

"Oscar called the first floor the Voyeur's Garden," Fabienne says. "Ten rooms, all equipped with windows facing the hallway. You can always see in, but it's up to the inhabitants of each room if they want to see out. Allows a little mystery."

Jasmine opens the first door and shows me the switch on the window that allows us to see out to the hallway. The room itself is sparse, nothing but a large bed sits in the center of the room. Dressed in white sheets that match the stark, bare walls. White... innocent, holy, virginal. All too familiar for me. My pulse speeds with memories of the 'special tutoring' I was given as a child.

You are not back at that place, Delilah.

"This is the White Room, for obvious reasons," Jasmine tells me before heading to the next room. I'm thankful we move on quickly.

Fabienne opens the door to the next room, black walls show

themselves in here. Like the White Room, the walls are bare, except for large steel rings placed in various locations around the room. On the walls, ceilings, and in a few spots on the floor. Fabienne flips a switch, and the room is drenched in darkness for a moment before a million twinkling stars brighten on the walls and ceiling, bringing the space to life under black light. It wouldn't be impossible to spectate, but it would be more private than the first room.

"The rings?" I ask, sheepishly.

"Are for securing someone where you want them to be. We have collars, cuffs, tethers, and leashes available. Though many subs come in wearing a master's collar already."

"Okay." I nod and swallow. Cookie has broken down some of the basics for me, I didn't walk through these doors completely blind today. That's not making it that much easier though.

From there, we move to the Swing Room, which has nothing more than a sex swing hanging from the ceiling. Fabienne and Jasmine take the time to demonstrate how it works, but they keep it lighthearted and fun. We're all laughing by the time we enter the next room down, and while this is still so far outside my wheelhouse, I feel safe here with these women.

"We used to call this the Red Room, but then *that* book came out so we've changed it," Jasmine says. I don't know what book she's referring to, and I don't ask. "It's the Moulin Rouge now."

If I had known a place like this could exist, I would have fantasized it as my dream room from a young age. It has a large crimson canopy bed with plush velvet bedding and wispy drapes. The walls are floral and another swing in the corner; this one simple and made of polished wood, like you'd find hanging in a tree. The rest of the space is cluttered with gilded mirrors and upholstered furnishings in arrays of reds and pinks.

"It's beautiful."

"Yes, it's our favorite," Fabienne agrees.

The last room on this side of the hall is bigger than the others and full of equipment. Some things look like they should be in a doctor's office, others look like gymnast equipment. Again, the two women show me how some of them are used.

"What's this room named?"

"Gluttony," Jasmine says with a grin, and I can't help the laugh that escapes me. "Oscar kept the rooms the same for over a decade, we've been changing many of them up and will keep doing that. Rotating themes should keep it more entertaining for all involved. Though this room will stay much the same."

"The rooms are attended; everything is cleaned in between use. Our dungeon master is the best in the world, if I say so myself. And we always have several dungeon monitors for this floor alone. Nothing goes without notice, so everyone plays safely." Fabienne opens a door at the end of the hall that has cabinets, washers, and dryers. "You okay to go up a floor? We don't want to overwhelm you."

"I'm good," I promise while doing a self-check to make sure it's true. It's a practice Dr. Price taught me. A moment of pause to check for signs of anxiety so that I don't rush into anything that may be triggering. "How many members are there?"

"Five hundred, with a waitlist of roughly twelve hundred."

"Seriously?" I ask, astonished by the high count.

Fabienne hums. "Nearly half of our members are not local to New Orleans. Same with most of the waitlist. We're a… destination."

"It's why we want to expand," Jasmine confirms. If they had something similar to this in a handful of large cities, it could be extremely lucrative.

"This floor is basically one big orgy waiting to happen," Fabienne says when we reach the second floor via a set of stairs. The room is huge and open, with the largest sunken bed you could imagine. It takes up most of the room, the perimeter is lined with banquets draped in pillows and cushions. The walls and ceiling are covered with antique mirror panels, no matter where you are in the room, you'll have a view. Fabienne points to the far end. "Over there are the restrooms and showers. This is where most clients congregate after leaving the salon."

One more flight of stairs takes us to three small rooms.

"You may have noticed the mirrors in each of our offices," Jasmine says to me, I nod that I did. "They aren't normal mirrors, dear. They're a looking glass straight into these rooms. Each must be reserved. You'll control the middle room. If you don't want it used at all, that's up to you. You can block it out entirely, or only approve the reservations you see fit. Oscar was the biggest voyeur I ever knew, he spent most nights in his office, just watching."

"What makes these rooms so sought after?"

"They're the only private rooms in the place," Fabienne says. "Well, semi-private, anyhow."

"I can't imagine ever using my mirror."

Jasmine and Fabienne smile conspiratorially, so at ease with the idea. As if it's a given that at some point, I'll be so integrated into this life that it won't be a big deal that people are copulating a thin wall away while I sit there crunching numbers and tracking stocks.

If I thought leaving the ranch would make my life less weird, I was so very wrong.

CHAPTER NINE

POPE

Lupus et Agnus has been closed for a month. The longest month of my depraved fucking life. The club has become a crutch for me, and I don't like being denied access to my favorite playground. Tonight is the grand re-opening under the new management of Fabienne Basquiat and Jasmine Parnell. Both incredible fucks from what I've heard. And seen.

I've never had the pleasure of sticking my cock in either woman's cunt. They're quite particular in their tastes. Fabienne says I'm far too old for her, Jasmine says I'm too young. I'm thirty-nine; I feel neither young nor old, but that's their business. We've played, however. *Touched and tasted.*

While Lucinda has kept my regulars in rotation these past few weeks, it's not the same as being here. Lupus et Agnus brings a sense of decadence that I crave, an edge of excitement I can't find with partners at my office or home.

Tonight, we celebrate with a masquerade. A stupid idea, if you ask me. However, I'll indulge the new owners in most anything since they're keeping this place open after Oscar retired.

As I punch my code into the pad by the front door, Sybil sidles up closer to me as if she's cold. She's not. She's fucking clingy. Sybil is up for anything, though, that's why she's my plus one tonight. Not her first time, though it may be her last as she's rubbing my very last nerve raw. Sybil knows what I like and has dressed appropriately, a silvery, strappy dress that I can tangle my fingers in. Her blonde hair is in a high, sleek pony that will be easily pulled. And her heels will put her ass at the perfect height for punishment or fucking. She dons a simple mask that covers her eyes and temples but not much else, she's too vain to keep much of anything covered.

To you has been given the mystery of the kingdom of... Sybil Winter.

"Did you reserve a third-floor room?"

"No."

"Too bad," she says, losing a bit of the excitement she showed on the drive here.

"You'll be sufficiently fucked regardless."

"I can't wait," she whispers in my ear.

"I didn't say by me." That brings on the pout that I love so much.

The hostess checks us both in, pressing the button to let us into the inner sanctum. Relief hits me directly. I sigh with it, relaxed for the first time in... years. Or so it feels. I head straight to the bar and order a bourbon for myself, champagne for Sybil. She's allowed only one. The rules of the club do not supersede mine and I take no chances that a woman will come back to me claiming I spanked her ass raw without consent. Besides everything she's signed for the club's protection, I've also made her sign a contract with me.

Whether or not it would ever stand up in courtroom has never been tested by anyone I'm acquainted with. The added layer is helpful, regardless. My father would be burning with shame if he knew that his son only fucks women who are under binding agreement.

Which only makes it more fucking fun.

The elder Mr. Blackwell is a good ole Southern Baptist preacher man. Christian to the bone in all his hate and hypocrisy. No doubt he's currently leading the charge of banning books and drag queens in the entire state of South Carolina. In the name of saving the children, all while he's armed with the knowledge that he beat his own children on a regular basis. He broke my jaw once. I was eleven.

He may have passed down some of his violent tendencies, but I'd never harm an innocent with the carelessness or abandon that he did.

"Mr. Blackwell?"

"Yes?" I answer to one of the club's employees, Micah.

"If you could spare a moment, your presence has been requested upstairs."

"For what purpose?"

"I'm not sure, Mr. Blackwell."

"Fine," I tell him. "Behave, Sybil. You're a guest, remember that."

"Yes, Sir."

"Lead the way, Micah."

Following him back out to the lobby, he enters the code to the stairway up to the offices but does not take the steps with me. The door closing behind brings a pressure in my chest that I don't recognize at first. Not apprehension, but not excitement either.

Fate leading me to my doom.

I was vetted for membership a decade ago and have only visited the offices a handful of times between then and now. Oscar would occasionally invite a member up to watch something he found especially titillating in the room on the other side of his office.

He was a curious figure. Well into his seventies, I'm unsure he's ever had sex himself. He prefers to watch from the darkness, hence all the black walls that used to hold this place up. They're gone now, in this hall anyhow. They're now covered in stark contrast.

Only one office door is open when I reach the landing. I knock and enter and quickly stop short as the woman sitting at the desk pops her head up to face me.

"Hello, Pope."

The sound of my name on her lips makes my blood rush. It's been five years since I threw her out of my house. Five years of no contact. Five years of keeping tabs on her as much as I could without her knowledge.

"Why are you here, Delilah?"

"I work here."

"Doing what?" I step to the opposite side of the desk, leaning over it and gripping the edge. I don't look but I'm sure my knuckles are as white as the newly painted walls.

"Making the club money. Or, trying to. Upstairs, here," she clarifies, sensing my distress. "I asked you up here to apologize. I tried reaching out to you after that night, but you never responded. When I saw your name check in, I took the opportunity. Perhaps it was heavy-handed of me, but I hope you'll forgive that as well."

Blinking away my anger, I take in the young woman in front of me. She's changed. Delilah never shied from being as direct with me as her shy personality could be, but the bravado she displays now is new. She's in control. It's sexy as fuck, which is something new for me. It's not at all what I look for in women. Quite the opposite really.

It was never my intention to cut her out of my life. In truth, I despised the idea of leaving her without someone to talk to about the faith-based questions she was having. It was a discussion I had with Noah's fist that made me see I was confusing her more than helping her. He didn't believe that I didn't encourage Delilah's... romantic attention.

I couldn't exactly argue with him, the man knows me too well.

She's changed in more ways than just attitude and maturity, though. The girl I first met the day of Noah's wedding never wore makeup and she let her hair fall around her face as a shield. Tonight, her hair is up and though she doesn't wear much, she has applied makeup to highlight her features. Delilah now looks more alive, vibrant in a way she could not have been in those early months away from the prison she grew up in. Her sable hair shines differently, her eyes are bright and not hidden behind hooded lashes, she sits tall and strong.

I can't wait to break her.

"You owe me nothing, Lamb. You never have."

The reaction I was hoping for is exactly what I get. Her nostrils flare at the moniker I know she hates. I give her kudos for tamping it down quickly, though.

"That's not at all true, Pope. I violated your home and your trust. It was wrong of me. Please trust that I'm not that same girl any longer."

I don't trust that at all. She's changed, of course, but I see the remnants of her innocence that still hang on her like Spanish moss. Delilah can try but she'll never be able to hide from me.

"Water under the bridge, Lamb."

"I'm not your pet, Pope," she says between tight lips. "Again, I'm not the same girl I was back then."

"Still pious?"

"Yes. But critical and honest with myself about my faith." Her chin rises in challenge.

"Good. And school? How was that?"

"Easier than expected for someone with the most basic of early educations." I knew this information already. Delilah was top of her class, a valedictorian candidate even.

"You're qualified for this position, then?"

"As much as I'm qualified for anything, I suppose," she says, annoyance back in her tone. "I'll follow you down."

She stands, allowing me a good look at what she's wearing. The top of her dress is unassuming with a high neckline and long sleeves. The dress is deceiving; it hugs her curvy hips and ass, flowing down to her calves. It's the slit that cuts up to her thigh that makes me move to block her path as she grabs a lace veil from the desk, ready to cover her face.

"No."

"Pardon me?"

"You will not be following me downstairs."

"Then you can follow me," she says, trying to step around me.

"Over my dead body, Delilah," I say, grabbing her elbow and leading her back further into her office. "You said you work up here."

"I have to learn the business, Pope." She scoffs. "This is my first opportunity to do so."

"No, Delilah. Not dressed like this, and not when the place is packed with people ready to fuck."

"Exactly why I need to be down there," she replies as confidently as she can manage, but I hear the waver. "Now please get out of my way so I can go do my job."

"After everything I've fucking done," I rage, catching the words and shutting them down. "You *will* stay up here."

Delilah flushes with her anger, her pale cheeks reddening with it.

Fucking exquisite. I wonder if her ass would turn the same shade from my palm.

"You just said I owe you nothing. You were adamant that my education was a gift. What have you done for me that makes you think I should listen to you instead of doing my job?"

I broke a boy's leg for touching you when you didn't want it. I made that shit of a boyfriend flee the state before he could sink his creepy little claws into you.

Of course I say neither. Nor do I tell her any of the other ways I've looked out for her wellbeing. All for her to end up here, in a den of goddamned vipers.

Like me.

"You don't understand what happens here. You couldn't possibly."

"I understand enough, the rest I'll learn when you move out of my way," she says with an annoyed roll of her eyes. "You don't have a say over me, Pope. Move, or I'll call Fabienne."

She knows exactly who would be most willing to kick me out of this place.

"You do not speak to any of the men. And you most certainly do not participate in anything. The people here won't fuck you the same way your silly little boyfriends have," I say, stepping so close to her that I smell the strawberry of her hair. She hasn't changed her shampoo in all these years. My dick practically weeps from missing it. Delilah doesn't shy away though, instead she tips her chin up even higher.

"I do what I want, Pope."

Not if I have anything to fucking say about it, you defiant little shit.

"That veil doesn't come off, or so help me I'll take you over my knee." Delilah lets out a soft gasp and her lashes flutter rapidly. "Say you understand."

"I understand," she breathes, agreeing as if it's the most natural thing to do.

"Good girl." She doesn't move, so I don't either as I stare down at her red heart-shaped mouth. I want it. I want to take it and more. "Let's go."

Delilah isn't meant for me. No matter how much fun I'd have with her. Her future holds marriage, family, *monogamy*. All things I've never considered for myself.

Shifting, I let her lead the way out of her office and down the stairs. Her ample ass teases me the whole way. Gone is the waifish body she arrived in this city with. Even as covered as she is, she's going to bring this lot of degenerates to their motherfucking knees.

Taking a hard breath and cracking my neck, I prepare for what's to come as we step through the door into the salon.

CHAPTER TEN

If I thought I was prepared to see Pope, to speak to him, I was wrong. So, so wrong. It's been long enough that I should be over my schoolgirl crush on the man, but he's more handsome than ever. He wears his hair similar, maybe an inch or two shorter. He still tucks it behind his ears, and now, it gives me a clearer vision of the tattoo on his neck. I swear the darn thing's eyes follow me through the room.

As soon as we entered the salon, Pope disappeared to the far end of the room and I went to my position at the bar. I'm helping Martin, the bartender, for the first hour or two. By help, I mean observe. I rarely drink and when I do it's usually a glass of wine or a cheap beer. I know little about mixing drinks. But I can be helpful in other ways; keeping ice stocked, cutting lime wedges, and such.

I'm doing just that, slicing citrus, when the woman who's been on Pope's arm comes up to the bar. She's gorgeous, of course, from what I can see of her face behind the slim red mask she wears. Blonde, which must still be his preference.

"Mr. Blackwell would like another whiskey," she says to me.

Martin is currently speaking with another client, but I do know how to pour whiskey.

"Certainly, do you know his preference?"

"Of course I do. I wouldn't be any kind of girlfriend if I didn't. He likes the Green Spot."

Girlfriend rings in my ear. I don't know why I didn't expect him to have one. Why wouldn't he? The thought never crossed my mind, however. Not that it should matter. He may not see me as the shy virgin any longer, but he still sees me as a childish lamb who can't hold her own. There's no future for me and Pope. Only a past filled with tangled memories and bitter regrets.

"Green Spot," I repeat. "On the rocks?"

"Straight," the woman says as if the word alone is titillating, as if it turns her on.

I'm so out of my realm here.

"Will that be all, Miss…" I let the question drop, waiting for her to give me her name.

"Winter. Sybil Winter. Though I hope for it to be Blackwell before too long."

"Oh." I fumble with the bottle and look over to where Pope sits with a few other gentlemen. Every one of them has their eyes on me, hard to miss even through my stupid sheer veil. Pope's mouth forms a pleased smile, but his eyes are full of warning. For me? For Sybil? Maybe for everyone here, maybe sending this woman for his drink was some sort of test. "Well, that would be lovely."

Lie.

"It would," she says with a wide smile, reaching for the glass I've finally finished pouring two fingers into. "What was your name?"

"I'm Delilah."

Her smile morphs into a pout. She's still attractive with a frown, to my utter dismay.

Stop that.

Jealousy and pettiness are still unwelcome emotions. Neither come natural to me and they certainly are not becoming of a young Christian woman. But then again, I'm not working a job very becoming of a Christian either. I'll worry about that later, though. Right now, I need to focus on making it through the night. It won't be long before the door to the Voyeur's Garden and the upper floors are open.

Then Sybil and Pope will only be a portion of my problem. Fabienne and Jasmine taught me what to expect, I'm as prepared for it as I can be. Though there is no way to know how I will react when truly faced with it all. I only hope nothing triggers anything from my childhood. Therapy has gotten me far, but it also brought to the surface some memories I had been suppressing or had simply forgotten. There may be more of them hidden in the dark corners of my mind.

"You have a wonderful night, Ms. Winter. Please let us know if you need anything else."

Sybil grabs the glass, a small drop of amber sloshing out on the bar top in haste, before she walks briskly back to her boyfriend. Who is still staring at me, and only me. Brushing it off, I get back to my duties and meeting the other members in attendance tonight. It's a full house, many of our non-locals have come to celebrate with my boss ladies. Jasmine warned me it will get rowdy. I'm not sure what that means exactly, as I expect most evenings here are active and salacious.

Cookie tried to help me prepare for the night, which was hilarious because she's never been. It's a part of her parents' life that she never wants to be exposed to. Understandably. Children shouldn't be witness to their parents' sexual escapades. A lesson I learned the hard way at too early an age. Bradley is here to support Jasmine in her new business venture, but he's assured me that they won't be partaking in certain festivities tonight.

I've become something like a daughter to them and while Jasmine tutors me in anything I want the knowledge of, she also respects that there are boundaries due to my close friendship with Cookie and Fig.

Fig is Cookie's enigmatic brother. He, on the other hand, would have no qualms performing any sort of debauched act in front of me. Or with me, for that matter. He relentlessly flirts with me, but never pushes me past my comfort zone.

Three years my senior and infinitely more worldly, Fig has become a confidant. A friend who watches my back with the same fervor as his sister. Fig was my first kiss. Only because I asked him to teach me before my first date with Andrew, but still. I know I'm safe with him and that's worth its weight in gold.

He's brought a plus one tonight as well. Damian March, his best friend and partner in crime. They're practically attached at the hip. Opposites in so many ways; where Fig is smooth, Damian is hard edges. When Fig is boisterous and laughing, Damian can often be found almost sullen. But they balance each other well in their odd pairing.

They come to sit at the bar, Fig offering up a smile for me, so I move to serve them.

"Hey guys, what can I get you?"

"Waters, please. It's Dame's first time here, and I'd like to keep him sober enough to remember it," Fig says with a laugh. His friend shoves him, amusement in his eyes even if it does not reach his lips.

"If Damian gets wasted on three drinks, he's a bigger lightweight than me," I say on a laugh.

"That's exactly what I'm saying."

"Shut up, Fig. I'm not that bad," he says, turning to me. "I promise I can hold my liquor. I just don't drink much."

"I get it, I'm the same way."

"Are you doing okay?" Fig asks.

"So far, so good."

"It's not weird for you? Being here?" Damian asks with genuine curiosity. He's in graduate school for sociology, his focus on fanatical cults. Someday, he's going for a PhD. I'm like a shiny toy for him, but I don't mind that he peppers me with questions; it's grounding and helpful for me.

"Are you kidding?" I laugh. "It's beyond weird and the night has only just begun. But I'll get through it. It's a good job, great

pay, interesting work. I'm not one to pass any of those things up."
I set two bottles of water in front of them.

"Yeah, I can see that. You've said before that financial independence means more to you than almost anything."

"Yep. Keeping the flock dependent keeps them scared and in place. I'm not giving that kind of control up, ever. I can handle a sex club if it pays all my bills."

"Good for you, Delilah," Fig says with a nod.

"Thank you." I smile at him. "You two be good... or whatever." They both laugh at that and stand to leave the bar. But Fig pauses.

"He stares at you a lot, you know?"

"I think he's just protective." I shrug, knowing who he means. I've confided in Fig about the infatuation I used to have with Pope.

"So am I," he enunciates slowly. "If you need me, you holler."

"Noted. But I'll be fine."

Jasmine and Fabienne enter just then to a round of soft applause and loud well-wishes. The people outside of here may look at this place as sinful, but all I see in front of me is a community of support. Well, except for maybe Sybil who still pouts while she side-eyes me. Pope has his arm draped around her, possessively, so I don't know what she's so upset about.

Fabienne begins speaking about the refurbishing they've completed in the inner sanctum. Jasmine joins in to tell everyone about future plans. Not only for the club, but the charity foundation they've set up to help marginalized communities in New Orleans and the surrounding area.

"We'll hold a fundraiser each year, starting with a bachelor auction which we will send details on very soon." This is met with more applause and no small amount of laughter. When my bosses first told me of the idea, I was somewhat horrified by it resembling the bride market within the polygamist community.

The more they explained it, the less apprehensive I became. They both assured me it's all in good fun and the men of the club would support it wholeheartedly. Based on the reaction, I see they were right. Several men in my vicinity are already volunteering themselves.

"With that, my darlings," Fabienne says. "Welcome back to Lupus et Agnus. Enjoy!"

Bradley opens the door to the hallway, allowing members to start their trek inside. I stay put at the bar with Martin and the dozen or so clients not yet ready to move further inside.

"Are you on the menu tonight?" a deep voice asks to my right, where I find a broad man, perhaps in his late forties. A salting of hair on his otherwise dark head sprouts at his temples, and there are just the beginnings of age around his eyes. A handful of clients are without masks tonight, this man and Pope included. It wasn't a requirement, more suggestion to keep some air of mystery to the evening.

"N-no," I stammer. The man is handsome, almost intimidatingly so, but it's the direct stare that makes me fumble over the tiny word. "I'm working tonight."

"Oh, did I suggest there wouldn't be work involved?"

"Enough, Halston. She's not here to play," Pope interrupts the conversation. "Let the lady do her job."

"You used to be fun, Blackwell," the man says before walking off, sending me one last look.

"Water, please," Pope directs to me. "For future reference, I like my whiskey on the rocks."

"What?" I ask, annoyed. "Your girlfriend specified the opposite."

"Fucking Sybil," he mutters barely loud enough for me to hear.

"It doesn't matter. I'll remember if I'm ever back at the bar again." I sigh, handing him a bottle.

"Good," Pope says, then he, too, leaves through the door. I wonder if I'm ever going to gain enough courage to walk through it.

Half of me wants to witness what sexual freedom looks like.

How people interact with each other when it's not a burden, not forced or coerced. I want to witness women enjoying the experience just as much as their partners. There is a need for me to believe that exists.

On the other hand, I'm so utterly terrified of it all. My fingers tremble slightly at my side with my mixed emotions.

"Hey." Fig suddenly appears behind the bar next to me. His hand takes mine, soft but reassuring all the same. "I'll go with you when you're ready. If you want?"

"Did your mom put you up to that?" I ask, turning my face up to his.

"Not really. We did discuss keeping extra watch over you, but I would have done it anyway. Cookie would cut my balls off if I let you have a breakdown. And I'd never forgive myself anyway."

"I just don't know how I'll react. You know?"

"I understand. If something bothers you, we'll work through it, or I'll get you out of there. Okay?"

"You'll explain if I have questions?"

"You know I will. You're like a sister to me, kid. One I'd fuck, but still."

"Stop it!" I laugh and cover the full smile on his mouth with my hand. It skews his silly plague doctor half mask, making me laugh more. This is why Fig is good for me, he has helped me get comfortable with talk like this. When I first met him, I would have flushed at the word and the tease. That's not who I am anymore. "Okay, then," I say with a heavy inhale. "Let's go."

Fig doesn't release my hand as he leads me to the door out of the salon, Damian joining us before we go through.

"Not the White Room," I whisper.

"Got it," Fig responds, pulling me past the first room. Plenty of patrons linger in the hall, taking up their positions as spectators to the show. Many must have already made their way into the rooms or up the stairs, as it isn't overly crowded.

The two men flank me as we walk further, me surreptitiously peeking into the windows as we go. A woman is being strapped into the swing, several bodies tangle together in another room as they shed each other of their garments. The sounds of kissing and soft moans come from every direction. My chest hitches with anticipation, a neediness starting in belly. Desire and pleasure aren't so unfamiliar to me anymore. I recognize them for what they are, and they're difficult not to feel in a place where the air itself is heavy with sexual tension.

Fig's thumb rubs over my knuckles. I think he means it to be calming but it heightens my want to be touched on other parts of my body. If he were someone else, would I pull him into a room? Place his hands where I want them to be?

Could I be so bold? With the right man, I think I could. I think I *would*.

"What do I do with liars?" I stop at the voice coming from inside the next room. The door is ajar, making it easy to hear Pope pose his question.

"You punish them, Sir."

"Do you want to watch?" Fig asks next to me, and I realize I've stopped moving. I run my self-check, making sure I'm in control and aware. Then I nod. Damian and Fig move with me to the glass that will let me see into whatever scene Pope is playing out inside this room.

He stands in profile, a woman is kneeling at his feet. Not Sybil. She's across the room, the man from the bar with her. Halston, I remember the name Pope called him. He's buckling leather cuffs to her wrists. Her mask now gone, I see the consternation on her face, perhaps even a sadness in her eyes.

"That's right. What punishment do you hate the most?" Pope asks as Halston reaches for a bar on the ceiling with one hand and pulls up Sybil's arm with the other. He follows suit with her other arm so that she's attached securely to the ceiling. She raises on her toes to gain balance.

"When you deny me," she says, her voice sounding small.

"When I deny you what?"

"Your cock."

"Right. I think I'll give it to Sarah instead," he says, peering down at the woman at his feet. Sarah smiles up at him as she undoes Pope's pants. "If you behave well enough while Mr. Halston paddles you, perhaps he'll fuck you instead."

"Yes, Sir," Sybil says, the sadness finally showing itself.

"Can he do that?" I ask Fig. "Give her to someone else?"

"If she's given consent to it beforehand, yes. It's called consensual non-consent."

"It's quite common," Damian adds. "In lesser forms like this, and in more taboo ways. Like, when people want to play out a rape fantasy."

The gasp that escapes me isn't intentional.

"It's not something you ever have to witness, Delilah," Fig assures me. It's the mere thought that people want to role play such a thing that shocks me. I try not to judge others, it isn't fair for me to. Nor is it my place. But having witnessed rapes, it's... well, it's a lot to think about. "It's not something that happens here at the club."

Sarah releases Pope from his pants, her hands encircling his length with both hands as she moves them in slow rhythm from base to tip. I remember with great clarity the two times I saw him before. Yet I hold new appreciation for him now. There is no longer a skittish need in me to divert my eyes and I don't flashback to childhood memories.

I watch. With rapt attention.

"Take me in your mouth, Sarah. Halston is going to give you a swat every time Sarah gags or chokes, okay, Sybil?"

"Yes, sir," Sybil confirms.

"You'll think about your lies while you hang there."

"Yes, sir."

"Now, Sarah." Sarah opens her mouth wide. Without warning, Pope thrusts forward, instantly making her choke. A hard slap sounds and I bounce my eyes to the wood paddle Halston holds in his hand. The same continues for several moments, until Pope takes a step back to shed himself of his clothes. "You can play with yourself," he tells Sarah as she waits.

Her hand dives into her panties and her hips sway forward. Halston moves, drawing my attention as he, too, sheds his clothing. Pope steps back into my line of sight and I still. He's been fit since the day I knew him but he's more defined in a new way. I had noticed new tattoos on his left hand earlier, some simple symbols that I couldn't decipher. Now, I see another new addition.

Along his side, just above his hip, is a giant moth. It stretches to reach his back and lower abdomen in beautiful shades of browns, blues, and dark reds. I would have noticed it the first time I saw him naked, if he'd had it back then. Hope, or maybe vanity, wants me to believe it's symbolic of the conversation we had so many years ago.

Lay not up for yourselves treasures upon earth, where moth and rust doth corrupt, and where thieves breakthrough and steal.

Pope Blackwell, the corrupter.

"You ready?"

"Yes, sir," Sarah purrs. Pope steps closer to her, his hands tangling in her hair as begins pleasing himself with her mouth again. This time he's in full control of the tempo and the depth as Sarah's hands fold behind her back.

"Do you want to stay?" Fig's voice is barely a whisper in my ear. I nod instead of voicing my answer. Damian moves behind me, his breath tickling the length of my neck, causing a shiver to run down my spine.

"It's exciting, isn't it? Watching and wanting." Damian places a hand on my stomach, pulling me into his chest. I feel his hardness against my back. "You can imagine it's you. Feeling the pleasure, giving the same to your partner. But you get to see it all from this vantage."

"Yeah... yes."

"Do you see how Pope's muscles ripple with every thrust?" I nod, it's all I focus on. His magnificent body. "And how Sarah's getting so worked up she practically bounces on her knees? She wants his cock somewhere else. Lower. Inside where she can feel it giving her the same sensation he feels." Damian drags his nose up and down my throat as he speaks. My legs weaken and I'm thankful for the arm he still has wrapped around me.

"What do you want?" *For you to fuck me*, my mind answers the question Pope poses to Sarah. Her words mimic my thoughts.

"What do *you* want, Delilah?" Damian asks. Turning my face toward where his rests on my shoulder, I see Fig staring at us both. He's not upset or concerned. Rather, he looks curious. "Do you want to watch him fuck her? Or do you want to experience…"

"Something else," Fig finishes. "Something of your own, maybe."

Damian leans forward and presses a quick, but deep kiss to my mouth. It's amazing. Dizzying and the best thing I've ever experienced, but I know it's because I'm here and that it has more to do with being face-to-face with Pope again than anything else. Maybe that isn't fair to Damian. Maybe he doesn't care.

But I do.

When I raise my vision back to Pope, it's clear he cares too as he shoots daggers at me and the men at my side. I hadn't thought they could see out to us. Clearly, I was wrong. It's stupid of me to care what Pope thinks about my activities tonight. He's currently repositioning his partner so he can sink into her in other ways. His feelings about what I do don't matter.

Except they do. They do to me and that makes me angry and sad. It makes me want to rage and to wail because I should be stronger. Deep down, what I really want to cry about is that I want to be Sarah. I want to be worthy of Pope's attention.

"I think I've had enough for tonight," I say to the man in the room, yet only loud enough for Fig and Damian to hear.

CHAPTER ELEVEN

In the past week since the grand opening, I've witnessed everything my naïve mind could imagine. And then some. Each day I pushed myself a little further into the club. Eventually, I made it up to the second floor. Fig was with me again that night, keeping near along the wall while I spectated. He's been an almost constant fixture here. Some nights he hangs out with me, others he doesn't. A few times, he's booked a private room, careful to pick Fabienne's, not mine or Jasmine's. I've kept mine blacked out anyhow.

I don't know what he does when he's not schooling me, I don't seek that out as it's a line I don't think either of us are ready to cross.

Pope has been back every night I've been working. I've even checked the logs to be sure. I rarely catch glimpses of him, but his presence is felt regardless. As if he's always near and watching. It's both unnerving and comforting.

Damien is back tonight as well.

"Full membership?"

"Yes."

"Did Fig tell you the cost of membership?"

"Yes," he answers. "I'm already vetted, and Jasmine has

waived the waitlist for me. The only thing left is for me to pay you."

"Correct. I just want you to be sure. You're still in school."

"I'm sure. School is paid for. I know you don't know this, because it's not something I talk about. But I have more money than I can spend in my lifetime, Delilah. Let me in." He grins boyishly and goofily. It's so different than his normally quiet, unemotional way.

"I'm not barring you. This is a friendly discussion, Damian."

"Is that what we are? Friends?"

"You know more about me than most after so many hours of using me for your thesis. I'd go as far as calling us good friends."

"We could be so much more," he says with a dramatic sigh.

"Now you sound like Fig." I laugh.

"Where you're concerned, Fig and I agree."

"I don't even want to know what that means."

"You sure about that?"

"I'm sure, Romeo. Give me your credit card so I can kick you out of my office." Damian laughs now, too, handing me his card. I enter it into our system and give it back. "Go have fun."

"Come down and have a drink with me when you're done here," he says on his way out.

Damian's kiss plays reruns in my head often. The list of men I've kissed is short, making Damian's unexpected one even more memorable. It was a heat of the moment type of kiss, something he desired so much he couldn't resist. Or so I tell myself. Because believing that evokes powerful feelings in me.

As if I could be so wanted that a man couldn't help but fall at *my* feet.

With a past like mine, I'm not sure it's natural to dream of a happily ever full of picket fences, beautiful children, and a doting husband. And I don't wish for all those things. My fantasies are different. They aren't those bright hopes of childhood when you don't know any better, when you don't know the evil that exists in the world. I've known for too long, and it is that knowledge that has shaped me. Warped might be a better word.

Cookie sometimes calls me The Enigma. Partly because of the views I already have established. Partly because she never knows what new ones I'll settle on next. My mission of self-discovery since I met her has been a roller coaster for us both.

When I decide on something, I jump in fully. Like taking the jobs I have. The first being at Jasmine's talent agency, which in some ways isn't so different than the life I ran away from. Selling people for their beauty. And now I'm at a sex club.

The line between my old life and this one is thin and blurry. I believe that's why it's so easy for people like my father, and my uncle before him, to convert people into their way of life. If there weren't similarities between this world and his, it would be harder to entice people over.

Like I do every day before I head downstairs, I double check the list of everything I needed to accomplish during my office hours. I rely on lists to help keep me focused and on task. When I first started school, it was still easy to let my mind wander. Dr. Price helped me create tools to help with that. Though I don't need them much anymore, it's a habit now. And healthy habits are good. My to-do list is complete, so I check my email inbox one last time and shut down my computer at the same time a text message notification chimes on my cell phone.

FIG

Heading your way.

My guardian.

ME

I'm about to go downstairs. Damian is here.

FIG

Okay, see you in ten.

It's quiet in the salon when I enter, not surprising for a

Tuesday night. Attendance picks up on the weekend and any night there is a special event happening. But Lupus et Agnus is open seven nights a week for their clientele's convenience.

Damian sits by himself in a darkened corner booth. A glass waits on the table in front of him, so I grab myself water before accompanying him.

"Always hiding in the dark, Mr. March."

"We can't all be shining lights of this world, Delilah."

"I'm hardly that," I laugh.

"You don't have a shred of self-awareness, do you?"

"I like to think I do," I say, feeling the crease in my brow.

"Forgive me, I shouldn't have stated it so harshly. You know yourself very well in some ways. Your inner strengths and brains, for sure. But you don't have a fucking clue the effect you have on people."

"Good or bad?" I ask with honest curiosity.

"Good. Of course good," he says, setting his elbows on the table and leaning toward me. "You have an uncanny ability to encourage hopefulness with every shy smile. You are more thoughtful than anyone your age should be, you don't rush to words or opinions. And in case you never look in the mirror, you're more beautiful than most of the women in this city."

"Are you drunk?" I laugh.

"No. I'm honest. It's your whole style," he says, waving a hand my way. "You don't overdo it; you rarely have makeup on, and you don't flaunt your curves with teeny clothes. You keep it a mystery to us all. Even here." Damian raises an eyebrow and drags his gaze down over my chest.

Once again, I'm in a dress that covers my chest and shoulders. I'm accustomed to showing more legs, but I rarely wear anything less than short sleeves or anything low cut. New Orleans has so much rich food that I've fallen deeply in love with, I'm not a thin woman because of it. My abundant curves have added to the anxiousness I've always had about showing too much skin.

"You don't believe him?" a deep voice asks behind me.

"No," I answer both Damian and Pope without turning around. He must have come in right after me. I know he wasn't checked in before I came downstairs. I know because I check all too often.

"There isn't a man in this place that wouldn't jump at stripping you out of your clothes," he says dangerously close to the shell of my air. Steeling myself against a visual shiver, I clench my body tight.

Aside from you.

"Well, no one has attempted that yet."

"Careful what you wish for," Damian says with a devious smile.

"It's bound to happen sooner or later," I say, shrugging. "It's a sex club and I'm here more than I'm at home."

"A moment of your time, Delilah," Pope requests from behind my back.

"Of course, Mr. Blackwell." Standing, I turn to find his eyes narrowed on me as if I've angered him. "My office?"

"That won't be necessary." He palms my elbow and leads me through to the hallway, heading to the first door on our right.

"Not the White Room," I rush the words, and Pope instantly deviates course to across the hall to another empty room. He shuts the door behind, not turning on any light. Unseeing, I'm pressed up against the door and feel Pope closer to me than he's ever been before. His breath wafts over my face and tickles the hair at my neck.

"What's wrong with that room?"

"I don't like it."

"Why?" He presses even closer, and I raise my hands to his chest. A mistake because it takes effort not to drag them down over the hard muscles beneath them.

"It's a reminder of something unpleasant," I whisper.

"The Offering Room," he says. He remembers. It's stupid that I cling to that. I do it anyhow, liking that he listened when I spoke.

"Yes."

"One day, that place will burn to the ground."

"I hope you're right."

"Have faith," he says at my ear again.

"What did you need to speak to me about?" I ask him before I get carried away by his presence. Whatever Damian thinks about me, I have the same feelings toward Pope. He's still somehow a candle in the window showing me the way.

"I don't want you partaking in the pleasures of the club."

Pope delivers the words with such calm ease, almost as if it's just a casual thing to say. It's nothing of the sort.

"Your want is noted, Mr. Blackwell. I'll be sure to file it away with all the other suggestions made by members."

"Don't fucking push me, Delilah." His shoulders pull up, asserting a dominant stance as he stands so many inches above me.

"Or what?"

"Trust me when I say, you don't want to find out."

Oh, but I do.

I'd do so much for more of this man's attention; I'd push every boundary and walk down every dark alley.

"I've told you before, I'm not afraid of you, Pope," I say to the bristly skin below his chin.

"And I've told you, you damn well should." His hands come to my waist, and I have a quick flash of triumph. Except his touch is only to lift me out of the way of the door. Once clear, he flies through it. Leaving me to catch my racing thoughts.

Pope spins me in circles with every short encounter we have. I hardly know him, truly. Yet it feels like he carries a piece of me with him every time he steps away from me, leaving an emptiness inside until he's back in view.

He isn't even kind to me, that alone should be enough to kill my girlish crush. So why hasn't it died yet?

When I return to the salon, it's to find Pope having a discussion with Damian and Fig. Neither of my friends looks at all fazed by the imposing figure speaking what looks like angry words to them. He walks off as I approach, leaving me curious.

"What was that about?"

"I'm sure it was about the same thing he spoke to you about," Damian answers.

"Are you okay?"

"I'm fine, Fig. That's just Pope," I say with some exasperation.

"You don't mind it," Damian says quizzically, cocking his head to the side as he studies me.

"No."

"I think we have a brat in our presence," he says with a grin to Fig.

"You just said I was a light in this world," I complain. "Now I'm a brat?"

They just laugh, completely at my expense and incomprehension.

"Where to tonight, Delilah?" Fig asks me.

"Are you accompanying me instead of running off on your own?"

"I think I'd like to hang out with you tonight, yes," he says with a conspiratorial look at his best friend.

"To the second floor," Damian says before downing his drink and taking my hand to drag me behind him with Fig following. I don't know what they have planned but I won't argue. If I don't like something, I know I'm in control and can walk away. Not a small thing, nor something I take for granted.

I am in control of my life. Not my father. Not Pope. Not these two playful young men.

Me.

So, when they find another dim corner for us to lounge in, I don't fight it. Instead, I enjoy the attention they're paying me and the words they say quietly as they describe the scenes and bodies in front of us. Teaching me the way in which that man is pleasuring his partner with his mouth, telling me the techniques involved. Or the tricks this woman is using while she performs orally on the two men she's with.

Damian and Fig tune me into the small details, the ones they promise me matter the most.

I don't leave when Damian's hand finds my knee or when I realize it's slowly inching higher, taking the hem of my dress with it. I barely notice that I've been lifted and shifted so that I sit between Fig's widespread legs.

They both check in with me, regularly asking if I'm okay.

I feel better than I ever have.

Free.

"What do you want, Delilah?"

"To be touched," I answer Damian as I watch a man play with a woman.

"Where?" This time, it's Fig.

"Like that."

"Say the words, be clear. There can be no misunderstanding between us."

"Touch my pussy, Fig." For a moment, I'm surprised I'm not struck down. There are no flames licking at my heels. God isn't here to smite me for my sinful, sinful desires. I know that He can't. That He wouldn't because so much of what's in this room is in the Bible, too. I've read it and re-read it so many times, each with a clearer mind. A mind not full of sermons and other's interpretation. God knows I'm a good person even if I experience this type of pleasure.

"Fucking hell, that was hot," Damien mutters.

"You're sure?"

"Please, Fig." I arch back into him, spreading my own legs open another inch or two. Fig's hand finds my inner thigh, soft and gentle. I want something harder, but I'll take what he gives. A hand on my breast and a finger tickling the edge of my panties. No time is spent wondering what this does for my relationship with Fig, or Cookie for that matter. I only focus on how nice it all feels. When the finger dips under the edge, sliding against my sensitive fold, I audibly make my sensations known.

The soft light from the center of the room shuts off, and I blink up to the darkness. Except, the lights haven't been turned off; instead, a body stands in front of me, blotting it out.

Pope.

He doesn't give me a chance to speak a word as he hauls me off Fig's lap and over his own shoulder.

"I didn't even have the chance to taste her, Blackwell," Damien complains. Though I should be mortified by it, I laugh instead. Which only prompts Pope to grip tighter on my thighs as he stomps to the stairs, not stopping until we're up on the third floor.

"Code," he demands, setting me down between his large body and the closed door of the room that shares a wall with my office.

"What?" I say, somewhat dizzy from the blood rushing back to all the places it's meant to be.

"Type in the goddamned code, Delilah."

I do and the lock whirls open. Pope quickly pulls me inside and latches the door behind us. The room is set up like any number of hotel rooms around the world; king-size bed, nightstands on either side, large mirror on one wall. Simple, comfortable, efficient.

"What did I fucking tell you?"

"I don't have to listen to," I begin but can't finish because Pope shoves two fingers in my mouth, depressing my tongue with them before sliding out the smallest amount.

"I will not stand by while you get gangbanged in the corner." He spits the words with such venom. As if there weren't people having sex all over that room, some in groups. He didn't haul any of them up, in fact, I bet he watched them with entertained glee.

The argument doesn't come though, it can't with my mouth full. I stare up at him and suck his fingers like the woman sucked on the two penises downstairs. Back and forth, allowing them to get wetter and wetter. Swirling my tongue around the tips, like Fig described liking.

Pope's eyes glaze, and I rejoice.

"I'm going to punish you," he says, and I hum in agreement. His eyes narrow even more. "I told you not to push me. Hands on the bed."

Pope removes his fingers and takes a step back, allowing me to move to the bed. A tremble runs through me, but not in displeasure or fear. It's anticipation. It's the manifestation of so many years waiting for him to pay me this sort of attention.

The dress I wear is on the shorter side, falling above my knees, but still raised from Damian's and Fig's ministrations and Pope's manhandling. I don't fix it, opting to instead raise my ass higher in the air as I lean over to dig my fingers in the sheets of the bed. A part of me doesn't trust that this is happening, that Pope will follow through on his threat. If he's meant to walk away from me tonight, I'm determined to make it as hard as possible for him. He's disappeared before; I'm not prepared to have it happen again. I'll push myself past every obstacle and take him along with me.

CHAPTER TWELVE
POPE

C *rimson.*

It's the only thing I see as Delilah lifts onto her toes, the heels of her shoes slipping off the back. That fucking luscious ass teasing me to bite it. It took every ounce of control I have to not throw fists in Parnell's face for touching her the way he was.

I know Delilah isn't the innocent young thing she was when I first met her, but she isn't part of this world either. Tonight, I'm going to teach her why she shouldn't venture out of that office of hers.

"Was I unclear earlier?" I ask her, pushing her chest down and raising her chin with a hand on her throat.

"I'm not yours to boss around."

I deliver a swat to her ass. Not hard, just a warning to her fleshiest part.

"What was that?"

"I do what I want."

"And what you want," I say, leaning over her body so I can say the words quietly in her ear. So I can feel her body under my own, "is to be bare and fingered in a room full of people?"

"It's not your business, Pope," Delilah says, but her voice has changed. Defiance flees to make room for need.

"I'm making it my business, Lamb." I reach a hand between us, easily finding the side of her panties and ripping them free as she gasps in surprise. "Who's doing this to you, Delilah? Say my name."

"Pope."

"Good, just like that. Keep saying it. Every time you feel my hand on you, you say my fucking name." I pull myself off her and immediately feel the loss. Delilah does things to me no woman has done before. She's dangerous. Yet too alluring to walk away from. Bringing her panties to my face, I indulge myself in the scent before I toss them next to her face. "Is that for me or for Fig?"

"Both."

Fucking brat.

Kneeling, I remove her shoes, setting them neatly aside as she digs her toes into the plush rug under her feet. Starting at her ankle, I slowly walk my fingers up the back of her leg, feeling every anticipated shiver she can't control.

"Pope," she whispers shakily. When I get to her now bare ass, I pull it apart just enough to drag my nose through her scent again. Delilah rewards me with the longest muffled moan, which I immediately follow up with another swat to her ass.

She flinches away, and I pause to see what she'll do next. What wins, fear or something else?

"What's my name, Delilah?"

"Pope," she whimpers.

"Who am I?"

"Pope." This time, I hear the strength she's had all night, and she shifts back into the position I placed her in.

"Why am I punishing you?" I ask her with another palm to her ass, this time the opposite side.

"I didn't do what you wanted."

Over and over, I deliver more and more. Each time she calls my name and rights her position again. There is no complaint, no cry, no plea to stop.

She is perfect in her punishment. Delilah is a wet dream in flesh and blood. I keep at it until both cheeks are the same pretty pink as her blush used to be. Her thighs shake with fatigue and her fists bunch into the sheets of the bed. She's spent and it's fucking gorgeous.

I pick her up gently and lay her on her stomach across the bed. Opening the bedside table, I find the arnica gel packets that are always stocked here amongst the variety of other toys and aftercare items.

"How do you feel?" I ask her while I warm the gel between my hands. Her system is already shocked, no need to add to it with cold cream.

"I'm okay," she says after a moment, brushing the hair off her face so she can watch me.

"I'm going to put this gel on you. It will help with the discomfort." I begin to rub it on the red blotches. I wasn't hard on her, but this is her first time. Or... "Has anyone done this to you before?"

"You know my father has; we've discussed that."

"That's not what I meant," I say through tight lips. If it's with my last dying breath, I will see that man bleeding out so I can bathe in his fucking blood.

"You mean for fun?" she asks with a devilish grin. "No."

"Was this fun for you?" I massage the gel deeper in.

"It still is." She still gets the small crease between her dark brows when she's calculating something.

"We're done," I say, removing my hands from her, though it takes effort when all I want is more of her under my fingers.

"That's it?" She sits up and winces when something other than air hits her ass. "You're just going to spank me, then leave? You're incredulous."

"You're overreacting," I say, sternly. "We're done with the arnica."

Her mouth shuts quickly and tightly, and I raise a brow at her while I toe off my shoes so I can move on to the bed with her. I lean against the headboard and adjust the pillows to my liking.

"Come here, Delilah." She's been watching me, wordlessly and unmoving, but at the command, she crawls toward me. I hold my arms out to my sides, letting her take whatever position she's comfortable with. She chooses to curl up on her side, her head resting on my shoulder allowing me to smell her strawberry hair. "How are you?"

"I'm okay, that wasn't a lie." Her voice has lost its stubbornness, and she sounds content. I don't trust that, though. Not with a past like hers.

"Have you had any problems working here? Other than the white room."

"Is this a therapy session?"

"It's called aftercare. We don't leave this room until I know you've come down from any euphoria or adrenaline rush that I induced. Until I know that you're clear on what happened here, and why." I brush the hair away from her cheek, wrapping a strand around my finger.

"But you weren't asking me about what happened in this room. Quid pro quo?"

"Question for question? You really are a brat." I laugh.

"First question. Why does everyone keep calling me that?"

"I asked first," I remind her.

"No, nothing else bothers me. I just stay away from that room and I'm good to go," she says with a shrug. "Now you."

"In this world, a brat is a submissive that is willfully defiant or disobedient."

"Then, are they really a submissive?"

"Yes, you can be submissive and purposefully naughty. You can be a submissive and a masochist, so you act out to for that purpose. I wouldn't consider much in the lifestyle as finite."

Delilah plays with the top button of my dress shirt. I don't push the conversation as I had in the past with her. She's older now, wiser, more capable of coming to conclusions on her own without prompt.

"Are you a sadist or a dominant? Or both?"

"I'm a bit of both, also neither. Not fully, anyway. I like to be in control of certain things, but it's not widespread. And while I don't have a desire to deal pain, I do like it on occasion." She unbuttons my shirt now, only the top two, but it's enough for her to rest her cheek on my skin.

There's an edge here, one I stand on with unbalance. One side leads to salvation for us both, the other is much more appealing. It's always been like this with her, not as easy to deny myself now though. Not with her constantly tempting me here.

"Have you continued with your therapy?" I rub my hands softly on her back, it's not where they want to be. I haven't had my willpower tested this thoroughly… well, maybe ever.

"Yes, so I don't need you to psychoanalyze me too. I'm of sound mind; a fully functioning, healthy adult," she says, dragging her words up the column of my neck. "What did you get out of spanking me, Pope?"

My hands on your body, finally.

"I got you away from boys that would rather defile you in front of others than correct your behavior," I say, frowning at her.

"That's it?" She sits up, straddling me so we come face-to-face. "You only wanted to teach me a lesson?"

"Yes," I say, but she shifts her hips enough for us both to notice how hard my cock is. She's a fucking minx, a goddamned siren moving on me like that while innocence still plays in the depths of her eyes.

"You didn't want to touch me?" she asks while she pulls her dress over her head. I didn't anticipate this; I wonder if I had, if I would have stopped her. Not likely, but I should, because she shouldn't be on this bed with me, bare cunt and barely covered tits. *"How much soever she glorified herself, and waxed wanton, so much give her of torment and mourning: for she saith in her heart, I sit a queen."*

"Are you asking me for more punishment?" She quotes Revelations with the ease of anyone giving sermon. Like my father, like me.

If she were nearly any other woman, I'd consider her my match. My other fucking half.

"No, Pope," she says, reaching behind her to unfasten her small lace bralette. "You gave that to me already. I'm asking for the sinful pleasure that should have proceeded it."

Digging my fingers into her scalp, I fist her hair and pull her face closer to mine. Eye to eye.

"I don't play by your Bible's rules, Lamb. You get pleasure when you have fucking earned it. Not before."

"Was I not good enough?" she asks from a pouty mouth, but this time, she isn't playing. I see how disappointed she is in herself.

Everything Noah accused me of plays through my mind. Delilah was trained to be this way. Groomed from the day she was born to be submissive to men in all ways. There isn't a way to know if she's here, wanting to please me, because it's nature or nurture. Would she be so impeccable if she hadn't been taught to be by her father? Would this have been a lifestyle that appealed to her at all? Likely not.

Would she have set her intentions on me if I didn't have so many of the same characteristics as those who brought her up? Again, likely not. It's a debate I hold with myself every time I see her. Neither side of it ever wins.

If I tell her the truth, that she was perfect, she'll expect her reward. If I lie, will she crave it time and time again until she believes she's perfected it? I suspect she would.

Both scenarios are rewarding for me. And again, I'm reminded of Noah, who I made promises to. Namely to not be selfish in my dealings with Delilah. A vow I've already broken by bringing her into this room at all. I won't apologize for that, not when she was walking the path she was on with Parnell and March.

"You were perfect," I finally say, resting my brow on hers. "But we aren't meant for each other, Delilah. Not that way. I can't be your father figure, your savior, or your lover."

CHAPTER THIRTEEN

Pope left me after those parting words. Immediately upon his departure, Fig rushed into the room. Seems he'd been waiting in the hall in case things became too intense for me. He found me sitting on the bed, naked and stunned. Then, in only the way Fig can, he made me laugh while he helped me pull my dress back over my head.

That's when the anger set in.

I never asked Pope to be a father figure or a savior. Maybe, a long time back, I treated him as if he could be the latter. But I never asked for it, and I certainly haven't asked for it now. The lover part, that I can't deny. That is my shame to carry. His is hauling me up to that room in the first place. His is thinking he could lay hands on me for what he needed and not expect me to have needs in return.

Pope can deny it all he wants, but I know the way he looks at me. I know how hard I made him tonight. I *know*. He wants me as much as I want him. More, even. I'm not the one showing up at his workplace to watch him every day, after all.

I let out a long, frustrated groan and Cookie sets a glass of wine on the coffee table in front of me. After I was dressed again, Fig brought me home. She takes a seat next to me, pulling the throw blanket off the back of the couch and placing it over our laps.

"What happened?"

"Pope Blackwell," I mutter, then take a large swallow of the red liquid.

"What did he do?"

I explain the whole sordid evening, not leaving out the details that include her brother.

"I'll scrub the image of Fig's hands on your lady bits from my memory later. With all the bleach I can find," she says, dramatically. "Did you have any flashbacks?"

"No, I didn't at all. Every time he touched me, Pope made me say his name. It kept me firmly in the room with him, my head didn't wander at all."

"Well, that's good. Did you like it?"

"Yes! So much, I wasn't anxious at all. It was exhilarating, Cookie."

"I'm still having a hard time believing you stripped down naked for him. And I'm pissed on your behalf that you didn't get off." Cookie laughs. "Remember how it took you weeks to even kiss Andrew?"

"Andrew isn't Pope."

"Right," she says, her eyes flitting between mine as she tries to work something out. "What is it about him, Delilah?"

"You think I have Daddy issues, too?"

"Of course, you do. Your dad is like the devil incarnate, or whatever. I'm not suggesting that you're drawn to him because of that. I'm suggesting that maybe you don't know that much about him at all."

"I know," I sigh and throw my head back onto the armrest. "I'm being a stupid girl. But I can't deny what he makes me want or how he makes me feel."

"How?"

"Safe, Cookie. And free, like I'm only able to do what I want when I'm with him. Which sounds dumb since he's so controlling.

But it's like, when he's near, I have the courage to do all the things I really want to."

"Because he's there to catch you if you fall," she says, and I nod. "Except he hasn't, has he?"

"You should be a shrink, not a nurse."

"I'd work better hours if I was," she says, and we laugh. Her schedule is brutal, but she loves it. "You know I'm not judging you. I'm proud of how far out of your shell you've come. And that you're making decisions for you. But I'm never not going to be protective of that girl I first met who still lives buried deep inside of you."

The girl that didn't understand the conversations that she heard all around her. She'd never been kissed, never touched by anyone with the intent to give pleasure more than receive. Honestly, I don't think Andrew ever touched me with that in mind either; he gave but not as much as I gave him.

"Is it me?"

"Is what you?"

"Do I encourage men to take what they want from me without thought of my desires, or even wellbeing?"

"Of course not," she says, her anger seeping in. Something rarely seen from her. Cookie is nearly always calm and levelheaded.

"Maybe this was God punishing me for my sexual immorality."

"Shut the fuck up," Cookie says, real mad now. "You are not immoral. Besides, doesn't the Bible say something about delighting in the Lord to receive your heart's desires? After everything you've been through, you haven't given up your faith, where's your damn reward?"

"I don't think it meant desires like orgies at sex clubs."

"You don't know that. The Old Testament is dirtier than anything that happens at Lupus et Agnus."

"You're probably right," I agree. I'm not as well-versed in that translation, but the Cleric never limited himself to any single edition. He cherry picked the verses from the books that best suited him in whatever endeavor he was hoping to achieve.

"So, what are you going to do? It's not like he's just going to up and quit the club."

What *am* I going to do about Pope Blackwell?

"Not a thing, just like I'd been doing before tonight. I put myself out there, he rejected the idea," I say. It hurts more than I would have expected. I've never experienced anything like heartbreak. This isn't what that is, I'm smart enough to know that. But it's something painful all the same. "I'll leave him to his life."

"But will he leave you to yours?" Cookie asks sardonically.

Great question.

Two weeks later and the answer is clear.

No, Pope will not be leaving me alone to live my life. Each evening I'm at work, so is he. Checking the guest logs reveal he doesn't come when I'm not here. He hasn't tried to speak to me and there's been no more hauling me off to private rooms. Though, I've hardly had time downstairs past the salon.

The details of the first charity event, a bachelor's auction, have been taking up all my spare time. When I was downstairs, he was there watching. Typically occupied with any number of random blonde women.

That too keeps me from lingering too long.

But it's Saturday night, our busiest of the week. I'm done hiding away doing busy work. I'm ready to get into some trouble.

Cookie and I went on another shopping spree. I was fed up with Pope's antics and came up with a plan. One that requires another push at my own defenses. I've never worn a dress to work that falls too far above my knees, never bared my shoulders, my midriff, or my cleavage.

Tonight, I bare a lot in a metallic, one shoulder mini with a cutout on the side. For how much it cost me, I should look less like someone held shiny, sheer silk out and let me twirl myself into it. Regardless, I feel more powerful than I ever have before. No wonder women dress like this regularly. I've been so concerned with staying unnoticed I had no clue.

Off duty for the day, I shut down everything in my office and head downstairs, saying hi to Hattie, the receptionist on duty tonight.

"Wow," Hattie says with a whistle. "Looking like pure fucking fire tonight, Boss Lady. He checked in about twenty minutes ago."

"Thanks, Hattie." She's closer to my age than any of the other staff and we've become friends. While I have not told her the details, she's aware enough to notice there is a past of sorts between me and the notorious Mr. Blackwell.

"You got it, Delilah. If you need help tying him up so you can trip and fall on his dick, I'm your gal." She winks and hits the button that automatically opens the door for me to enter.

"You're bad." I laugh, walking through it.

"In all the best ways." I hear her sing before the door shuts behind me.

If my life were a movie, this would be the part where the music stops, all conversation ends, and every head turns my way to witness the birth of the new and improved Delilah Simms. I don't feel new, though. I'm the same woman I've always been somewhere inside. The improvement is that I'm not hiding her anymore.

During my session with Dr. Price last week, I filled her in on my last encounter with Pope. She asked how I felt about it after. When I said that later that night at home I had a moment of shame, she told me something that stuck.

"Shame is the brother of fear. I've never known you to be afraid, Delilah."

"You're looking fierce tonight, my darling," Fabienne says, stepping up beside me. "Does this have anything to do with Mr. Blackwell?"

The woman sees and knows everything, I swear it.

"No, ma'am. It has to do with me."

"Bravo, Delilah. If I teach you anything, it's this; never make a man your main reason for anything."

"I take a small amount of offense to that," Paul, her partner, says.

"Of course, you do, dear." Fabienne laughs, pulling Paul away toward the bar. "Enjoy your night, Delilah. I'll be here if you need anything."

Paul is much younger than Fabienne, thirty to her sixty something. They've been together for over a decade and have a relationship I admire. It doesn't fit the societal norms, they don't fit into any box, and they're proud of how they've made it work. With a strong mutual respect, communication, and a deep love for one another.

Glancing around the room, I don't see Fig or Damian, though I know they're here. I don't see Pope either. Making my way to the inner rooms, I greet several of the members I've become acquainted with these past weeks. Many smile at me in knowing ways, and one woman winks. I'm beginning to think everyone knew this night was coming.

Delilah's metamorphosis.

Whatever it is, I'm ready as I leave the salon. Somewhere in here, I'll find Pope in some form of pleasurable state with a blonde woman. Or three. It doesn't take any time at all to find his hiding spot tonight. He's in the white room, sitting with his back against the headboard, his shirt unbuttoned only at the top. A nude woman with mink colored hair sits atop his lap, grinding on him. His pants are still on, and from this angle, I can't tell if they're undone, but the way she moves and moans tells me they are. The all too familiar scene makes my stomach drop. This room, of all the places this club holds, is where he chose to inflict this pain. I want to rage at Pope giving this woman exactly what he so easily denied me.

I don't know how to rage, though. It's not an emotion I've ever held in my possession. Anger is even difficult for me to muster most days. I'm very much feeling it right now, but I can't channel it into something that allows me to walk through that door and lay it all at Pope's feet.

Besides, him recreating this way tells me things about him. It screams he wanted it as much as I did. More, even, because he sought out a woman he could pretend was me. She's filler, a stand in for what he was too cowardly to take for himself.

Pope makes eye contact with me through the window, his face visible over the woman's shoulder. I know he can see me when my smile grows, and his eyes narrow on it.

Yes, I see you, Pope. *Game on.*

I head straight up the stairs and to the corner my guys usually end up in. Sure enough, they're there. Damian's inked chest is on display under his open shirt, arms thrown over the upholstered bench seating as he watches Fig's interaction with a woman I've seen here regularly. Shanna, if memory serves. She's one of Pope's blonde playthings.

"Do you want to do more than watch tonight?" I ask Damian, stepping between his widespread legs. He blinks up at me, letting some of his lustful daze fade, only to reignite when he takes me in.

"Holy fuck," he mutters.

"Is that a yes?"

"What are you offering, Delilah?"

"Teach me how you like your dick sucked." I'm sure my cheeks are flushed; I can feel the heat of them. Saying words like that are not something I'm accustomed to. The act isn't new to me, it's one of the things Andrew and I did together. That, and the tips I've learned here, should put me in a decent position to get Damian off.

I hope.

Damian's head tilts, observing me for a moment before he reaches for a cushion and drops it at my feet. Holding a hand up to me, he helps me while I get comfortable on my knees.

"Delilah?" Fig calls from behind me.

"I want this, Fig. I want Damian in my mouth. Now."

"Jesus fucking Christ," Fig mutters as Damian smiles proudly at me.

"I don't know what's gotten into you," Damian says, "but it looks good on you."

"The dress?" I ask, looking down.

"No, love. The attitude." He kisses me then, heated and forceful with his fingers under my chin. My hands reach for his waist, pulling the shirt out of his waistband before I begin unfastening him. Our tongues duel, his tasting like cinnamon.

Getting his fly down, I reach a hand in to find no further barrier, just smooth skin. Hard and ready.

"This won't be like that nice boyfriend you had," he says the words into my mouth.

"I didn't ask for nice, Damian."

"Say my name again, I like it."

"Let me taste you now, Damian," I whisper to him, feeling the precum bead at his tip. I rub my thumb through it, then bring it to my mouth to lick it clean. Damian, too, licks at it, sending heat through every vein I have. Everything else fades away. All I see are his bright eyes, all I hear is the pounding of my own blood.

Damian has always been appealing; mysterious and edgy. There's never been romantic feelings between us, but sexual tension isn't lacking at all tonight. Maybe that's spurred by my determination and hurt, or maybe it's just about damned time.

I won't spend any more time questioning it. I want this and that's all that matters.

"You'll tell me if I do something wrong?"

"Sure, but I don't see how you could."

"I'm not that experienced," I admit.

"I know, Delilah. So, I'll go a little easy on you," he says with a grin that says otherwise. Pushing him back into the seating, I get my first good look at him. He's a little longer than Andrew and fills my hands more. "Start at the base, lick your way up."

I do it slowly, savoring his scent and how the slightly salty taste mixes with the spiciness from the kiss. Keeping one hand around his girth, I move the other to fondle lower. All while peering up at him through lowered lashes. Damian's stomach clenches but the sound he makes lets me know it's in pleasure, not discomfort.

"Again."

Starting lower this time, I run my tongue around my fingers, then trail up his length. When I get to the tip, I swirl my tongue around it before taking it in my mouth. A hum finds its own way out. Damian's appreciation shows when his hips push up into my mouth. His hands come to my head, one on either side and his thumbs brushing gently over each cheek.

"Right there, love. Be noisy, gag on it. Okay?"

I nod and let Damian take the lead. He was right, it's nothing like it was with Andrew whose movements were all subtle and he didn't take any control. For him, it was my job to please him to the end, my job to do all the work. Damian takes what he wants, how he wants it.

Yet, I don't feel used. He doesn't break eye contact ever and doesn't stop moving his fingers over my face in a gentle, almost reverent way. He's treating me like I'm the most precious person in this place. As if he's not giving me as much as I'm giving him.

He might not know, but with each time I swallow him down, I grow stronger. More confident and more controlled. I'm not being debased, I'm being enriched.

"Fig's going to take care of you with his mouth, okay?"

I hum again, nodding as much as I can within the confines of his hands. Fig scoots close behind me, running fingers down my sides to the hem of my dress which he pulls up over my hips.

"I'm going to lie and you're going to lower on to my mouth. But you don't take your attention off Damian."

"Mmhmm."

The heat at my back disappears and only a moment later I feel the tickle of Fig's hair against my inner thighs. Fingers pull my lace panties to the side.

"Lower." I do and then lose my mind, not even sure who made the demand. Fig wastes no time as a finger pulls me open and his tongue plunges in. My core tightens. I want to cry at how the sensation travels through every limb at once.

"Feel it, Delilah. Listen to your body, fuck Fig's face while you choke me down."

My body does what it wants, finding the movements that feel the best. Hips swaying forward with each lick of Fig's tongue. The closer I get to the edge, the farther I push on to Damian's dick and the more natural it all feels.

I exist in this moment alone.

Fig reaches up, pulling the dress down to bare my breast so he can massage and pull at it. I lean into his hand, the movement dragging my clit in such a way that it sends a shock through me. I shake with it.

"You're close," Damian says, picking up pace. "Finish her off, Fig."

Fig's hand leaves my breast, moving lower. Fingers join his mouth, plunging in while he sucks. It gets harder and harder to catch my breath, my chest pounding so hard as the adrenaline and anticipation escalate me higher.

"Fuck, Delilah," Damian curses, his eyes still boring into my own. "You're so fucking good."

I break over his words, the praise and appreciation of them. Everything they're doing to me feels amazing but it's the knowledge that I'm giving him the same thing that sends me soaring over the cliff of an orgasm. In a rush, Damian stands, pulling out of my mouth. I scream with the loss, but it's forgotten within my own climax. He still has a hand on my head that I grasp it, tangling my fingers with his to tether my soul to my body. His other hand works himself up and down.

"Open that mouth for me, Delilah," Damian says, voice hoarse.

As soon as my tongue starts to poke out of my mouth, he

explodes on it. More than I can contain, some drips down my chin and to my breast.

"Gorgeous," Fig says. I hadn't realized he'd even moved, but he's at my back again, a hand rubbing Damian's remnants into my skin.

"You are nothing less than exquisite when you come," Damian says, trying to find his own breath. He tucks himself back into his pants, partially zipping his fly, then squatting down in front of me. "How do you feel?"

"Amazing," I gasp. "Is it always supposed to be that way?"

"Yes," Fig says, his chin dropping to my shoulder. "I'm sorry it's taken you this long to experience it."

Damian pulls my dress back over my hips. Before covering my breast back up, he presses a small kiss to it.

"It will be better for you now that you know what it can be like. You won't settle for anything less." Both men rise, pulling me up with them so we can settle back on the seating.

That's when I see Pope. Just as I find a comfortable spot, safely cocooned between my friends, Pope's large figure comes into focus from across the room. Fabienne stands with him, her back facing me, she has a restraining hand on Pope's shoulder as he glares my way.

"I forgot there were others here," I say, almost embarrassed at how easily I was able to tune everything out. There was no self-conscious, doubt, no worry. Most importantly, there were no thoughts of Pope. Just me, just Damian and Fig and the pleasure we gave each other.

"Again, that's how it should be," Fig says, wrapping an arm around my shoulder and pulling me closer.

Fabienne turns to give me a knowing smile before she disappears, and Pope takes the first step toward me. There's danger in his eyes, but like always, he doesn't scare me.

CHAPTER FOURTEEN

"How's work?" Noah asks.

It's been a month since my night with Damian and Fig. Everything changed after that. Sure, Pope still watches me constantly and I've twice more found him having sex with the brunette. But never in the white room.

I still play on Saturday nights. Only with Damian and Fig and only with mouths and hands. That hasn't escalated, despite the guys' willingness to.

Pope still watches that, too. But he doesn't haul me off afterward anymore.

"It's going well. The initial investments I made are showing stable returns and we've been able to cut some fluff expenditures that the previous owner indulged in."

Lorelai called family dinner tonight. She had an announcement she wanted to make. None of us had the heart to tell her we already knew she was pregnant again. Instead, we pretended to be surprised. Our excitement is genuine though, she's a great mother.

"Get lost, sucker!" Olivia yells at the television in the next room. She's playing a video game where she's a survivor trying to escape killers from horror movies, a love she's gotten from

Lorelai. Olivia's probably too young for the game by societal standards, but she isn't exactly the typical ten year old.

I remember the day she was born. Everyone thought Martha was past her childbearing years. She was revered by the congregation as one of Cleric's most cherished wives because she'd given birth to the daughter he'd coveted the most and had lost. The tale of Lorelai, or Abigail as she was known there, was a fable told to scare us all about how the Gentiles outside of the ranch wanted to steal away everything we held most precious. They'd take us away and sacrifice us to the evil sinners in the world and we'd never reunite with our families in the Kingdom of Heaven.

So, when Olivia was born with the same molten steel eyes and hair like frosted wheat, the Cleric was once again enamored. Olivia was trained from birth until the day she was ferried off the ranch, still a toddler, to be the perfect homemaking wife. Because of her worth to her father, she would have been priceless as a bride.

She is priceless; intelligent, fun loving, and incredibly kind. The biggest blessing I've ever witnessed was her escape from the ranch so she can be all those things and more, on her own terms.

"That's good, you should be proud," Noah says, rolling his eyes at Livi's trash talking. "What about the rest?"

"It's okay, Noah. I've found my comfort zone." Before Lorelai came back into his life, Noah was a member of Lupus et Agnus. It's how he met Pope. Also, it's where he met Fabienne, the only other woman he's ever had a relationship with. They were together for a few years. Noah said it was a very open relationship.

It sounded a lot like polygamy when he first explained it, so we had a long discussion about the difference between that and polyamory.

"And Pope?" Noah is aware of the girlish crush I had on Pope; he knows it was a concern of mine when I took the job. I don't know how much else he knows, but I'm sure it's a lot. Noah seems to know everything all the time.

"He leaves me alone, mostly."

"Don't lie to me," he says.

"Fine," I sigh with an eyeroll of my own. "He watches me but doesn't speak to me. Not anymore. Not since he said he couldn't be anything to me."

"What do you want him to be to you?"

"A friend, at least. I miss talking to him."

"At least?" Noah prompts, letting me know he's not letting me out of this conversation so easily.

"My reaction to him hasn't changed," I say, falling back into the corner of the sofa dramatically. "I can't explain it, but he's always in the back of my mind. Like the other day, I got a statement for one of our accounts and the profits were better than expected. It's Pope I wanted to share that with first. Not Jasmine and Fabienne."

"You want him to be proud of you," Lorelai says from the doorway. "Piper is in bed, reading her book until you come up to tuck her in. Beck's fast asleep."

"Worn out from chasing after his favorite visitor," Noah says, smiling at me. It's true; that boy is attached to me whenever I come over. I don't mind it though. "Do you think that's it? You want him to be proud of you?"

"I guess that could be part of it. Another is that when I'm around him, I feel like I can be the woman I want to be."

"Because he makes you feel safe," Lorelai says, taking a seat next to Noah and giving him a pointed look that I'm not sure I understand. He returns her look with an uncomfortable one of his own.

"What am I missing?"

"I may have convinced him it would be to his benefit to stay away from you."

"When?" I ask him, but I'm sure I know the answer.

"After the night you snuck into his house. I don't regret it, regardless of how you're both looking at me right now," he says, leaning forward with his elbows on his knees. "I know Pope in ways neither of you do. You were freshly out of that hellscape in Utah, and I wanted you to have a chance at independence."

"You didn't think I could do that with him in my life?"

"No, Delilah. You were groomed by the men on the ranch and Pope would have groomed you in another way, even if he wasn't doing it with intent."

"You mean as a submissive," I say, and he nods.

"He's also quite a deal older. At the time, I didn't think it was appropriate for there to be such a connection between you."

"I was eighteen."

"Yes, but did you feel like you were an adult?"

I don't answer that. We all know I questioned every decision that needed to be made in life because I'd been able to make so few before.

"And if he's what I want now?"

"I trust in your capability to make decisions for yourself, Delilah. You've done one hell of a job of it these past few years. You were confused about so much back then; I didn't want him adding to it. I do apologize for being heavy-handed in my protection of you, though."

"It's kind of your specialty," Lorelai says to him.

"I forgive you, because you were right. I wasn't ready for Pope in my life back then. But you don't get to mettle anymore."

"No more interfering, I promise. Unless he, or anyone else, hurts you. Then all deals are off, Delilah. You are family and I protect that at all costs," he says definitively.

"And I appreciate you for that," I say before giving hugs to everyone and saying goodnight. Being mad at Noah just isn't something I can be, there's no telling where I'd be if not for him and Lorelai. Besides, I meant what I said, I wasn't ready for Pope or the obsession I had with him at the time. It made me want to make bad decisions without thinking of the consequences to follow.

It's a night off for me, and I promised I'd spend it with Cookie. She's infatuated with an indie rock band that's playing at some dive bar in the Quarter.

The bar scene isn't something either of us is particularly versed in, we're homebodies at the core. Meeting her back at home, I find her panicking over what to wear.

"Keep it simple, Cookie. What are you most comfortable in?" I ask, trying to hide my amusement. She's never been this worried about her wardrobe before.

Her shoulders drop in surrender as she scans the clothes strewn over her bed. After a moment she grabs a blue vintage band t-shirt and a skater skirt. Knowing her, she'll pair it with her high-top Converse and look fabulous doing it.

"Hey, did you hear about the Orion constellation?" I ask her.

"No, what about it?"

"They're removing it as a constellation. They claim it's just a waste of space."

"Who the fuck decided… Oh, my god. That is such a shitty joke." She laughs.

With my job complete, I go to find an outfit of my own. Beck wiped a third of his dinner on me, I probably smell like slobber and broccoli beef. I change into one of the dresses I've been wearing to work recently, nothing super revealing but it is short.

It's becoming more and more comfortable for me to show skin. It's not the only thing I'm more skilled at now with my Saturday nights still spent with Fig and Damian. That's not anything we'll be discussing tonight. Cookie doesn't mind that Fig and I play around, but she sure doesn't want to hear about it.

The bar, a place called Santos, is located under a sign bearing a big mouth with fangs. Cookie gives me a lopsided grin as we show the bouncer our identification and head in. The inside of the bar also sports fangs, this pair is in neon. Another bright sign flashes 'girls, girls, girls'. It's the one that says 'do shots, hail Satan' over the bar that Cookie apologizes for.

"It's fine. You know I'm not that kind of Christian," I reassure her.

"Which type? The pushy kind or the judgmental kind?" the bartender, a man not much older than us with long dreadlocked hair, asks me.

"I'm neither," I say. "What's your favorite drink to make?"

"The Corpse Revivor," he says with a wink.

"We'll take two." I laugh along with Cookie.

Not long later, the band comes on stage. It's easy to see why Cookie has become so enamored with them, the lead singer is exactly her type. Tall, dark, and broody. She can't keep her eyes off him and in this small of a space, he notices her too. If she could blush, she would, but I've never seen her do it. She does surreptitiously tangle her fingers in mine each time it happens though.

By the end of their set, he spends most of the time singing while staring at my best friend.

"I guess we're not going home right away, huh?" I ask her when we take a bathroom break after the last song.

"Do you mind?" she asks me hopefully.

"Of course not, go get yourself a man."

"Thanks, Delilah!" She throws her arms around my neck and gives me a big, if not a little drunk, hug.

"Come on." I take her hand and pull her to the door. "Let's go see if the band is around."

Sure enough, the band is at the bar. The singer glances around the bar until he spots us, and a smile grows on his face just as big as Cookie's. She ends up talking to him, Logan, for the next hour while I end up chatting with their drummer. Lucy, Logan's sister, is tired of getting hit on by every guy at every show they put on, so we find a table in the corner and try to stay out of the mix while keeping an eye on our two smitten loved ones.

It's been a fun night, but it's clear as the place starts to empty, that Cookie and Logan aren't ready for it to end. Neither of us has ever brought a guy back to our apartment, but Cookie is giving me big puppy-dog eyes, so I don't deny her. The band is crammed into two hotel rooms, being that they're all from Lafayette, the only chance at any privacy for them is our place.

I put the headphones on to tune them out. While I lie in bed listening to songs about love and hope, I'm only filled with a deep disappointment that I can't have the same from the only person I've ever wanted a more meaningful connection with. It wouldn't be so infuriating if I didn't think Pope wanted it too. And it only makes me more determined to get it.

For all my self-lectures about taking control of my life, I've still only taken baby steps toward it. Cautiously dipping my body into the deep end one inch at a time, still letting the faded voices in the back of my mind tell me I'm a sinner. An abomination that God will send away on the day we meet at Heaven's gate.

I'm not a good girl. I should have stayed sweet and obedient, they say. If I focus on them, the anxiety that I've buried so deep creeps back up to wrap itself around my ankle and pull me back under.

But I'm stronger now, pushing it back into its cage gets easier and easier with every day. Because I refuse to live in that kind of fear anymore.

For God gave us a spirit not of fear but of power and love and self-control.

Eighteen years I spent playing mouse to feral cats backing me into corners. Now… I bite back.

CHAPTER FIFTEEN

For two weeks, I've had my plan in place for tonight. Of course, I have little control over the most important aspect of it. I have determination in spades, though.

Tonight is the first charity auction for the foundation Jasmine and Fabienne founded. The bachelor auction will raise money for a local domestic abuse women's shelter. Fabienne found it especially pleasing to sell men for the benefit of women who've been hurt by men.

The men have all gallantly volunteered. While we opened ticket sales to the general public, most have been bought by current club members or potential members patiently waiting for their name to make it to the top of the list.

There is plenty of chatter as I walk around the venue greeting the people I know and introducing myself to some I don't. Halston's name has come up a lot, as have Fig and Pope. All three are hot commodities from the brochure alone, it seems. My competition is likely steep.

The bachelors will be brought out when all the guests have arrived and are seated. There's an empty seat at each table. The men will pick a table, eat one course, then move to another table for the next course. It allows for some mingling while dinner is served, and everyone is suitably plied with booze. Being a little tipsy helps them loosen their wallets.

"Hey, love. You're looking delectable tonight," Damian says, stepping up beside me, handing me a glass of champagne.

"I'd hope so for how much I paid for this dress." The dress itself is simple, strapless without embellishments; it hugs my curves and slits up the thigh in a metallic white that makes my eyes sparkle. Or so Cookie said. I've kept it all simple, light makeup, my hair hanging in waves down to my waist.

"Worth it," he says. "You look like a drop of icing ready to be licked up."

"You wish," I tease him.

"You know I have a sweet tooth for you," he banters back.

"Will you go find us some seats?" I ask, handing him my auction paddle. "I'm going to let Jasmine know we're about ready to start."

"You got it," Damian says, pecking me on the cheek before he saunters off.

In the back room, I find Fig with his mom.

"I'm nervous, Delilah. What if I go for the least amount? Do you know how that will bruise my ego." He smiles so I know he's partly joking, but I can see his tension.

"I came back here to tell you a time travel joke, but you didn't like it."

"Jesus fucking Christ, I hate your stupid jokes," he says, but he laughs too.

"You'll be fine, son. Your ego is big enough to take a hit or two," Jasmine says with a sympathetic pat to his shoulder. "Are we ready?"

"We are."

"Okay, then. We'll be out in just a moment."

I find Damian at a table filled with only other women; I laugh as I take the chair he pulls out for me.

"Why didn't you volunteer for this, you charmer?"

"You know me, love. I'd rather tag along on Fig's date and just watch," he says with a cheeky smile. "Do you plan on bidding tonight?"

"We'll see." I give a shrug just as Fabienne comes out to greet everyone.

"Good evening, my darlings," she calls from the small stage set up at the front of the room. She's lavishly dressed in all royal purple and looks amazing. "Thank you all for coming tonight. The Chastain House is a shelter I've worked with for years and Jasmine and I are honored that you're all here to help us raise much needed funding for them."

Fabienne speaks for a few minutes about the charity and why it means so much to her. Her ex-husband was abusive, and it was a similar shelter that gave her security when she left him back in the days when women struggled even to get checking accounts and credit cards on their own.

Parts of her tale remind me of things the men at the ranch did, small things that seem innocuous but are designed to control and keep us needy to be clothed, housed, and fed. Fabienne had every means to take care of herself slowly removed by her husband, one by one. Until all she had was him.

At the ranch, we were never given anything to begin with, it was all removed before birth. I'm not sure which is worse; never knowing there could be more or knowing and having it all taken away.

She crawled her way out of a horrible situation with every ounce of strength she had and only wants to make it easier for others to do the same. The story makes me love and admire her more than I did before the night started.

"Enough seriousness. Let's introduce you to tonight's auction items."

One by one, the men are introduced and find a table to sit at. Pope started toward our table but changed course when he saw me. It sends a pain to my heart each time he does such a thing, but I've found that I can be quite stubborn when I put my mind to something.

Tonight, its sole focus is him. He won't be able to avoid me easily tonight.

Fig sits at our table for the salad course, Halston for the main. Every woman at the table is starry-eyed over the prospect of a date with either of them. But the woman directly across from me makes it clear that her sights are set on Pope, who carefully did not come near our table.

"Did you sit us at the thirstiest table in this place?" I whisper to Damian.

"Of fucking course," he answers. "What do you have up your sleeve tonight, anyway?"

"I'm going after what I want." My voice doesn't waver, even though my nerves are starting to kick in. There's no way of knowing how high the bids will go until it all gets started. There's a firm number in my head that I don't want to go past. I will if I must, but it will take a big chunk of the money I have set aside for future endeavors.

"Atta girl," Damian says with hints of both excitement and amusement. "I don't know what your ceiling is, but you go as high as you need. I'll front you whatever you need."

"I... I can't let you do that." I'm shocked he'd even offer. It's always been my impression that he possesses a large lack of respect for Pope.

"Yes, you can. And you will if any of these vipers try to outbid you. I've got more money than half this lot combined and I'd pay a lot of it to see you put that prick in his place."

"Hopefully, it won't come to that."

"We're about to find out," he says with a nod toward the stage.

Jasmine brings up the first bachelor, starting the bidding at one thousand dollars. He goes for multiple times more. As does the next, and the next. Halston is next who goes for a cool twenty grand.

A couple more men are sold off before it's Pope's turn. Jasmine starts the bidding at the same number as all the rest, and I let a handful of women make their bids before I get involved.

Including the lady sitting at our table. She bids nineteen thousand; the response from the rest of the room is a silent pause. Everyone is waiting to see if anyone will push it up.

I raise my paddle to a shocked Pope. Jasmine, to her credit, doesn't show any surprise at all. The look on her face is something more like pride. Looking back to my prize, I finally understand the saying if looks could kill. Because I'm pretty sure Pope wants to strangle me right now.

"Twenty-one," the other woman says.

"Twenty-five," I say, still watching Pope, his hands fisting tightly at his side.

"Twenty-six," the woman says, shooting me a glare of her own.

"Thirty." I raise the paddle again while Pope mouths the word stop to me.

"Drop the paddle and I'll fuck you here tonight for free, sweetheart," Damian says to the stranger on the other side of the table. In her shocked stupor, the bidding ends and I'm declared the winner.

As anticipated, Pope beelines right for me. Before he can reach our table, I stand, letting him follow me to a back hallway.

"What the fuck are you doing?" he snarls the words in my face as he pushes my back up against the wall.

"Each of you should give what you have decided in your heart to give, not reluctantly or under compulsion, for God loves a cheerful giver."

"I am not your abundant blessing, Delilah." Pope's hand wraps around my throat, keeping me firmly in the place he wants me to be.

"Maybe I'm yours."

His head dips down, and for an exaggerated second, I float on pure euphoria that he's finally going to kiss me. After so many years and so many more daydreams, I'm going to taste his taste.

Pope pulls away and the loss of that inch of space feels like a mile.

"Where are you going to get the money?"

"I have it, you actually came cheaper than I expected," I say with a sweet smile to his narrowing eyes.

"You bought a date," he emphasizes the word. "Nothing more."

"Of course," I say. "No one here is being prostituted. I do expect you to show up, though. And you could at least be cordial, I've paid enough for that."

"I'm not cordial to brats." His thumb runs along the column of my neck, over my chin, stopping when it lands on my lower lip. Like I did at our first coffee meeting, I stick my tongue out. This time wrapping it around his thumb in the same manner I would do to him elsewhere, if only he'd let me.

I see how I affect him. The heavy rise and fall of his chest, the slight tilt of his head as he struggles to not give in, the flare of his nostrils when his body leans into me on its own accord—say enough.

"Sometimes I'm a good girl."

I've never felt more powerful than I do in this moment, feeling how hard he is when I push my hips forward. Pope removes his thumb from my mouth, only to quickly replace it with two fingers. He pushes them in roughly, and it's a struggle not to gag on them, but I keep my composure, just barely.

"Are you good for your friend out there?" I nod my head, unable to speak with his thick fingers still firmly inspecting my mouth. "Does he like it when you're good?"

Another nod and his fingers push further in. Digging my fingers into the shirt at his waist, I pull closer. Body to body that I wish was skin to skin.

Pope and I are fated. We're God's will, or we're written in the stars. I'm not certain why, but I am certain we are meant for each other. If the look in his coffee eyes tells me anything, it's that he knows too. He's angry with me right now, but there's more I see. Like regret that he didn't take this sooner. He can't hide it from me when we're so close, when we're this connected.

"You don't know what you're getting into." Finally, the fingers leave, and I can take a full gasp of air. A palm to my cheek steadies me as I regain my bearings. Yet another sign that he cares more than he wants to show.

"You'll teach me."

"So much confidence for a little lamb."

"I've changed since you first met me, Pope," I say, stretching up to lick over the body of the black dove. "You should find a new pet name for me."

"We'll see. I'll show up for your little date," he says, fingers tangling in my hair. "But remember this, Delilah. You get what you fucking pay for."

"I'm counting on it." In response, his laugh is devilishly low. A threat, a warning that I should scamper away from someone so dangerous. Pope forgets that I've known and suffered worse. "I'll send you the details."

"You do that," he says, then walks away with one fleeting glance.

CHAPTER SIXTEEN

POPE

Before I even made it home last night, Delilah texted me an address and a time. My day was busier than I'd planned. Something I've been working on for years finally broke loose and needed my immediate attention. Because of that, I'm late when I walk up the path of the address in Bywater.

I don't know who lives here, certainly not Delilah and Cookie. Their shoebox size apartment is in the French Quarter, amid all the drunken frivolity. The home I'm about to enter is a two-story shotgun style home in the suburbs surrounded by a canopy of old growth trees.

She doesn't answer my knock immediately, though, I'd guess she's been waiting anxiously for the last twenty-five minutes for my arrival. I could have texted her regarding my tardiness, but that's not quite my style. Delilah needs to learn she doesn't make the rules. Not where I'm concerned, at least.

When she finally opens the door, I lose my damned mind for a bloated moment. She's wrapped herself in a sheer bloodred dress. If it were made of a less revealing fabric, she'd look almost demure with the long length and sleeves, even with its plunging neckline. This material lends itself to revealing that she's barely covered in straps and bits of lace underneath.

148

"You're late, Mr. Blackwell," her matching red lips speak.

"Apologies, there was a pressing matter that couldn't wait."

"More pressing than my investment?" she asks, turning to lead me into the well-appointed house.

"I believe you'd think it was," I say, confident she would if she only knew. "Whose place is this?"

"It belongs to a friend. I've borrowed it for the night."

"A friend you fuck?"

"I don't see how it matters." She steps to a bar and pours me the drink she remembers I like. Between us is a dining table, every inch covered in serving dishes. "Please sit."

She places my drink in front of me before she takes a seat herself.

"What's all this?"

"I made dinner, it's probably getting cold," she says, and I hear the disappointment she tries to hide. She cooked for me, and I couldn't even give her the respect of showing up on time. She's too kind to say it to me directly. Despite her new stiff backbone and sexual awakening, her heart is the same as it has always been.

Too good for me.

"Delilah," I say so she pauses in uncovering a dish near her. "I apologize. It was more important than you could know, and it was rude of me not to let you know."

She blinks her shock away. Good, she should be shocked. Apologizing isn't something I do, but I promised myself I wouldn't start this night off with anger. Especially after today.

"Okay," she concedes. "I wasn't sure what you liked, so I went with French." She points out Salad Niçoise, Quiche Lorraine, Savory Crepes, and a Beef Bourguignon that looks delicious enough to be served at the best restaurants around.

"This is enough food to last a week," I say, beginning to dish us both up, the table small enough for me to reach most items. I serve a small amount of everything until her plate is full, then I move on to mine. "You made it all?"

"Yes, I've been cooking for as long as I can remember. I don't get as many opportunities to do it anymore, but I still enjoy it."

"Do you want to say grace or a prayer?" I ask curiously when she lifts her fork. The younger Delilah would say a silent prayer before she took a sip of coffee, I don't think she even realized she did it. But I noticed every time.

"No."

"Why not?"

"I don't do that any longer." She shrugs it off as if it's not an important detail and takes a bite of her salad. I do the same, savoring the bite as I wait to see if she'll elaborate. She doesn't though.

"Why, Delilah?"

"It began to feel, I don't know, performative. Back at the ranch, if someone said I'll pray for you, it meant something. It meant they would. Out here, people say it so often it's lost meaning. They pray for no rain, or for their kid's baseball team to win a game. Then when something they say they prayed about comes to fruition, they thank God. As if God has time to make all those minute things happen but doesn't listen when one of us prays to save a child from cancer or to end world hunger."

"So, no prayer at all for you now?"

"I think God knows I'm thankful without me having to say grace and I don't pray for anything selfish or self-serving."

"It's that simple?"

"It wasn't simple at all, Pope," she says, looking up from her plate to meet my eyes. "It took me a long time to come to the conclusions I have."

"But at least they are *your* conclusions," I say, and she hums in agreement. "This is delicious, Delilah. You've got quite a talent."

"Thank you." Her cheeks turn rosy, and she sits up straighter.

"My mother used to make this." I hold up a bite of the quiche.

"Did she?"

"It was one of the few things she made well, so she made it

often. My father berated her if he didn't find something appetizing. It limited our menu."

"That's an awful way to live." Delilah blinks rapidly, her eyes shining with wetness.

"It is. You know something about that, of course. She left when I was in middle school. I guess she couldn't take his temper any longer."

"Pope," Delilah says, saddened.

"Stop it. It's not worse than what you went through."

"It's not a competition. I can be sad for both of our childhoods simultaneously." I watch her take another bite. I could watch her always. Fuck, I do watch her nearly always. More than she knows, surely. "Do you think bad childhoods are the norm, not the exception?"

"It often feels that way. We both survived them, though."

"Did you ever see her again?"

"No."

"I'm sorry, that had to be hard."

"It focused my father's abusive behavior on me. I never missed my mother. I never made a habit of craving to be around people who don't want to be around me in return." Sadness settles on her face, and she doesn't initiate more conversation until we're done eating.

After I've helped her clear the table and load the dishwasher, I pour myself another drink. She watches me from the other side of the room, not the same confident woman she was at the auction. Delilah is second-guessing whatever she had planned.

"Is there a comfortable spot here to talk?"

She gestures with her head for me to follow, her bare feet silently padding across the hardwood floors. We end up outside. The back patio is mostly a swimming pool, but a plush seating area is set up in the corner.

Delilah sits, pulling her knees up and wrapping her arms around them. Vulnerable and small, it's how I've always seen her. Except the childishness is gone now.

"What's wrong?"

"Nothing." She shakes her head and adjusts her dress to flow over her legs and cover her toes.

"Do not lie to me, Delilah."

"How do you do that?"

"What?"

"Put so much force into your words that I immediately want to obey?"

"Practice. Don't change the subject." I lean forward, grasping her hands that she's now wringing atop her knees.

"You said earlier that you don't want to be with people that don't want to be with you. Now I'm second-guessing all of this, because you didn't want to be here. I forced it."

"Why did you do it?"

"I'm tired, Pope," she says, resting her temple on our tangled hands. "It's exhausting to feel the things I feel and have you walk away from it night after night."

"What is it you feel?"

"You. I feel you with me all the time. It's a connection I can't deny or shake away. Most of the time I think you feel it also but are too cowardly to act on it."

Too cowardly.

She'll pay for that.

"It's not cowardice, Delilah. It takes great goddamned strength to let you live your life the way you do."

"Then stop doing it," she pleads. "I spoke with Noah. I know he told you to stay away from me. But that was then."

"Yet nothing has changed, Delilah." She sits up, pulls her warm hands away from mine. "My life isn't suited for someone like you. I don't want marriage or kids. I don't even want monogamy."

Now she stands, pacing the few steps to the pool's edge where she stops and tips her head to the emerging stars. My eyes follow, wondering which she's so focused on. When I bring my gaze back to her, she's letting the dress fall off her pale body.

"I'm not asking for any of those things."

"Delilah." She's the biggest temptress I've ever met and all by merely existing. Though the barely there panties she's wearing help.

"Tell me you don't feel it. Tell me you don't want me, Pope. Tell me that you don't crave to be Damian or Fig every time I have one of their cocks in my mouth."

I grab the straps crossed under her breasts and pull her to me. She stumbles at the force, but I don't let her fall.

"Watch your mouth."

"Shut me up."

"You'll only get hurt, Delilah."

"Then I get hurt," she says, holding her palms up. "I know the risks, Pope. Maybe I just think the rewards in the meantime are worth it."

Delilah isn't the first woman to throw herself at me. She is the first one to approach it with a thoughtful argument. She is the only one to ever make me feel like she wants me and not just my money or my dick.

I don't trust everything she's said. Delilah, like so many before her, will eventually want what I can't give. But maybe she's right. Maybe the in between, the space after we start and before we end, will be worth our eventual fallout.

As if she can see I'm about to give in, her small hands land on my shoulders and she crawls onto my lap.

"All I'm asking is that you give it a try."

"There are so many rules," I say, letting her drop her brow to mine.

"Teach me." Her sweet words land on my mouth and I can do nothing else but take hers. I'll teach her how I like it all, starting with this. I start the kiss easy; a lick of her lips is all. She gasps as a shiver wracks her spine.

So affected by something so simple.

I deepen it, pushing her back so she has to wrap her hands around my neck to hold on. When I finally push my tongue inside to meet hers, she moans, her body sagging as if the kiss is a relief she's needed for a lifetime.

My hand finds her ass, middle finger following the crease under her. Another gasp leaves her, and I pull back just enough to speak.

"Show me the bedroom."

Instead of climbing off me, she latches onto me tighter. Keeping my hand on her ass, I stand and adjust her in my arms.

"Inside, up the stairs," she says almost dreamily. An innocence I want so desperately to corrupt. I take the stairs and easily find the main bedroom with its king-size bed. My plan was to talk to her first, but as soon as I set her feet on the carpet, Delilah turns to place her hands on the bed. Her ass high in the air.

She's fucking perfect.

"What are you getting spankings for tonight, Delilah?"

"I bought you and I called you a coward."

"Do you remember how this works?"

"Yes. I'm to say your name with every spank." She looks over her shoulder at me.

"Do you know why?"

"So I know it's you. So I know I am safe."

I lean down to kiss her again; she pushes that round bottom into my crotch.

"You are safe, but it's still going to hurt."

Delilah takes the first handful of swats like a champ before she starts to falter. Her toes dig into the rug as she gets increasingly more uncomfortable, yet there aren't many other signs. She still calls my name; she still rights her position after each flinch. After a dozen or so, I let her off the hook and pull her up to stand. I can't take much more myself, I've been rock hard since I walked into this house. If I don't sink my cock into her soon, I'll lose my fucking mind.

Pulling off the bedding, I pile it in a corner of the room before I return to her. I don't want anything in the way, nothing between her and I.

"Remove your underwear. The rest can stay."

Wordlessly, she complies. She's dressed just right in a black lace bra that barely contains her and straps that crisscross both over her shoulders and down around her abdomen. It makes it easier for me to position her however I please.

"Come here," I call, sitting at the corner of the bed with my legs spread wide enough for her to get close. "We'll be using condoms. Are you on birth control?"

"Yes."

"Are there things you don't want to do?"

"I'm not experienced enough to know." Of course she's not. She's only been in one relationship, and I doubt that twerp of a man was at all creative. From what I've seen of her in the club, it's been kept to oral. Still enough to make my eyes bleed, but we'll get to that. "You'll need to start me off on the bottom rungs."

"I can do that," I say, a little amused. "If we do this, if I claim you, there is no more Damian. No more Fig. No more anything that doesn't involve me."

"Okay."

"Be certain, Delilah." I lay my hands on her bare hips, unable to keep her out of my grip any longer.

"I am. They're fun, I've learned a lot from them. But they were never my first choice."

"Good," I say, pulling the cup of her bra down so I can work at her nipple with my thumb. "I'm your teacher now and nobody touches this body without my fucking permission."

"Yes, Mr. Blackwell," she says in a teasing tone, making my dick twitch.

"Lie on the bed. On your back, knees up. Face right here at the very edge." Like she's done every time tonight, she follows instructions without question. As I strip my clothes off, she watches with rapt attention. Her eyes hooding, her chest flushing pink. "You like watching."

"As much as you like watching me."

She's wrong. I hate watching her. I'm compelled to, but I hate it all the same. Delilah wasn't wrong earlier when she said I wish it was me in her mouth.

"Open your mouth," I tell her, one hand moving on my already fully erect cock. She turns her face toward the side of the bed and opens wide, sliding her tongue out without direction. "Eager?"

"Mmhmm."

The bed is slightly too low for my height. Brushing her hair aside, I prop a knee up to gain a better position. Then I slide into one of the only places I've wanted to be for weeks. Years, even.

"Fucking hell."

She hums again, and I feel it through my balls as they bounce off her cheek.

"Spread your knees," I say, lightly smacking the one closest to the edge of the bed. It gives me a great view and access to her pink cunt. Walking my fingers down her sternum to her belly button, every muscle they touch twitches. When I slide my middle finger over her clit and through the slit of her pussy, her legs start to pull back together. "No."

She whines but complies. Every sound she makes amps up my need for her, spurs my hips forward to plant my cock further down her mouth. In return, I slide my finger around and around, heightening her own need. Edging her closer and closer and closer. When she gets too close, I stop, slap her cunt and let her gag as she gasps at the unexpected attention.

This continues until there's a stream of drool trailing down her cheek and she's so wet my finger slides inside her with such ease I'd think she couldn't feel it, but she's tight as she clenches around it. I can't wait to taste her, but I know once I do, I'll be there for a while, and right now... I need to be inside Delilah.

"It's time, Lamb."

CHAPTER SEVENTEEN

He bends to take a condom out of his pants pocket and sheathes his veiny dick. How many times has he done this? The difference between us is a vast, vast sea. My nerves act up. Things I never planned to say settle on the tip of my tongue.

"Pope."

With so much ease, he picks me up and repositions me. Still on my back, my butt just at the edge of the bed. He loops his arms under my knees and grabs hold of my wrists, lifting my lower half into the air. I'm so shocked by the quick change; I forget that I was trying to convey something. Information, importance, warning.

He doesn't know.

It's too late to tell him as he thrusts in, and I choke on a sob and scream inwardly. He instantly tries to pull away, and I struggle to lock my legs around him, wanting to keep him in place.

"No," I say through the panic and searing agony that rips through me. "No, Pope."

Tears well up, shocking me. I'm not much of a crier anymore. I haven't cried since the day Jillian called me to tell me she was out.

Before that, I don't know how long it had been. Maybe it's the pain, but I know I'd weep if Pope left me right now.

"What the fuck have you done?"

"I did what you said," I plead. "I waited for someone I cared about and who I trust. That doesn't come easy to me."

Andrew didn't believe in full-on sex before marriage. Which was fine because I never wanted to have sex with him. Fig and Damian have both offered, but that didn't feel right. Even after all the things I've done with them, to them, taking this step didn't feel right. I could never seem to want this with anyone but the one man who I offered it to and who repeatedly declined.

Pope's fingers pull at the hair on either side of my head, his body falling atop mine. He doesn't pull out of me though and I bare the pain like I've borne everything painful in my life. Silently and alone.

"I didn't know," he breathes heavily, staring at me with eyes so blank; I'm terrified. Not of him, but *for* him. "I thought you had with *that* Andrew."

"It wasn't his to have," I whisper, wondering how he even knows about Andrew.

"Fig and Damian?"

"It wasn't theirs either." He blinks, and a little light comes back, but he's not fully here with me. I bring my hands to his face, trying to make him see me. "Pope, it was always you. The only man I've ever instinctually trusted. Please, please accept it. Finish what we've started."

"Delilah." His fingers tighten and I'm grateful for the pressure there taking the bite of the sting elsewhere. "I don't know how to do this."

"Yes, you do."

"No, I don't," he snarls. "I want to fucking throttle you by the throat, but at the same time, I want to be gentle too to ease your discomfort."

"I was going to be in pain one way or another tonight. It's just not the way you expected."

"Stop taking it so lightly. This isn't how it should have happened. You should have been prepared better," he snaps. "Fuck! I need to move, Delilah. I can't be in you and not move."

"Then move, and I'll move with you." Before the words have a chance to fade, his mouth is on mine. A hand moves to my breast, gently massaging at the same tempo as his tongue. Mixing pleasure with pain, confusing my senses. He still hasn't moved his hips or his cock.

Tentatively, I slide my leg against his, raising it, shifting to find a position that might feel better. Pope flinches, dragging some hard part of himself against my clit.

There it is.

I groan into his mouth, sucking his tongue further. My hands land on his sides, and I move them slowly to his ass so I can push him against that spot again. He catches on, taking the hand from my breast and moving it between us right where I need it. He's still so tightly wound around me, he's barely moving, and I can barely move.

"Pope, I'm okay. Move like I know you want to."

At the same time, he thrusts two fingers in my mouth and pushes his hips forward hard enough to fully seat himself inside me. I gasp at the overload of sensations.

"Stop talking, you can't possibly know what you want."

If I could laugh with fingers shoved halfway down my throat, I would. There are so few things I've wanted in life; I know very well what they are. The amusement in my eyes grabs his attention and he glares in return. Ever my big grumpy brute. I suck my cheeks in, drawing his fingers in further; something we can focus on. Slowly, he begins to fuck my mouth with them, and as I make more and more pleasurable sounds, the more the tension in his jaw begins to relax.

But then he's gone from both above and below.

"Pope," I protest.

"Shh. Give me this, then I'll give you what you want." He props himself up on an elbow and inserts his fingers where his dick just was. My chest lifts with his gentle ministrations. He soothes as much as brings me closer to the brink I had been on before that small innocence was breached. "This is for me, Delilah. It's mine, this orgasm you're about to have. Not Damian's, or Fig's, or anyone else who watched you light up the room with your ecstasy. I wanted to murder them that first night. Fabienne had to talk me down. I'd never felt such rage."

"I wished it was you, but you were with someone else," I say with shortness of breath. I'm so close, nearly there.

"I was wishing she was you, too. Then you were there, watching, and I couldn't do it."

"What?" He pushes the pad of his palm against my clit and pushes me toward my dive.

"I thought I could pretend she was you. But I didn't fuck her that night, because she couldn't compare."

My air hitches, then vanishes altogether. A billion tiny orbs of light reflect into Pope's eyes as wave after wave hits me. He doesn't stop working me until I'm nothing but a puddle lying under him. His attention moves away from my face. I don't mind the chance to admire his profile. I push a lock of stray hair behind his ear. This is the most intimate I've ever felt with him. Everything about us has been so intense, so loud, I revel in this small, quiet moment.

When I look at what has him so somber and quiet, I see he's rubbing his fingers together. My release, stained red.

"Oh," I exclaim. I hadn't considered I'd be bleeding. Pope looks back to me, bringing his finger to his chest, and then he draws a cross over his heart.

Then his fingers tangle with mine as he pulls my arms up over my head. He parts my knees, then… he's back. The sting persists, but so dull in comparison to the feel of Pope as he moves with me while he stares into my eyes.

I take my earlier claim back; this is the most intimate. The most real. The most intense and important moment that's ever been there between us. The vacancy in his eyes is now gone so I can trust he's here with me, too. Feeling what I feel.

Fated.

I pull my legs up to lock around his waist. He rolls his hips, and I've never felt so many things. Everywhere, all at once. If I died in the next moment, I'd meet my maker with only the regret of not doing this sooner.

"Pope," I cry repeatedly. It's too little and too much all the same. I'm insane with need and completely clear that this is where I'm meant to be. We're contradiction but truth. Feeling and no thought. "Pope."

"Come with me, Layla."

I do on a scream punctuated by his moan. We still to nothing but heaving chest against heaving chest. Still, he doesn't let go of my hands. My heart hopes he never does.

Layla.

"Stay," he murmurs before getting up to enter the bathroom. He turns on the water and then he's back, gently lifting me in his arms. He drops me to my feet in front of the toilet while the bathwater rises. "Urinate. After every time you have sex. Understand?"

"I'm not a child, Pope."

"And I'm holding on by a fucking thread, here. Can you just do what I ask?"

"Are you going to watch?"

"Fucking hell," he curses. "After what just occurred… pee."

"Fine."

He doesn't watch, but he doesn't leave either. Instead, he tends to the bath he's running. When I finish, he steps into the tub and holds his hands out for me to join him. Cautiously, I toe into the water, sinking down with him and wincing as the heat hits my behind.

Resting my head back against Pope's chest, I take the moment to reflect on what we've just done. I always knew my virginity was of too much importance to others, including Pope. For me, it's a milestone in my relationship with him. One that may set us back if he can't see past it. But it's not significant in any other way to me; it's just biology. A first try at something I hope to improve on.

Pope sets his arms on either side of the tub, staying silent.

"You're mad."

"I'm processing."

"Can you do that with your arms around me?"

"What do you think this is?" he asks, fisting the wet tangles of my hair and pulling it so that I look up to him.

"Aftercare, I know that. While I expect you to be a grump about it all, you aren't cruel," I answer, seeing the twitch of his lips that he fights.

"You have no idea what you're talking about."

"School me then, Mr. Blackwell."

"You'd probably hate me if I did."

"Try me," I taunt. He hesitates for a long minute, maybe trying to convince himself not to believe I can handle him at his worst.

"I broke that kid's leg."

"Which kid?"

"The one who went to Tulane with you. Aaron something."

"Why?"

"He didn't heed my warning." He turns his head to the side, no longer looking at me.

"About what?" I reach up, bringing his eyes back to me.

"What do you think, Delilah? I gave him clear instruction to leave you alone, but he didn't follow."

"So, you broke his leg?"

"Yes. And I put one of his father's businesses in financial ruin."

"Huh." I spin to my side, wrapping an arm around his waist as I snuggle closer.

"That's your reaction?"

"That kid was horrible. You know he used to introduce himself to women with *you're pretty, we should bone*? He deserved it, and more. Wait, you thought I'd hate you for that?"

"It's not very Christian of me," he says.

"You're not a Christian. Besides, I've never asked you to be anything you're not."

His arms finally come around me, one trailing down my side to my butt.

"How do you feel?"

"I'm good, Pope."

"You're going to be sore."

"Then I guess we can't do that again right away."

He laughs and it's a revelation.

"Why are you so calm about any of this?" I'm not sure if he means about losing my virginity or learning that he's capable of violence toward others.

"This was something I chose, Pope. You, in my life, is something I choose." He quiets again, it's worrying if I let it be. One moment he's almost relaxed and talkative, the next he has one foot out the door in his attempt to run away from me. "You called me Layla."

"It rolls off the tongue better." He's trying to be dismissive, but I know better. He didn't call me a biblical philistine, or a betrayer. Instead, he gave me a name of my own. He doesn't understand what a gift it is to me.

"I liked it." I run a finger over the ink on his hip, along the jagged edge of the moth's wing. "I like this, too."

"Don't read into it," he says, which I take to mean I should.

"I do what I want, Mr. Blackwell," I sing, sliding down further into the warmer water.

"I hope that's true." The words sound vacant, I glance up to see he looks it, too.

"What does that mean?" I move again, facing him now, his large thighs shifting to make more room for me.

"How familiar with the story of Samson are you?"

"As familiar as any of the Bible stories, I guess. It was used more often on me—don't be deceitful like your namesake and whatnot."

"Delilah isn't given a masculine link in the Bible, no husband, no father. Just Delilah, the only woman in the story to be named. It's a Hebrew name that means delicate but is derived from Layla which means night. Samson is derived from Shemesh, meaning the sun," he says, leaning to rub his nose against mine. "The delicate night who overtakes the mighty sun."

"Have I overtaken you?"

"Since the day I met you. There is a connection between us, created by some shared experiences. When Noah came to me, suggesting I back off, I knew he was right because that connection could lead to influencing your decisions. You needed life experiences on your terms."

"I did that."

"Not entirely. You didn't get this one, because of *me*. I'm the night in our story."

"Oh, fuck off, Pope!" Almost tripping on the ledge of the tub, I scramble out of the bathroom. My calm is gone completely as I rummage through the overnight bag I have stashed in the closet. Clothes being my first priority, armor before I kick him out. My underthings have disappeared into the depths of the bag, but I grab the other dress I had as an option for tonight. Red again, not see-through. It's a struggle to get it over my wet skin, but I manage.

"Stop," Pope bellows from the door of the walk-in closet. I hate myself for obeying.

"You stop," I say, feeling defeated. "You stop, Pope. I'm not a child, you didn't groom me, you didn't coerce me. I chose this, I decided when I was ready. *I bought you.* If anyone here is the night, it's me, damnit!"

"Curse at me one more time and see what happens," Pope says, crowding me. He's still naked, water dripping over his pecs. Anger aside, I want to lick it up. His cock pushing into my stomach tells me I'm not alone.

"Fuck you, Mr. Blackwell."

The dress I've had on for only seconds is torn off my shoulders in one quick movement. Another and it's split down to its short hem to barely hang off my body. Skin to skin, we meet again.

"The way you fucking challenge me…" Pope hauls me onto his shoulder. One of his arms securely around my thighs, while the other swats my still burning cheeks, as he walks me back out the bedroom. "You don't get to walk away from me."

I'm not sure how he maneuvers me so easily, but within seconds, my back is slammed against the wall, my legs are over his shoulders and his face is buried between my thighs.

"Oh, God."

He moans into my core, his fingers pulling me apart as his tongue dives in. So far I think he's trying to climb inside and take up a home. Digging my fingers into his hair and pushing my shoulders into the wall, I begin to roll my hips. He gives me another sound of approval that sends tingling sensation through my chest. My chilled skin suddenly burns with flames.

"Pope," I cry, unable to keep his name out of my mouth. His head tilts so he can look up my body through eyes darkly laden with desire. He winks at the same time he pushes closer, his nose giving my bundle of nerves the pressure it needs to explode on his tongue. It's embarrassing how quickly he makes me come.

Carefully, he slides me down his rigid body until I'm an unsteady, panting mess standing before him.

"If that's my punishment for foul language, expect more of it," I pant.

"Your punishment is sucking my cock until your throat is so filled with my cum, you're choking on it and can't talk back to me. Now kneel."

CHAPTER EIGHTEEN

He comes, yelling Layla.

He then picks me up and takes me back to the bathroom to shower. Only minutes ago, he had forced his manhood so far down my throat I gagged and cried. Now, he shampoos and conditions my hair before meticulously washing every inch of my bruised body.

Hard and soft, the man is a miraculous contradiction.

Though he's silent throughout the process, he pauses to kiss my lips, the back of my neck, the inside of my thigh. When he has us both spotless, he dries us off and leads me to bed.

"I have pajamas in my bag," I say.

"No," Pope says. "We'll sleep naked."

"I've never done this."

"Slept in a bed?"

"Funny," I deadpan. "Never with a man."

"I never have either." I'm not sure what to do with this side of him. Usually so serious and stern, I like the playful side, but I probably shouldn't get used to it. "Climb in."

I crawl on the bed, and he picks up the comforter from the pile he'd made earlier on the floor before getting on the bed and covering us both. We lie face-to-face in silence for several moments.

"There's something I wanted to talk to you about."

"What?"

"Your family is about to be out of money."

"Noah?"

"No, not your family here," Pope tells me, a palm cupping my cheek.

"How?" Honestly, I'm shocked at the possibility. The agents working to take down the ranch have been forthcoming in that my family has a seemingly unlimited amount of funds. It's how they've paid off all the law enforcement in the area, it's how they've stayed protected for so long. His eyes bounce between mine rapidly. "Pope?"

"Me. I'm how."

"I don't understand."

Pope wipes at my cheeks with his thumb.

"Your father is good with money, as good as your uncle was before him. I'm better. Though it's taken me years to find it all."

"Years?"

"Years," he confirms. "I started working on it shortly after I met you. When I started finding relevant information, I passed it to Lorelai, who in turned passed it to that agent."

"Agent Daughtry?" She's now the lead on the case and has been working on it since before I escaped. She's also the one that has been willing to bend the rules to keep the new girls safe.

"I assume that's the one. I've known about most of his accounts and investments for a long time, but there was one I couldn't find. It holds the bulk of his wealth. The money is clean, as far as I can tell. It's not a path the Feds can take. But I can."

"How? Legally?"

"No," he laughs. "It won't be entirely legal, though some of it can disappear by lawful means."

Pope leaves me with a lot to unpack. My gut reaction wants me to tell him to do it, take it all away. Except where does that leave the innocent that rely on that money? If there are no funds, will some leave on their own? I'm doubtful it would be many. I have many siblings, mostly older who are so entrenched in the life that I'm not certain they can ever come back from it. The younger ones have the chance if there's a way to remove them from it, but that's proven to be most difficult. Even without money, their parents still have rights. That's not even considering my cousins. There were hundreds of people living there when I left.

My father would use it as another lesson in the evils of the outside world. However, financial ruin is a step in the right direction of taking them down.

Then there's Pope's involvement and what that could mean. I can't have him taking risks that could end up with him in trouble or prison.

I can't lose him now that I've barely gotten him. It's maybe the most selfish concern I've ever had. I feel the shame of it as if it's burned on my skin.

"I don't want you to do anything that can get you in trouble."

"Shh, Layla." He kisses me deeply but not with the hunger he's shown all night. "You don't need to worry about me. I'll do what I can legally for now. When the time is right, I'll ruin him."

We don't speak about it further. After such an emotional night, I easily fall asleep with his arm wrapped around my back and my leg thrown over his hip.

I wake in much the same position, thrilled that he didn't sneak off in the middle of the night. He's hard again when we wake, and I snuggle close.

"No," he says sleepily. "Touch yourself."

I do and wince. He raises an eyebrow pointedly. I guess I'm out of commission for a day or two.

"I've got to go," he says. "I'll text you some instructions."

"What sort of instructions?"

"You'll see." He presses a kiss to my forehead. "Remember what I said, you do nothing without my involvement."

As if I even want to.

I clean up the house before anything else. It's one of Fabienne's, which she normally rents out. After that, I head straight to Lorelai, the only person that will fully understand my concerns regarding my father's money.

She's also the first person I want to talk to about what happened between Pope and me.

"What's going on?" she asks, setting a mug of tea in front of me.

"I spent the night with Pope yesterday." No point in sugarcoating or delaying, this is Lorelai. I've always been honest with her.

"How do you feel about it?" She's worried; the crinkle around her eyes is evident.

"I'm good, Lore. I promise. It was what I wanted, and you know I've put a lot of thought into it."

"I know you have. How was he with you?"

"He was how you'd expect Pope to be," I say, with a side smile and a shrug. "Bossy, a little mad at me, but caring and sweet, too."

"Why mad?"

"He thinks he did something that made me think I couldn't have done that with anyone but him."

"When it was really just him being him," she muses. It's a subject we've discussed in the past. My crush on Pope was never about replacing my father with him. My father never made me feel safe, quite the opposite. There was always a deeper force at play. "Is he still upset about it?"

"I don't think so. We argued about it some, but by the end of the night, his attitude had changed. He calls me Layla."

"That's pretty, but why?"

"I think it's his way of giving me distance from a name so commonly associated with a whore."

"She wasn't, but I get your meaning," Lorelai says, taking a sip of her own tea. "You have him figured out pretty well, don't you?"

"I'd like to think so, but only time will tell."

"You'll be okay, no matter what happens with Pope. Remember that. You're the strongest person I've ever met, never letting anything stand in your way. Never letting anything scare you off. I've often admired your determination and your thoughtfulness. I wish I'd had a fraction of it at your age."

"You've always given me too much credit."

"I have not," she disputes with an attempt at looking stern, but she's never been able to pull that off.

"You have. I'm more calculated than thoughtful."

"Are you in love with him?" she asks me after a few beats of silence.

"I don't know what romantic love is, Lore. Even if I did know him well enough to be at that point, which I don't," I emphasize, "how would I even recognize the signs?"

"You'll know," she says, almost sadly. "You'll know when things feel… more."

"When it starts to hurt?"

"There's that thoughtfulness," she says, the sadness washing away some. "But I hope that's not how you figure it out."

"Enough about me, there's something else," I hedge.

"What?" One of her hands covers mine. This is the Lorelai I know, the one that's always ready to soothe everyone else's hurts and concerns.

"Pope says he's found the family money. He can take it away. All of it."

"He's finally done it, huh?"

"Yes, but what will it mean if he goes through with it? What happens to everyone? What happens to *him*?"

"They won't be homeless," she starts. "The Cleric owns the property free and clear, that's not something Pope can take away. The families all get by on so little, for the most part, it won't take a big toll on anyone but your father and the other council members.

They won't have the same leverage inside the ranch or outside of it."

"They won't be able to pay off the police."

"Exactly. Without that, maybe whatever price my mother is paying will reduce enough to get even more girls out."

She watches the tea in her cup as she swirls it. When Martha smuggled Olivia out of the ranch, it cost Lorelai a small fortune. Every penny she had went to saving her small sister. When Martha got me out, nobody ponied up money. At least that we know about. Same with Jillian and the others. We can only guess at the deals Martha is making and what she's giving up saving girls.

She doesn't have anything but herself to give. It's not a fact any of us like, but we aren't able to get in touch with Martha, either. She knows how to contact Lorelai but hasn't since Olivia was three.

"And Pope?"

"I don't believe Pope would do anything in a way that puts him at risk, do you?"

That's what I want to believe, but it's not something I can put much blind faith in. I'm not very good at that sort of thing anymore.

Lorelai fills me in on new developments with the FBI, which aren't much. When Noah and the kids get back from the park, I play a couple rounds of chess with Olivia. We're learning the game together, though she's already much better than I am.

"Checkmate," she says again with her toothy grin.

"Well, I've had enough nonsense. I'm going home," I dramatically say the line from *Alice in Wonderland*.

"If I had a world of my own, everything would be nonsense," Olivia barks back.

"When I get home, I shall write a book about this place!" It's how we often part ways. Olivia, like me, has a love for stories. Alice being a favorite of both of ours. She runs off as Noah walks to me to the door.

"Tell me you're okay."

"Lorelai filled you in that quickly, huh?"

"Of course, you know how we are."

"Partners," I confirm.

"Yes. Something more important than just lovers, we're a team unit. No battles are fought alone here."

"Is that what I am?"

"No, sweet girl. You've never been anything but a joy. She just worries for you, always will."

"I know, but I'm good."

"Glad to hear it. But if he's not willing to be your partner, you kick his ass. Being dominant or domineering doesn't mean he gets to run all over you. Understand me?"

"Understood."

The life Lorelai and Noah have isn't my ideal. I've never pictured myself with a fancy home and a bunch of children running around. I love kids. Other people's kids, though. Motherhood isn't something I dream of.

There's still a freedom I crave that seems harder to obtain with children in tow, for one. But I have other reasons, too. What I do want is the sort of trust Lorelai and Noah have. It didn't come easy to either of them. But now that they have it, it's unbreakable. It's the opposite of what I was raised around. Now that I've witnessed it, I won't ever settle for anything less.

"Have you spoken to Jillian lately?"

"Yes." I smile. "She's doing okay. Carlotta has her studying most of the day, and she seems to like it."

"She's still excited to move out here?"

"She is. I'm not sure she believes me when I tell her Olivia and I are doing so well. Seeing it for herself will go a long way."

"I'm sure you're right. Just a couple months."

"I've said it before but thank you again for all you do for them."

"Anything for family, Delilah."

CHAPTER NINETEEN

*J*erk.

That's all the text read. It's been two days since I last saw him, but he's checked in each night. Mostly just to check that I behaved myself, but still, it's something. At least it means he thinks about me, too. There are no nerves when I walk up to his house this time. I'm ready for whatever Pope plans to throw at me.

In fact, I'm hoping to throw some things at him, as well.

After pushing the button of the keypad by his gate, I check the time on my phone. I'm five minutes early, which is late for me, I'm habitual about never being late. The gate opens with a click. Walking through it, I find not much about the courtyard has changed. The plants have matured but the space is still lit up with dim, twinkling fairy lights.

The front door of his home is wide open. This time, instead of creeping up the stairs, I go right where I can see the back of Pope's head as he lounges on a chair in the living room. Pausing long enough to drop my bag, remove the long jacket I have on, and toe off my shoes, I pad into the room.

Watching Pope for weeks at the club has given me some insight as to what he likes. I won't be going blonde for him, but I can take up some of his other preferences.

Kneeling at his feet, just to the side, I rest my cheek on his thigh.

"What's this?" he asks, trailing his gaze down my body.

"Just something I had lying around," I tease about my mesh bondage set. The mesh covers my shoulders, arms, and lower lady parts while thin red straps cross around my abdomen, hips, and thighs. Small O-rings hold it all together and offer some functionality for cuffing. It's a new purchase, one I made with him in mind.

Plus, I know I look amazing in it.

"Stand, let me see." He holds his hand out to help me up. I spin in a circle, so he gets the full view. "Do you want to eat dinner with me with your tits hanging out?"

"I don't mind. You didn't say what tonight would be and I didn't want to be presumptuous."

"I'd say this outfit is very presumptuous."

"Then allow me to clarify," I say with an eyeroll. "I didn't want you to think I assumed this was a date."

"Because you don't think you're more than a fuck?"

"I know I'm *worth* more than that, Pope. I also know you haven't stated you're looking for anything more than that."

"Fair enough," he says. "But I saw that eyeroll. Turn around, bend over and grab your ankles."

As soon as I'm in the position, the first spank lands. Luckily, it was not hard enough to topple me as my hair sweeps over the hardwood. Perhaps an eyeroll is a minor offense. Pope only delivers three before his hands grip either side of my hips.

"You didn't say my name each time."

"I know where I am. I know I am safe." He can hide behind

brutishness and bravado all he wants, I see him. I know it's not all possessiveness. This man cares about my well-being.

"How is the soreness?"

"It's mostly gone," I say but stop when Pope's nose drags over my seam as he deeply inhales. I go lightheaded, certain I'd collapse if not for his hands still holding me still.

"Fucking exquisite," he murmurs, sending a shiver through me. "Go upstairs. Find my bedroom. Pick a shirt out of my closet. You can cover up while we eat. Otherwise, we won't make it to dinner at all."

"Okay." A smile takes over my face as I stand.

"Find me in the kitchen when you're ready."

Pope's bedroom takes up most of the upper story, and a bed takes up most of the bedroom. The space of the walk-in closet smells like him, and I take a healthy inhale and try to memorize it. Flipping through the row of shirts, I can't help but wonder if others have been in this same position. It doesn't feel like jealousy. More just a curiosity about Pope and if he treats all his women this same way. Something tells me he doesn't.

I pick a black shirt, buttoning only a few buttons and tying it at my waist. When I find the kitchen, Pope is checking something in the oven.

"It smells great," I tell him.

He looks over his shoulder at me and laughs, something he does so rarely. Every time I pause to bask in it. The man is breathtaking when he's this relaxed. Comfortable and relaxed in his own space, he's sexier than I've ever seen him. His chin-length hair is slightly tousled and the normal rigidness in his stance is gone completely.

"You just can't help it, can you?"

"Help what?"

"Pray that you will not fall into temptation."

"Are you saying I tempt you, Mr. Blackwell?"

"You know exactly what you're doing, Layla," he says.

Holding my hips again, he hoists me up to sit on the countertop. "Keep me company while I finish up."

"I didn't expect you to know how to cook."

"Why?"

"I don't know, I guess you just seem like the type of guy that exists off fine dining in dark restaurants."

"You're not wrong," he says, eyeing me curiously, then he drops a quick kiss to my lips. "I do that mostly. But after my mom left, I learned quick enough. I enjoy it when there's a reason."

Butterflies take flight in my stomach at being Pope's reason for anything. That's a dangerous train of thought to follow, so I ignore it instead.

"Well, I appreciate it. Unless I'm at Lorelai's, I'm the one cooking, but it's not often that Cookie's schedule aligns with mine. It's hard cooking for just one, so I opt out of it a lot. Plus, this city has amazing takeout."

"You cooked a lot as child?" he asks as he moves to my side and chops a tomato.

"Do not give your strength to women."

"That's the scripture they used to justify child slave labor?"

"One of them, anyway. There were tons more," I answer with a humorless laugh. "Can I ask you something?"

"I'll allow it."

"How did you know Aaron harassed me?"

"Pass."

"Did you have anything to do with Andrew ghosting me?"

Pope shoves two fingers in my mouth, his signature move to shut me up. I suck the tomato juice from them.

"Are you asking me questions you already suspect the answers to?"

"Mmhmm."

"I have zero qualms chasing off the unworthy men in your life. Understand?"

"Mmm." He pulls his fingers out and goes back to salad preparation. "That was sexy, Mr. Blackwell."

I notice that he stumbles on the next chop. It feels like a win in the nameless battle we wage against one another.

"Did you play sports when you were younger?"

"That's a random question. But no. If I wasn't at school, I was expected to be at my father's church. I, too, was used for free labor." Pope says it so nonchalantly, so void of any emotion, that I don't believe for a minute he doesn't hold some animosity about it. It's a tool I've used as well. Pretend hard enough that it didn't bother us and maybe one day it won't. "What about you? Was there anything at the ranch that wasn't about teaching you to be a good child bride?"

"No. Everything led to that in one way or another. Even the things they made us feel were special treats just for us, like dance classes. But I wasn't pretty enough for those."

"Pretty enough?" he asks, his nose crinkling in disgust.

"Only the prettiest, most prized daughters got to go to special classes. Lorelai did, Olivia would have had they not gotten her out. My father didn't think I would catch him a high enough price to put in the extra effort."

"Evil motherfucker," Pope curses. Moving to stand in front of me, his hands push my knees apart so he can step in closer. "Two things; one, you're beautiful. Two, how are you so well-adjusted?"

"Tons and tons of therapy," I joke. "There were only so many directions I could go. I guess most would expect I'd end up on one extreme end or another. Either so wrapped up in the teachings of the congregation that I couldn't find my way out, or full-on self-destructing with booze, drugs, sex, and poor decisions. It shouldn't really be a surprise that I ended up somewhere in the middle. I had an extreme childhood but I'm not an extreme person."

"It's hard to believe you're the same girl who was embarrassed by a painting of the statue of David. You're quite wise for your age, especially considering your circumstances."

"Good thing since I'm hanging out with a forty year old."

"Don't fucking remind me of that, Delilah. Besides, I'm not

forty yet," he says, once again checking the oven. This time, he pulls the dish out.

"I asked you once, but you never answered. Is Pope your real name?"

"Not from birth. It's a nickname I earned in college, it stuck, and I eventually changed it legally."

"Will you tell me? I think we've confirmed I'm not a fairy," I say, hopping off the counter so I can help carry items to the table.

"The fuck you aren't." I take that as a firm no.

We plate the food with light conversation about how he's prepared the roast chicken and vegetables. It's evident he likes talking about it as much as he enjoys the actual cooking of the food. Hopefully, I'll be able to give him more opportunities to do this. But again, pinning plans on him probably isn't my safest move. He hasn't gone this long as a non-monogamous bachelor for no reason.

Before he takes his first bite, he reaches for something sitting on the seat of one of the empty chairs and places it next to me.

"You need to read over that and tell me what you don't consent to. We can re-evaluate it in the future, if needed."

"This is a list of all the things you enjoy?"

"Some are. Others are things that can come up, I need to know your boundaries."

"You have all your partners go through this?"

"To varying degrees, yes. It's for both parties' comfort and safety. It's something you should do with all your future partners, as well."

Future partners.

Because this situation won't last forever. One day, Pope will bore of me, so I better enjoy it while it lasts.

"I've never done anal, but I'm cautiously open to it," I say, reading down the list. "Breath-play is fine."

"Noted."

"No caning. No consensual non-consent."

"I assumed as much," he says, casually eating his dinner.

"No humiliation. I don't even know what figging is, so that's a no."

"That's saved for particularly bad slaves anyhow."

"I'm not anyone's slave," I say, anger pouring out with the words.

"Also noted," he says calmly. "Eat, before you get too agitated. Nothing on that list happens without your consent. That's why we're going over it now."

"I'm sorry," I say without necessarily thinking about why.

"There's nothing to apologize for. Eat."

I eat, reading through the rest of the list. Not much else stands out except one thing. The food is as delicious as it smells. I try to imagine a teenage Pope, motherless and sad, learning how to cook on his own. He's so strong and independent that it's hard to picture.

Maybe that's another thing we'll have in common and someday people will view me in the same light. Too in control of my own life to have ever been a pawn in a religious cult. Too strong to have ever been such a meek, weak thing.

"Finish up, so I can fuck you." Pope stands to clear his plate, then the rest of the table. I watch in silence, eating the last of my meal. I take my own plate, and the list, into the kitchen.

"Anything else?" he asks me.

"Explain partner sharing."

"I can give you to another man or woman. You've seen me do that before."

"I'm the only one that can say no to that, right? You've already said you won't be monogamous, so I assume you'll take other women at will."

"That's correct. The same rules don't apply to me," he says.

"Do I get to put any restrictions on you?"

"You can try. That won't be one of them."

"I don't consent to you giving me to anyone else."

"Noted. Anyone that joins us is for me and me alone. I assume you'll agree to other men watching, if I don't let them participate."

"I trust you, Mr. Blackwell." Pope's face relaxes for the briefest moment, then goes right back to the rigid mask he normally wears. *I see you.* "You can fuck me now."

"Upstairs, to my room. I'll be there shortly."

I rush off, shedding his shirt. Awkward with this sort of situation still, I'm not sure what to do with myself while I wait. Do I stand? Lie on the bed? Does he even have those type of expectations of me?

Deciding the safe bet is to kneel, I do that at the foot of the bed. And I wait.

And wait.

And wait some more.

There's no clock in here, but I'm guessing it's been about thirty minutes by the time he finally appears holding a small bag.

"I have a gift for you. Stand up," he says, reaching a hand down to help me up. "Bend over, hands on the bed."

He pulls my panties down, slowly trailing kisses behind his graze. After so much time in here alone, anticipating so much, the small ministration sets me aflame. He touches my feet one at a time for me to step out of them, then tosses them on the bed next to my face.

"Can you smell yourself?"

"Yes."

"Sometimes it's worth the wait," he says, pulling the items out of the bag. "This is a small anal plug. We're going to start with it, and we'll work our way up to a larger size."

"I'm familiar with training kits," I say, eyeing the plug. It's a few inches long, shaped like a tiny penis with a ridged head, not large yet still intimidating. Much less intimidating than Pope's own appendage, though.

"Good," he says, pulling out two small leather cuffs. He buckles one to each of my wrists, then pulls them to my lower back and attaches them to the straps that hang down over my hips. I still have mobility; it's just very limited now. "Are you good?"

"Yes, Mr. Blackwell," I sing, wiggling my rear.

"You should be more apprehensive. You have no idea what may come next." Pope has that dangerous tone in his voice now, the one he uses when he's being the big dominant. It's meant to scare, but it's never had that effect on me.

Dr. Price once asked if perhaps I don't find anyone capable of hurting me more than what my father, and uncle before him, were capable of. Since I survived that, I may have a false sense of security. It gave me something to think about, which was her point. It's not a propped up feeling with Pope, my faith in him is real.

"I trust you."

"Grab your ass, keep it spread for me."

Shame tries to worm its way into my head as I open such an intimate place to Pope. I recognize the signs, the warmth on my cheeks, my crinkled brow. Blowing out a long breath of air, I center my mind on the situation. I chose to be here. I am not frightened. I'm safe and I have nothing to be ashamed of. I'm not doing anything wrong.

A mantra that took me a long time to perfect.

Pleasure isn't shameful.

"Perfect, that's perfect," Pope praises, relaxing me even further. He spits. It hits me and it begins its path downward before a warm wetness breaches my entrance. The tip of Pope's tongue working around and around, enough to make the room disappear, for all sound to silence except the approving sounds he makes mixing with my own needy ones.

"Pope," I cry out, trying to spread wider for him.

"Good, Layla. That's good." His tongue dives right back in, and this time, he slides fingers into my pussy, too. My knees try to give out, so I dig my toes into the shaggy carpet to hold myself up, not wanting to give him any reason to stop what he's doing. It feels better than anything has before. "I'm going to use my finger now."

"Mmm." Not able to form words just now, I nod my head. His fingers, now slick, pull out and slide up. He massages my tight hole before one begins to push in.

"There you go, don't fight it. Good," he says, softly, as I release my tension. The sting is slight, not enough to cause much discomfort. He continues his appraising words as he works his finger in further, spitting a few more times to help. After a moment, the pressure eases, and he must feel it too. "Okay, now a second one."

This time, he drops a bit of cool lubricant on to his fingers, then tosses the bottle on top of my panties. The bottle reads Tush Cush, and I laugh.

"Fuck me," he curses. "Remind me when my cock is finally in this ass to make you laugh. I'm going to put the plug in now, get it wet for me."

Pope holds it to my mouth so I can suck it into my mouth, getting it as wet as I can. Then he removes it and I feel it below.

"Bear down a little. Good, just like that." Applying pressure little by little, it works its way slowly. "Okay, relax now."

It fully seats, and I let out another long exhale, moving slightly to get used to how it feels.

"That wasn't so bad," I say. Pope hoists me to standing, and I grimace.

"You took it like a champion," he says, bringing his lips to mine in a searing kiss.

"A champion of butt plugs, that's me," I tease.

Pope laughs, but eyes me curiously as well.

"Follow."

I tip-toe behind him, down the hallway, my butt twitching strangely with each step. At the opposite end of the house is another door that he holds open for me.

"I want you to see what I do to you," he says. The room's darkly painted walls are covered in antique mirrors hung in no certain design or order, all gilded gold. No matter where I look, I find us in the reflections.

"What are you going to do to me, Mr. Blackwell?"

"I'm going to fuck my maddening obsession with you out of my system." Pulling the hair at my nape, his mouth lands on mine again. I pretend I'm forcing his harsh words back into his body, erasing their very existence with my tongue. Pope isn't forever, I know that, but damn his reminder.

CHAPTER TWENTY

POPE

Delilah tastes like fruit and honey. Like sunshine and sustenance. But also, like prison and demise. Never have I craved the way I do her. She brings me to my knees without knowing and I fear her for it. What I wouldn't lay at her feet to make her mine. No price too great, I'd give her everything. But at what cost?

Her mouth alone drives me to a state of delirium. Delilah's body... so different from the waifish thing she inhabited when she was younger, is nothing short of divine. Lustful curves in all the right areas. Like the heavy breast currently weighing down my hand as I acquaint myself with every corner of her mouth.

She fights none of it. In fact, she takes it all with the stride of a much more experienced woman. How? Why is she capable of such an easy sexuality? It goes against all odds.

Yet here she is, mewling into my mouth as if she can't get enough of me either. A man nearly twice her age.

How?

How do I leave this beguiling creature be?

Breaking free, I stare down at her searching for any sign of fear. I find none. She's excited, as excited as I am.

Grasping one of her cuffs, I guide her to the end of the padded bench set up in front of one of the larger mirrors. A cushion rests on the floor. Without direction, Delilah kneels, watching me strip out of my clothes.

She thinks she enjoys watching me as much as I watch her, but she has no idea how much I've seen these five years. How many shadows I've hid in to feed my obsession, and to keep her safe.

None of that matters here in this room, however. Not what we've done, or what we've been through. Who we are or were. Our vast differences, or our remarkable similarities.

Only her body and mine. Only this.

Straddling the bench, I position myself in front of her with my legs spread wide. She tries to reach up for my erect cock, forgetting that her hands won't rise past her waist with the cuffs on. An adorable pout marks her mouth.

"Open your mouth, I'll help you get there." When she does, I palm the top of her head and bring her down on me. Further and harder than she likely expected, but she needs to learn. I won't always be so enamored with her. I won't always be kind and good. I'm not with anyone else, so it's only a matter of time.

Fuck me, her mouth is magic. Her tongue worships my dick like it's her lord and savior. Maybe it is, maybe she'll get a communion of a different sort tonight.

"Did you get this good by sucking *that Andrew's* little dick?" I spit at her. She looks up at me and shakes her head as I drive it back down. "Damian's?"

Delilah blinks rapidly. She doesn't need to answer, I know. *I saw.*

"Stop." She pulls her mouth off with one long, slow suctioning movement. "You like sucking cock, Delilah?"

"Yes," she says, with some hesitation.

Going to the small chest in the corner, I pull out a decently sized dildo. It's equipped with a suction cup on one end, which I use to attach to the mirror.

"You can watch yourself, then. You'll suck on it as if it's Damian while I fuck you," I tell her, pushing the bench out of the way before I detach her cuffs from her harness. "On your hands and knees."

Delilah crawls to it but doesn't place her mouth on the dildo. Squatting beside her, I position her how I want her. Legs closer together, arms wider, hair pulled over one shoulder. I slide on a condom and still she doesn't move.

"Open wide, Delilah. Show me what you'd do if it was his hard cock bouncing in front of you."

Watching me in the mirror, she leans forward and licks from the fake sack to the tip where she pauses to suckle and lick. Again, she does this, but then she takes it into her mouth, letting the head bulge at her cheek. Her eyes never leave mine. I reach back and wiggle the saucer of the plug, watching as her titanium eyes glaze with fire.

Moving behind her, I wait until she's just started to pull back from the cock in front of her to thrust my own into her cunt, hard. She gags and groans, but like always, she recovers beautifully fast. Me, not so much. Even the smallest plug makes a big difference when I'm inside her. She's unbelievably snug.

I'm relentless with her tonight, unconcerned by lack of experience. Even with her ample curves, her hips fit between my thighs. With my hands on her waist, I pull her back on to me and push her back on to the imposter before her. She braces a hand on the mirror, eyes still on mine. Never leaving, never giving up any of the power she has over me.

"Are you full?"

Her head bobs up and down, forward and back. Our skin slapping is the only sound. It's not enough. I will never have enough.

I stop, and she whimpers.

"Pull it off," I command. Once she has it in hand, I sit, bringing her on my lap. Lowering her back on my cock, I lean back on one arm and kick our legs out in front of us. "Watch in the mirror but don't quit sucking that cock."

My other hand goes to her clit, picking up a slow rhythm with both my fingers and my hips. Her shoulders relax, her head dropping back to relax her neck but not enough that she can't watch. Her cunt reddens, and her nipples grow harder. All the while she feeds herself the cock. She must be feeling sensation everywhere, from my cock, my fingers, the dick in her mouth, and the plug riding in her ass. Yet she keeps up with me, watching intently in the mirror through a hooded gaze.

"If you let me share you, you could have this for real. His dick in your mouth. Fig's in your cunt, and mine in your ass," I whisper in her ear. It's a bold-face lie. I don't think I could ever allow that with her. I already want to strangle them for their past touches. For daring to taste what was always meant to be mine.

She's not repulsed by the idea though, evident by how she works her clit against my fingers. The fantasy of three men at her disposal intrigues her.

"You like the idea. Your body doesn't lie, it likes this feeling," I tell her, and she moans again. It's the most beautiful song. "You can come now. Do it all over my fingers and my cock."

She wastes no time. I knew she was close but within seconds her body is convulsing with her orgasm. Her heels dig into the floor as she grinds her ass in stuttered movements against me.

Still, she doesn't stop sucking, even after she's come down and she's gasping for air around it.

"Perfect, you're so fucking perfect," I hiss in her ear, sending a shiver down her spine. Sliding my dick out, I replace it with my fingers. Gathering up some of her fluid, I bring it to her lips. "You can stop now. Taste this instead."

Delilah tosses the dildo halfway across the room, and I struggle not to laugh. Immediately, she sucks my fingers into her mouth. Like every time they've been there before, she runs her tongue over them almost lovingly. It's always meant to force my will on her, but she never takes it as any sort of punishment.

Always trying me in one way or another.

"You'll suck the real thing now." Scooting her off, I dispose of the condom. When I turn back, she's ready and kneeling on the cushion again.

A goddamned dream.

"Chin high, mouth open. Tongue out." She complies so I can drag my sack over her tongue. Delilah sucks it into her mouth without instruction. I work myself to a frenzy at watching her enthusiasm. "Fuck, Layla. Fuck!"

I come with a grunt as it rains down on her never flinching face. Delilah catches what she can and licks what else she can reach, a small smile on her face.

"Are you enjoying yourself?" I ask her.

"Very much, Mr. Blackwell. Though, I'm ready to take this micro penis out of my ass," she says with a slight wince.

Once again, she's found a way to make me laugh.

***

"You call me Layla when you're sweet. Delilah when you're not," she says while we bathe.

"You only curse when we're fucking. What's your point?"

"No point," she laughs, snuggling closer. Her arms wrap tighter around my neck. "Just an observation."

"How do you feel?"

"Amazing," she murmurs into my neck, sleepiness setting in. I've never allowed a woman to stay over. Honestly, I hadn't planned on that tonight either. Yet I'm not ready for her to leave. I can't keep her forever; she has a whole life to lead that I won't fit into. But I'll enjoy her while I can. Before my own fairytale ends and reality washes it all away. "How long have you lived in New Orleans?"

"Since I was your age. About a year after I graduated from University of Pennsylvania."

"That's where you went? I assumed it was somewhere down here in the South."

"Because of my Southern drawl?"

"Something like that," she says, smiling against my skin.

"Growing up, all I wanted to do was get away from the people down here. From the culture that's so steeped in the religious beliefs that allowed my father's abuse. At some point, I decided that felt like running away from it when I really wanted to stand up to it."

"That makes sense. I wish I had the power to stand up to my father."

"That's different, taking down your father takes more than just one person."

"I spoke to Lorelai about the money," she says, shivering slightly so I sink us further into the water. "She thinks it's a good idea to take it."

"I'm not as concerned with Lorelai's opinion as I am with yours. There is the possibility that he finds out who's behind it. It could lead him here. To me. Then to you."

"How likely is that?"

"Depends on how talented his own money people are." Frankly, I'm not at all worried about anything her father tries to do to me. However, if I'm the reason he finds a way back into her life, she needs forewarning. "It's not a decision that needs to be made right now. Think on it, let it settle."

"What do you do when you aren't working or having sex?"

"I have hobbies, if that's what you're asking."

"I'm asking what your hobbies are, you grump."

"Keep calling me names and my only hobby is going to be spanking that ass of yours," I tell her.

"Promise?"

"How are you so comfortable with all of this?" I ask, still amazed by her attitude.

"I just am. I like what I like. Some things I don't know I like until I experience it. Other stuff I try and decide never to do again. Being denied so much early on makes me want to experience more now. And it isn't as if I'm out snorting cocaine or anything very harmful."

"Spanking hasn't triggered anything for you?"

"No," she says decidedly. "Caning might, because Father always used a willow branch. Which is why I said that was out."

Noah must have paid a fortune in therapy bills for her to be this self-aware.

"Roller coasters."

"What about them?" Delilah asks.

"That's my hobby. I want to ride all the best ones in the world."

"That has to be a lie," she says in awe.

"The getting of treasures by a lying tongue is a fleeting vapor and a snare of death."

"Really? Roller coasters?" She sits up, straddles my waist, and wakes my cock back up.

"Really. Is it that hard to believe?"

"Yes. Absolutely." She nods emphatically with a cheesy grin. "I've never been on one."

"Well, we'll have to change that and see if it's one of the things you like or dislike." It breaks my heart some that she didn't get to experience parking lot carnivals or full-on amusement parks as a child. "Noah said you didn't celebrate birthdays in the congregation."

"No, we didn't. Well, except the Cleric's. The first birthday I celebrated was my eighteenth, the day Lorelai flew me here from Nevada. Noah and Olivia had a cake waiting."

"Even my asshole dad remembered my birthday."

"It was a calculated measure to make sure we never forgot our place. Insignificant and only there at the Cleric's will."

"Not your god's will?"

"God isn't there at that ranch. Nothing wholly is. I see that clearly now."

"You seem to see a lot pretty clearly these days."

"I see you clearly," she says, her tone flirty, but I know it's the truth. And I have no fucking idea what to do with that.

CHAPTER TWENTY-ONE

Tonight is the first night we'll be together at the club as anything more than acquaintances. Not a couple, not slave and master... I don't know what to label us. Playmates? Whatever we are, tonight feels monumental. Like a milestone. Or a test I haven't studied for.

I've watched him enough to know what he likes. And enough to know what I will and won't do. I've seen how easy it is to lose yourself in a relationship with a man. It's how places like the ranch begin in the first place. No matter what Pope makes me feel or how much I want him in my life, it must be give and take. I won't allow such a lopsided balance of power, regardless of his preferences.

Lupus et Agnus is built on a foundation of safety and trust. I have faith that Pope will respect the boundaries I put forth. Yet something tells me tonight... here, he'll be different than he's been the other times we've had alone together. I'll be Delilah, not his Layla.

I'm dressed for the occasion but not like I was at Pope's house the other night. Instead, I'm in a pale pink, tiny babydoll dress that I paired with a black half bunny mask.

When I see on my screen that Pope has checked in, I shut my computer down and lock up my office. Fabienne is propped up in her office doorway, waiting.

"You look ready. How do you feel?"

"Empowered." The first word that comes to mind, it rings true. Maybe some would see it as a strange turn of events for someone like me. Some others would think this is my way of coping with trauma I've yet to deal with. Except I have dealt with it. The scars remain, they always will. But they don't rule over my life decisions. I haven't succumbed, I've overcome.

"That's what I love to hear," she says with a shining smile. "You keep that attitude, darling. I'll be around for a while yet, if you need me."

"Thanks, Boss Lady."

"Anything for you, Delilah."

Pope is chatting with Halston on the other side of the room when I enter the salon. Stopping by the bar, I pour him a whiskey before heading to where he sits. I hand it to him. He and Halston pause the conversation to watch me, then I kneel at his feet. I face the room, like I've seen his other women do. I stay silent, like his other women have.

I am not those women, even if I play one here tonight.

"Good evening, Delilah," Halston says to me. I look up at Pope, who raises an eyebrow.

"Good evening, Halston."

"Well done. Thank you for the drink," Pope leans down to whisper in my ear.

"You're welcome, Mr. Blackwell."

"I don't know what this asshole did to get your attention, but if he fucks it up, you come see me."

"He's very sweet to me, but I'll keep that in mind," I tell Halston, who laughs at Pope's pursed lips.

I look back to the room and see Shanna glaring at me. She's

only a few feet away and obviously very upset that I'm the one at Pope's knee tonight. He's mine for as long as I can have him, her bad feelings don't make me feel anything but annoyed that she's putting them on display for everyone in the club to see. It's not the sort of drama we encourage. I send her a sweet smile. It makes her scowl worse, but it's worth letting her know I see what she's doing. My workday is done, but the care for my workplace never ends.

Pope's hand strokes down my head a few times before settling at the nape of my neck. The men continue to talk about business. Stocks, specifically. I listen quietly for the first few minutes, until Halston brings up a tech company based in North Carolina.

"I would pass on that one if I were you," I say, dropping my chin to rest on Pope's thigh. "I can email you the data I have on them."

"How old are you?" he asks.

"Twenty-three. My current return on investment for the club is eight percent. It's higher for my personal portfolio because I tend to take more risks with my own money."

"Delilah may not know her place, but she knows her investments." Pope's words come out harsh, but I'll take a little punishment if it saves Halston some money.

"Sorry, Mr. Blackwell," I playfully pout, making Halston laugh.

"Send me what you have, I'll take a look."

"You'll have it before the market opens tomorrow," I say, keeping my head down. I do it for Pope, trying to keep up with the preferences he's told me he has. We spoke about it at length yesterday when he expressed his desire for me to accompany him in this way. If I'm his pet for the night, I'm to follow his lead. Ask permissions I wouldn't normally. Speak when spoken to, etc.

It isn't hard, I just have to revert to my childhood behavior, really. What's difficult is setting aside the hard-earned attitude, abilities, and pride I possess now that I never did then. I suppose it's a good thing I like his punishments, since I'm likely to get them often.

Their conversation turns when a woman I've never met enters the Salon. Tall, curvy, dressed in a demurely sexual way with enough covered to keep it a mystery while still being alluring. Of course, she has long blonde, wavy hair.

"I didn't realize Tabitha was back in town, did you?"

"No," Pope says. He sounds, I don't know, wistful maybe. The thumb that's been rubbing back and forth on the column of my neck stills.

Who is this woman?

She circles the room, speaking with various people. All the while the two men in my company watch.

"Maybe tonight is my night," Halston muses. "You wouldn't mind, surely?"

"I have no hold over her," Pope responds coldly.

"No, that was a long time ago. But out of respect..." Halston lets his words fall into the void.

"She's the best I've ever had, Halston. Count yourself lucky if she lets you in her cunt."

Halston stands, leaving us to pursue his quest. Goosebumps cover my flesh, suddenly cold and apprehensive for reasons I don't fully know. There's a sharp pain in my chest, dull but noticeable. Is this jealousy? It wasn't there before he said she was the best he'd had. Maybe it's just bruised ego, because I want to be that for him. It's hard to label the things I've never had experience with.

My palms sweat. I move them from my thighs to cross over my hips, lightly grasping the silk of my dress. Trying to work through the prompts Dr. Price has given me to check on myself. *I am safe. I am safe.*

"What's my name?" he whispers in my ear, tickling the hair around my neck.

"Pope."

"Good girl." Instantly, my body begins to relax. "Give me a kiss."

I am safe.

The kiss is small and soft, not the usual hungry one. No less pleasurable. He repeats it a few more times, the thumb at my pulse picking up movement again.

"If you're a weakness, it will be exploited. Understand?" he whispers. I nod, but no… no, I don't understand what he means.

Until he pulls away and I see Tabitha walking our way.

"It's good to see you, Blackwell." Even her voice is beautiful, deep with a sexy rasp to it.

"Tabby."

Her eyes narrow on him, not liking the nickname. Or maybe not liking the familiarity of it.

"I'm in town for a few weeks. I thought I might find you here," she says. She doesn't look at him, opting to instead watch the swirling red liquid in her wine glass.

"You know I'm a creature of habit. I've never been hard to find." The bite in his tone grabs her attention. They stare at each other for a few long moments. Equally awkward and fascinated, I do my best to not study the silent showdown. It's difficult, but I keep my chin tipped down and only my eyes stretch up to watch every few seconds.

"That was deserved," Tabitha finally says. "I was hoping we could speak."

"Not tonight. Contact Lucinda, she'll let you know when I can fit you in."

"Of course," the woman drawls, as if she was expecting that exact reaction. The lie of it is written all over her face. "Who's your pet?"

"Just a new kitten," Pope says more blandly than I knew him capable of.

It burns, so keenly and deeply. For eighteen years, I was nothing but currency to men. This feels too familiar; only now I'm currency in a match of wills I know nothing about. The only thing keeping me from standing and fleeing is the thumb still gently massaging. Serving as reminder to not be a weakness.

The game is something I don't understand, but the rules are clear.

"Does she play well with others?" Tabitha says with a hint of a hiss, kneeling in front of me and tipping my chin up with her long fingernail.

"No, I tend to bite," I say in a gut reaction. Pope's fingers press down into my skin, a warning that comes too late.

Tabitha smiles, and it's anything but friendly. "Mouthy, isn't she?"

"Yes, but you know how I enjoy punishing the new ones."

"Mmm, can I watch?"

"Of course, go find a room. We'll be along after I finish my drink."

She saunters off with a natural sway that I doubt I'll ever possess, looping her arm through Halston's as she does.

"Damn it, Delilah," Pope curses.

"I'm sorry," I say on a sigh. "Who is she?"

"Someone who will know if I take it easy on you."

"Then don't," I say simply.

"You don't yet know what that means."

"You must not know me at all," I say, fire of my own in my voice. "Whatever you have to do to save face in front of *that woman*, will not be worse than what I've already endured."

"I won't show you kindness in there, Delilah. You'll be alone in your pain."

"I've been alone with it my whole life." He flinches back an inch or so. Pope doesn't know what to expect of me any more than I know what to expect in whatever room Tabitha waits. He roughly grabs either side of my face, bringing his so close. Close enough to kiss.

"Don't push me in there. Please," he pleads.

"I'll do my best."

"Fuck me." He's gentle as he pulls me behind him. Until we

walk through to the hallway. Thankfully, Tabitha hasn't picked the white room. We find the couple across the hall in a room equipped with a couple benches that remind me of something a gymnast would vault over. I haven't yet learned the terminology for everything. The walls are equipped with tethers, and a case in the corner is stocked with various toys.

Pope leads me to the case, first to buckle cuffs on my wrist. Then he picks up a small ball gag. He contemplates it in his hands until I grab it from him and open my mouth. Again, he's shocked. I see it, thankfully his back is to Tabitha and Halston, so they miss his hesitation.

"Remember who you're with," he says, barely audible, as he buckles the gag.

I am safe.

My wrists are hooked to either end of the bench in front of where the woman watches intently. My only choices are to look directly at her, or to rest my cheek. I'm too stubborn to look away.

"You took your time," she coos at Pope, her hand on Halston's knee. He looks near boredom next to her greedy eyes.

"My pet needed to understand her offense." Pope removes my mask, weaving the strings of it into my fingers. "Don't let it drop."

"Does she understand now?" Tabitha directs the question at me, even if she's not addressing me. I nod, trying my best to seem contrite. I'm not at all. I don't like this woman, which is a very rare reaction from me. Everyone gets a chance, the benefit of the doubt. Not Tabitha. If it takes being chained and my ass beaten raw to get rid of her, it's an easy price to pay.

"She knows why she's being punished." He words it so I know it's more because of her than it is because of my behavior. Still, I'd like to know what power this woman has over him that it's led to this.

Pope enters my field of vision, once again over at the cabinet. He picks up a flogger, weighs it in his hand before he disappears again. The tassels of the flogger brush my bottom as he lifts the hem of my dress over my hips. Snapping the thin strap of my nude panties, he leaves them in place.

Then the sting comes, the blow landing on the tender flesh just above my thigh. I suck in air around the ball in my mouth, the feel of the flogger vastly different than Pope's hand.

Tabitha's sea blue eyes narrow on mine. Determined to not give her any satisfaction, I wink at her. My experiences in this room aren't for her pleasure. They're mine. Partly, they are for Pope, but I wouldn't have walked here with him if I didn't get something out of it that I want, too.

I want to learn about this world. And I want to learn it by Pope's hand. If at the end of the night I decide I hated this, then I'll know to never let it happen again.

Halston smiles at me knowingly. Tabitha may have walked in here with one game in mind, but I'm here to play my own.

Pope starts a lazy rhythm, as if playfully twirling the flogger in a circle and my ass just happens to be in the way. It smarts each time it lands. On its own, it wouldn't be too much to handle, it's the repetitiveness on the same spot that causes the eventual throbbing. My toes curl and fists clench as my muscles start to tense in defense of the next slap.

It's not until my vision clears on the woman in front of me that the pain of the flogger takes a backseat. Tabitha is enjoying what she sees. While she never takes her eyes off Pope, her hands pull her own dress ever higher. She hitches a leg over Halston's lap, taking his hand and placing it between her thighs.

She throws her head back on a moan and Pope's flogger hits harder. Still, I take it, not making a sound.

All four of us are locked in a game of stares. If I had been born with eyes on the back of my head, I'm sure they'd show me that Pope's watching her.

It's the only detail in this room that causes me offense.

He isn't doing anything that he hasn't already laid out as a possibility. He is not a monogamous man, I know this. Our time together is tenuous and temporary. I *know* this.

Tabitha pulls her dress over her head, her bare breasts bouncing with the effort. The flogger hits minutely harder.

The problem isn't that Pope is reacting to Tabitha, the problem is that he isn't here in this moment with me. The problem is that I don't think I'd be here at all if it wasn't for wanting to be with him. That's the thought that breaks through my defenses, no matter how many times I remind myself that he told me this would happen.

Halston undoes his pants; I watch it numbly. Then he slides on a condom, and with ease, he lifts Tabitha onto his dick, and I watch it exactly like Pope said I would. Alone. My punishment was supposed to take center stage, but Tabitha is the real star attraction here.

Pope lets the flogger fall to the floor. It thuds and bounces a few feet away from us. His hands find my panties, and I flinch at the touch, at the thought of what it is he wants to do. Pausing at my reaction, I use the moment to force my legs closer together. A clear signal that I don't want what he's offering. My mouth can't speak the words, all I can hope is that he understands my body language.

It screams at him that I will not be the vessel for his pleasure that is derived from her.

His hands leave me as he takes a step back. The rustling of his movements is distinctly heard behind me. He's undoing his own pants now.

Alone.

I am safe.

I know, I know, I know.

I repeat the chants over and over as I let my mask fall from my fingertips and finally turn my head away, resting my cheek on the cold, hard surface, as I try to block out the sounds around me.

CHAPTER TWENTY-TWO

Time passes indistinctly when you lose yourself inside your own mind. Maybe only five short moments have passed, though it feels far greater by the time the room quiets. Two bodies leave, I assume Tabitha and Halston. The buckle of my gag is loosened, but I don't open my eyes to confirm it's Pope. I'm exhausted and the effort seems too costly a price to pay.

One of my hands is uncuffed, and I grip the edge of the bench to steady myself as the other one gets unbuckled. Hands touch to lift me…

"No," I say softly.

"You're spent, let me carry you."

"No. I'll walk out of here on my own." I do just that. Not stopping until we've reached the reception area and Hattie gets my coat and handbag from the closet. "Thanks, Hattie, see you tomorrow."

Hopefully, my feigned cheerfulness fools her. Pope leads me to his car, opening the door for me as I sit as carefully as possible. My skin burned the entire way out here, but I tried so hard not to let it show.

"I'll take you to my house," he says when he enters the driver's side.

"My place is closer."

"You aren't likely to have what I would like to treat your skin with," he argues.

"Take me to my house, please."

He ceases talking for the short drive from one end of the Quarter to the other. Pope helps me out of the car and up the stairs to my apartment and waits while I unlock the door and open it to a dark space. Cookie must be out with Logan.

"You don't need to stay," I tell Pope who tries to follow me inside.

"The fuck I don't," he curses, flipping the light switch just inside the door. "Where's the bathroom?"

I lead the way, still too tired to fight with him about it. My bathroom is tiny, as is most everything about our apartment. Pope has to rub against my backside to get to the shower-bathtub combo. I hiss and he sighs reaching for the tap.

"No bath." It's the last thing I want. Besides, I did nothing to soil my skin tonight.

"Why?" he asks. It's how we always end our nights, after all.

"I don't need one," I say. "I have this cream, it should help." I take cooling gel out of the medicine cabinet and hand it to him.

"Fine. Show me your bedroom."

Turning, I walk out and to the next door in the hallway that leads to my cramped bedroom. It doesn't fit more than my full-size bed and a dresser. But it's my own space, decorated with furnishings I picked out and bought myself. That makes it my favorite place in the world.

"Lie down on your stomach."

The gel doesn't cool me under the fiery touch of his fingers.

"Talk to me," he says.

"I'm fine, Pope."

"I didn't say lie to me."

"It's not a lie."

Pope finishes with the gel and lies next to me, side by side, face to face.

"Is this because of what happened at the end?" His brow furrows.

"That she helped you jerk off onto her chest? No, it's not about that." I was despondent and done with the situation long before that moment.

"You've always known I would be with others, Delilah," he argues. "That served a purpose you don't understand."

"It's not about sharing, Pope. I was born to do that. I was *bred* for just that."

Horrified, his jaw tenses so hard I wonder if he'll crack a molar.

"You weren't," he says with such conviction that I could almost believe.

"I was." Pope stares at me like he might be able to change my mind by his will alone. It's the truth, though. He knows it, I've known it since I was old enough to understand. I was never meant to be 'the one' for anyone. I'm supposed to be one of many, un-special, and insignificant.

"Then what happened?" His hand pushes away the hair falling over my cheek.

"You did what anyone expected you would have done, Pope. You took the pleasure you wanted from where you wanted to take it from," I say with a sad smile. "I want my pleasure to come from you, but be because of me. Does that make sense?"

"You think I wanted her."

"It's not about what I think. It's about what I know and what I feel. It didn't need to be me in that room tonight. Any body would have done. I had a lifetime of that feeling; it's not something I'm eager to experience again."

"It was you I wanted with me tonight, Delilah." His thumb traces my jawline.

"I was with you." I don't say the rest. No need to remind him that it was he who wasn't with me. "I'm tired, Pope. You should go."

"That doesn't sit well with me; leaving you like this. There's a lot you don't understand."

"Do you want to explain it all to me?" I ask, and his expression stutters. "Go home, Pope. I'm ready to sleep."

"The next few days will be busy for me. I may not be around, but I'll check in," he says, still sounding concerned.

"I'll be fine."

Pope kisses me on the forehead before he leaves. When the front door shuts, I let the tears fall. There aren't many and they aren't for Pope. These are for me, for the strength I wish I had tonight but didn't. For the strength I had to show when I didn't want to. For letting the empowerment I felt at the beginning of the night flee so easily.

Mostly, I cry for the lie I told him and myself. Hearing Tabitha finish Pope off bothered me more than I'd ever admit to him. It may have even broken something inside me.

For the first time in a long while, I shut my eyes and pray that I'll have the power to overcome the sun.

"Seattle?"

"That's what he told Fig," Cookie says, sounding as shocked as me at Damian's sudden desire to move across the country. "He didn't say anything to you?"

"Nope. But I haven't seen him in several days." It's been three nights since I've seen Pope. He hasn't been back to the club. I've not been downstairs, either. I've lost the desire. For now, anyway. So, I finish my work and go home at the end of the day. Which means I haven't seen Fig or Damian, either.

True to his word, Pope checks in with me by text daily. My responses are always short.

"What will Fig do without his sidekick?"

"I don't know," she says. "Probably the same thing as always. Work, fuck, sleep, repeat."

We're at our favorite bistro sharing a charcuterie board and a bottle of wine. Thankfully, it's located around the corner from our apartment with patio seating for nights like tonight. Not too hot, but warm enough to enjoy the fresh air under the white twinkle lights they have hanging from all the umbrellaed tables.

"He'll miss him, I'm sure."

"Oh, yeah. They've been a hive mind for as long as I can remember. I'm not sure they'll function on their own. They have a few months before he leaves, though."

"That makes me sad for both of them." I take a bite of unidentifiable cheese; it tastes sort of like coastal cheddar but creamier. "This one's really good."

"You seem in a better mood," she hedges. Cookie doesn't know all the sordid details, though I did tell her the basics.

"I needed to evaluate things, I guess. Things have moved fast the past couple of months and instead of moving at my own pace, I tried to keep up with everyone else's."

"Should I be worried? Because I have been."

"I'm sorry, that wasn't my intention," I say, and she smiles as if it's all fine. "You don't need to worry. I think that part of the lifestyle just isn't for me. Or, at least not like that."

"You mean you want a one-man one-woman relationship?"

"I'm open to others participating in play. I've done that with Fig and Damian, and it was great. The other night was different."

"Because it was balanced more equally with Damian and my brother?" Cookie mimes gagging. "Or because you're in love with Pope?"

Am I in love with Pope? Probably.

"I don't know what being in love feels like."

"It feels sad when they are your priority, and the sentiment isn't returned. Love makes you excited for life. Or something like that." She laughs, because she doesn't know any more than I do.

"You're right about the balance of power. I enjoy submitting to him, but not at the expense of feeling unseen. As for being in love, maybe I was heading there. I don't know about all that, but I do know I won't be any kind of sister wife."

"What if that's all he has to offer?"

"Then he's not the man for me. It hurts, but it would hurt worse later," I say then finish up what wine I had left in my glass. Cookie is quick to add more for me.

"I'm sorry, Delilah. You've earned happiness."

"I have that," I tell her. "With you and with my family. I don't need a man for that."

"I'll fucking drink to that." We clink our glasses and finish our meal talking about subjects much less sad. Like how much time Cookie has been spending with Logan.

She's never dated much, not since I've known her. Logan must be a special guy to gain so much attention from her, they see each other several times a week.

While we wait for the check, we both scroll social media on our phones. I don't have much of it, in an effort to keep a low profile, but I like Instagram which is mostly just pretty pictures and little to stress about.

"Who's this?" Cookie asks, handing me her phone. It's a post from a local magazine called *Moxy*, something about an uppity charity event happening in the city tonight. The picture shows a few well-dressed couples.

"That's her. Tabitha." Who's standing arm in arm with Pope. He is in a perfectly tailored suit the likes I haven't seen him wear since the first day I saw him, while she's in a glamorous blue dress that shows off her curves. Both ensembles are accessorized with bright smiles.

"Did you know they were going to this together?"

"No. He said he had a full week. It's not really my business anyway."

"Fuck that, Delilah. I don't believe you were nothing but a toy to him." I don't believe that either, but that doesn't change a single thing. In fact, it makes it worse.

"Whatever I am to him, I won't be chasing him around like

some pick-me girl. If I start acting stupid, I'm counting on you to rein me in."

"Ride or die," she says, holding up her knuckles for me to tap with mine. "I got you."

Before the night ends, there is another text from Pope.

POPE

I want to see you tomorrow.

I shut my phone off without responding. He knows how to find me.

———

Tomorrow came and went without seeing him. The next day as well. Now it's Saturday, my day is winding down and like I do most Saturday evenings, I should be making my way downstairs. I've been stalling and Fig has been firing off text messages to me for the past twenty minutes. He's brought a guest tonight that he wants me to meet.

When I finally make it downstairs, he's in the salon with Damian and a woman who looks to be about my age. She's pretty with fiery red waves and lightly freckled cheeks. Like me, she's conservatively dressed for a Saturday night at a sex club. I didn't feel the need to be vampy tonight and opted for ankle length trousers and a slightly cropped top. This woman is in snug black jeans and a simple white tank top.

I like her instantly.

"Hey, guys," I greet them.

"There she is," Fig says, standing to hug me. "Delilah, this is Bree."

"Hi, it's nice to meet you."

"You too," she says with a big smile. "Fig doesn't shut up about you."

"Yeah, yeah. I'm pretty sure she was my twin in another life or something." It's not the first time he's said this. Fig thinks that because I fit in so well with him and his sister that it means something more. He's a lot like his mother that way, spiritual in a non-religious sense.

"You help run this place?"

"On the financial end. I know little about the workings of things down here."

"That's not entirely true, and you're learning more every day," Damian says.

"Well, surely you know more than me. I'm as virgin as it gets to a place like this."

"That's why I wanted you two to meet. Bree's curious about the lifestyle," Fig says.

"And bi-curious," she chimes in.

"And that. Also, she recently left the religion she was raised in."

"Oh," I say, intrigued. "What denomination?"

"Jehovah's Witness."

"I don't know much about them, if I'm honest."

"It makes sense you wouldn't," she says. "There aren't many to begin with and they have a horrible retention rate. About two-thirds of the people raised in it leave when they become adults."

"Wow, that many?"

"Yeah, it's a lot. Fig said you were raised in a strict religion, too."

"I didn't tell her the details, figured it wasn't my place," Fig says, throwing his arm around me from the chair next to me.

"I was. It was sort of a form of Fundamentalist Mormonism."

"Like polygamy?" she asks, wide eyed.

"Just like that," I confirm. "I got out right before I turned eighteen."

"Good for you! It took me until I was almost twenty, mostly because I didn't want to leave my younger sister to suffer alone. But she's out now, too."

We talk for another half hour or more, the guys saying little but not seeming bored by the topic. Eventually, we decide to show

Bree the rest of the club and we end up where we often do. Comfortable in our little corner banquet of the second floor, I rest my head on Damian's lap, sleepy after a long week. Bree is doing the same with Fig as we all chat about the random happenings in front of us.

"I think I've always been bisexual," she says. "I remember thinking girls were pretty when I was really young, but you suppress all that when it's pounded into you how wrong it is."

"Doesn't look wrong to me," Damian says, intently watching two women have a make-out session on the other side of the room.

"Right? It looks hot as fuck. I've just never had the balls to approach a woman in a flirty way. Let alone ask one if I can kiss her."

I roll over so I can see Bree better, draping my arms over Damian's thighs. He drops his hand to my ass and I send him a playful eyeroll.

"I don't think I'm into women, but you can kiss me. I mean, if you want to. Maybe having that under your belt will help the next time you meet a woman you want to flirt with."

"Really?"

"Yes, please," Fig says, and we all laugh.

"This isn't for you, sir," I scold. "It's for Bree."

"You're sure? I don't want to step on toes or blur any lines. Or fuck up what has the potential for an awesome friendship."

"I'm sure. It's just a kiss between friends. I've kissed both these guys; it hasn't ruined anything for us." She looks to Fig for some reassurance, probably because she knows him better. If she decides she wants to try, I'm not apprehensive about it. I'm even curious about it myself. There are plenty of members here who aren't straight, this is something I've been exposed to enough to wonder how different it would be with a woman. "What did the wall say to the other wall?"

"What?" Damian asks with a cheesy grin, while Fig lets out a long groan.

"Meet you at the corner." Everyone gives their own commentary about how bad the joke is, but it takes some of the pressure off Bree while she considers.

"Okay, let's do it," she says, showing excitement now.

I smile at her and prop myself up on my elbows while she moves to mirror my position over Fig's lap. Bree moves closer inch by inch. I don't know if it's to give herself time to change her mind, or for me to. Neither of us do. When her lips touch mine, it's tender and tentative, but not unpleasant. Bree opens her lips and I follow her lead, letting her deepen it at her open pace. After a short moment, her tongue darts out to lick my bottom lip. Even her tongue feels different than any man I've been with, the movement softer and more feminine.

Raising on to my hands and knees, I move closer and open my mouth enough to let her explore further. Her hand situates at the column of my neck, tipping my head to where she wants it. I let her take and take, get her fill.

After a few moments, she pulls away, a little out of breath.

"Fuck, Delilah. You're hot," she says, and I laugh.

"It looks like your kitten has found new playmates." I look up to the voice that's invaded our dark bubble to find Tabitha. Flanking her, Pope wears an expression that's hard to interpret. Pleased, perplexed… I can't say.

"She's right; that was fire," Damian says, swatting my ass for effect.

Then Pope's face takes on an all too familiar look.

Pissed.

CHAPTER TWENTY-THREE

POPE

"A word, Delilah," I grit out the words. She hasn't responded to my texts in days and the first opportunity I've had to come find her, this is the scene I walk in on. Damian's hands all over.

"Ooh, did we make Daddy mad?" the stranger who just had her tongue tangled with Delilah's, asks. I balk at the comment. *I'm not that fucking old.*

"It's fine. I think it's his default." Delilah laughs while she untangles herself from Damian's limbs. "I'll be back, this shouldn't take long."

Completely ignoring Tabitha and whatever she's trying to say to me, I grab Delilah's forearm and march her upstairs to the private room I know she still hasn't let anyone use. Compliantly, she types in the code without me having to ask.

"I think I was clear when I said no Fig or Damian?" I bark as soon as I have her in the room with the door securely shut behind us.

"I thought our agreement was over."

"Why would you think that?" I back her up against the wall, so she has no choice but to look up at me. Crowding so close to her I can smell her shampoo; I want to bury my face in it. It's been too long.

"Because I want it to be over."

So many words she could have spoken, none would have cut as deep as those.

"Please don't say that."

Delilah blinks at me. I'm not ready for us to be over just yet. She's so young, she'll be done with me far too soon as it is. I need what little time I have.

"Why do you care? It's been, what, a week? You've certainly been fine without my companionship. There are plenty of other women here that would gladly take the place at your feet. Ones more suited to your lifestyle. Women who won't care how you play or who else you play with. Women more your type. Blonde women! You don't need me."

If she only knew how untrue that was.

"I want you."

"Funny," she snipes with a tilt of her head. "It's not me that walked in with you tonight. And it wasn't me with you at the event the other night. Lie to yourself, but not to me."

"You don't understand," I say, snaking my fingers in her mouth. It's always been effective at getting her to quiet enough to listen and get her to relax while she focuses her attitude somewhere else. Tonight, though, she doesn't suck my fingers in, and her tongue doesn't play. Instead, she thoroughly relaxes her mouth like a dead fish, waiting for the hook to be removed. I pull them back out and take a step away from her.

"Here's your chance to explain."

How to explain Tabitha Monroe?

"Can you just trust me, please? Give me some time and keep Damian's hands off you in the meantime."

"Sure, Pope," she agrees, finally seeing some sense. "As long as you keep your hands off Tabitha and anyone else. Deal?"

Fucking hell.

"That's not how it works."

"New rules," she says with a shrug.

Obviously, she's not going to concede without some explanation. It's not that I blame her for that, I admire it. I'd do the same.

"She's not a subject I like discussing, Delilah."

"Then don't discuss it and leave me be." She turns to the door, and I know it's my last chance to keep her here.

"She was my fiancée," I blurt in a last-ditch effort. One that works, because Delilah stops.

She doesn't turn back around. She's like Lot's wife maybe, wanting to turn back to the carnage, but afraid of what she'll suffer if she witnesses my sin burning up in flames. Tabitha is that… a part of my sinful past that needed repentance.

"What does that change?"

"Nothing," I say, moving behind her so I can wrap my arm around her chest and keep her from running. "It's the start of an explanation. I met her when I was too young, when I was still very angry with the world. Neither of us cared much for other people and we bonded over that. She called it love and I naively believed her. She wasn't a good person, Layla. I bolstered that; I propped up her worst traits and supported her while she did horrific things."

"What type of things?"

"We often played with other people. One woman showed me a little too much attention and Tabitha hyper focused on it. Did everything in her power to ruin the woman's life. She drove her to attempt suicide," I say into the curtain of her hair. "I wasn't aware of it. Tabitha hid it well, and the other woman was too scared to come to me about it. When I found out, I cut it off with Tabitha. Told her she needed therapy, and I would pay for it, and that I'd help her through it. She started it, but after a few weeks, she packed up and left New Orleans."

"Had you seen her between then and the other night?"

"Once. A few years after she left, she showed up without warning. She seemed different, better. But I couldn't trust that it was true."

"And this time… you're just picking up where you left off? With the best you've ever had?"

"No," I tell her, forcing as much conviction into my voice as I can. What I said to Halston was a lie, and I should have expected such a reaction from Delilah. "She's not the best I've ever had, and we haven't picked up anything."

"Don't lie to me, Pope." Her shoulders slump. She sounds so tired, and I hate that I have a part to play in that. Not just a part, a starring role.

"I'm not. Will you look at me? Please?" She turns into my arms, raising her face to mine. There's a sadness there that I'm the cause of. "I'm keeping an eye on her while she's in town. That's it."

"Sounds good. Hope you have a great time."

"Damn it, Delilah. I don't want you on her radar. Or anyone's radar, for that matter. Including Halston's, but mostly Tabitha's. If that means I let her trail me around for the few days she's here, that's what I'll fucking do."

"I'm not that fragile, Pope. Is that not clear yet? Quit making excuses, it's not my business who you have sex with anyway, right? And now it's not your business who I have sex with."

"I'm not fucking her."

"I don't believe you," she says with an incredulous laugh. "You think I don't know you, Pope? That I don't see you? How often do you go a week without sex?"

"It's rare," I say, barely opening my mouth for the words. "But it does happen."

"Yeah? How rare is it that you go without a blow job or making a woman come?"

I don't owe her an explanation if we stick to the rules of what our relationship has been so far. Really, what I don't want is to hurt her. If there was a way to surround her in a protective bubble for the rest of her life, it's exactly what I'd do.

"More rare."

"Right, it's more rare," she whispers, eyes glittering with

wetness. This fierce, brave woman breaking down for me. "Then you're at least getting some of that."

"I haven't had my dick out for her since that first night here, if that's what you're asking."

"I didn't ask what you do *for* her."

"That was poorly worded. Nothing I do is for Tabitha," I say, tipping her head up to me again. "I'm trying to protect you. The only way I know how."

"I never asked for that, either."

"No, but you've always had my protection, regardless."

"Why? Why have I had that?"

"Because I'm fucking in love with you, Layla," I rage at her, finally losing any patience I had left. Picking her up by the waist, I take her to the bed. Laying her down, I stretch out on top of her, pulling her arms up over her head. "Since the first words you spoke to me in Noah's library, I've wanted to keep everything and everyone away from you. It's only grown since then. You are my obsession, my fucking addiction."

A tear streams out of the corner of her eye. It's the most vulnerable I've seen her in a very long time. She always used to look this way, shaking and held together by a thread. That isn't who she is now though. The Delilah that took a job at a sex community is fearless, sturdy, and strong.

Like the devil I am, I turned her into this.

"You *know* what it is to live a life unloved. It's a desolate and lonely existence, Pope. You don't get to offer me something like love without a full understanding of what that is. It will hurt too much if it's not real. As wonderful as it is to hear the words—" She pauses to collect herself, hitching air into her lungs. "I believe you know the meaning even less than I do."

"I don't agree," I say simply. She's wrong. I know with every drop of black blood being pumped through my body by my once dead heart that I love Delilah.

"That's not good enough for me. Words mean nothing when you've been behaving how you have this past week."

"Delilah."

"No. Let me up, please," she asks with such a weak voice I can't refuse. "Figure it out, Pope. Until then, you need to leave me alone. And know that if we never go any further, I won't ever regret the short time we had together. I'll cherish it, always."

"Delilah," I call again. It's too little and far too late as she pushes me off her and walks out of the room.

Falling back on the bed, I stare up at the blank ceiling to evaluate the situation and formulate a plan. Women don't challenge me, ever. Yet she does with every conversation. Every woman I've had any sort of relationship with since Tabitha, I was careful to keep tight control on, leaving no room for a repeat situation.

Delilah is the first one I don't want to control. She wouldn't be her if she let me have that, and I don't want to change her. I want to inspire her the way she inspires me.

Which only makes her right in the fact that my behavior has been all wrong. While I've been appeasing Tabitha's worst habits, what I should have been doing is supporting all of Delilah's efforts and aspirations. Instead, I've hidden her away. In part to shelter her, and partly to preserve my own reputation. I'm still uncomfortable with how much older I am than her. With that comes a deep fear that she'll grow out of me. Why wouldn't she? I have hair starting to gray as she's in the prime of her life. I won't be able to keep up with her when in a decade, I'll be facing fifty and she'll still be a handful of years younger than I am now.

Jesus.

It's goddamned terrifying.

What I've failed to consider is how frightening it all is for her. Yet everything I asked of her before that night Tabitha walked back into my world, Delilah faced with a strong backbone and lack of fear.

I trust you... how many times did she say that? And I still let her down. Repeatedly.

I am a stupid, stupid man. So proficient at it I could lecture advance studies on how dumb a man can be.

Noise at the door breaks through my lament. Hoping it's Delilah coming back, I drown in disappointment when I see Tabitha standing in the doorway.

"You're not allowed in here," I bark, sitting up.

"I saw your pet flee. When you didn't come back down, I thought I'd come find you."

"She didn't like what I had to say, it seems."

"Maybe I can make you feel better," she says with that sneer she perfected so long ago.

"Go home, Tabitha. Back to Miami. There's nothing for you here. Leave my life and everything in it. Understand me?"

"I'm not the same person. I can share," she starts. I don't let her finish, crowding her until she backs out of the room and against the far wall of the hallway.

"No. You will never have a place in my life again." I'm an inferno ready to burn her to the ground if she makes one wrong move. She senses it, her shoulders slumping under the tension. "I have spent days keeping an eye on you because I will never trust you not to cause more harm. That is the only reason. Now it's time for you to leave. Do not come back, do not interfere in my life in any way. Do you understand me?"

"You're not the same person, either," she says after a moment. "You're different, softer."

"I'm not sure if you meant that as a compliment or insult. Either way, I am who I am, and I am not your concern," I practically yell.

"Understood." Her voice shakes on the single word, and she retreats back out of the room.

I don't trust that she'll leave New Orleans quietly, but after the past week, I don't think she's lying when she says she's not the same person she was. Tabitha is still selfish and vain, but the diabolical part of her has faded to a dim flame.

Regardless, Delilah is right. I haven't given her credit for how capable she is of standing up for herself.

There isn't any reason, or time, to dwell on Tabitha and the mistakes I've made there. My focus is solely on the brunette that has turned my world upside down. Who's made me want to be a better man, one less selfish and hard.

The bible story of Samson and Delilah is most often told as a cautionary tale of a treasonous woman who beguiled the mighty Samson. Nagging him daily for the secret of his strength, which he was reluctant to divulge, until he was 'vexed unto death' and finally revealed it to her. Knowledge that she then used, along with his Philistine enemies, to steal it away, blind, and imprison him.

God, being so benevolent to one of his chosen men, gave Samson his revenge in the end by giving him enough strength to destroy the Philistine temple and the thousands that were inside it. He warned Delilah to run. She refused, instead choosing to die at his side.

It's not how I choose to see the story though. Samson spent decades as a judge in a battle zone between 'good and evil'. Perhaps by the time he met Delilah and fell in love, he was tired of the fighting, the hate, and turmoil. What if the story was seen from the other side? A man of such physical strength choosing to give it all up for a woman who had been born into so little of her own. A woman abused by the men that held the power.

In my mind, it makes more sense that Samson willingly gave Delilah his secrets because she was the one daily hounded by his enemies, and he'd do anything for her. In Samson's last act of rage against a nation that wouldn't let him and the woman he loved survive together, he sentenced them to loving eternally in the afterlife.

I don't believe in such spiritual things, but if there were such a thing as fate, I'd say it sent Delilah to me. I'm not softer because she's stolen my strength. I'm softer because I've chosen to lend it to the woman I love when she needs it. I won't use it on her, but I'll destroy anything that comes for her.

Delilah is not the delicate night who overcame the mighty sun. She's the brave creature born into darkness that only needed a small ray to light her path out. She's the balance, dimming me when I burn too scalding.

Delilah isn't my weakness; she is my reason.

I wish I had recognized it sooner, but I'll prove it to her now.

CHAPTER TWENTY-FOUR

"No, it's not like that for me. I still believe in a higher power, but I don't believe in religion," I say to Bree as she helps me wash up the dishes from dinner tonight. Cookie and I invited her over; she's been spending more time with Fig lately and we thought we'd get to know her better.

Bree fits in well, and honestly, it's nice to have someone to talk to about this sort of thing. Not many people I know can relate. Lorelai does, of course, but she's been out of it for much longer. Jillian brings it up often when she calls me from Nevada, but I try not to influence her too much.

It's important that she finds a pace that suits her best. Noah has already said he'll pay for her to start seeing Dr. Price when she moves out here. The other girls that got out with Jillian haven't yet committed to moving here, but if they do, he'll set it up for them too. I'm not sure where they'll go if they decide New Orleans isn't for them. Carlotta doesn't have the room to keep them all for too long, since she's a safe house for more than just one organization that helps run away youth.

"I can understand that, I guess. I'm not sure that's the normal outcome when people start to deconstruct, but it only makes you special."

"Thanks."

"I do understand, though. It's the things done in the name of any given religion that cause the trauma, right? If people just believed in their chosen deity and kept it between it and themselves, the world would be a much different place."

"Probably. Besides, I don't know where I'll end up a decade from now. Maybe the more I learn, the more I analyze it all, the less and less I'll believe. But for now, I'm happy where I am and that's what matters most."

"Agreed. For what it's worth, you seem very well-adjusted, all things considered."

"She is," Cookie chimes in, bringing in the empty bottle of wine from the kitchen table. "She's brilliant, she's caring, she's strong. And braver than anyone else I've ever known."

"Plus, she has amazing friends," Bree replies with a wink.

"The best," I agree.

"What about the hot-ass Daddy at the club the night we met? Is he a friend?"

"Oh, did she just call Pope a Daddy?" Cookie laughs with wide eyes. "I bet Mr. Grumpy Pants would hate that."

"About as much as he'd hate hearing you call him Mr. Grumpy Pants."

"Yeah, well, if the handcuff fits or whatever."

"I don't know what to call Pope. We're complicated, at best."

"The plot thickens," Bree says.

"The plot is stalled right now," I tell her.

"What about you, Cookie? Is there a complicated story line in your life, too?"

"Most definitely. We're still in the first chapters. Logan's in a band, and they're off to play in Nashville for a few weeks."

"Oh, good for him though."

"Yeah, great opportunity, but bad time to start a relationship." Cookie's been a little blue since Logan left a couple of days ago. We're making quite the pair lately. It's been a couple of weeks since I've seen Pope; he's kept away from Lupus et Agnus, and

I've tried to keep myself from the assumptions about why. He hasn't stopped texting me, every day I get a light message from him. "Do you have any kind of relationship with your parents?"

"No," Bree says somberly. "My dad would have at least tried with me after I left the congregation. My mom is a hard woman, it wouldn't have been as easy for her. But when I told them I didn't think I was strictly straight, that threw her over the edge. She thinks I'm depraved."

"Better morally depraved than orally deprived, my mother always says," Cookie says, patting Bree on the shoulder.

"I can't wait to meet the rest of your family," Bree says with a laugh. Fig is enamored with the newcomer, but he's yet to bring her home to meet the family. Hopefully, he'll see tonight as a first step.

"Okay, all cleaned up," I announce. "What cheeseball movie is on the list tonight?"

"*The Crush*, a cult classic from 1993."

We settle on the sofa with a fresh bottle of wine to watch Cookie's latest pick. We're about halfway through it when the parallels of the young girl in the film being obsessed with an older man hit me.

"I don't know if I like your choice tonight," I pout next to my friend.

"What? Why?"

"Was I that crazy?"

"Oh, fuck no. Not even close," Cookie protests.

"Wait… did you have a teenage obsession?" Bree asks.

"Yes. In my defense, I was barely eighteen and fresh out of the cult. But man, I was so dumb about it."

"Who was the guy?"

"Daddy Pope," Cookie teases.

"Oh, fuck!"

"Yeah," I say dejectedly while I continue to pout at their laughter. "At least you guys can find humor in it."

They only laugh harder at my expense.

"We've decided the next charity event will benefit another local shelter. This one caters to LGBTQIA youths who've been displaced," Jasmine tells me during our weekly meeting. "I'll email you the details and potential dates when I get back in my other office tomorrow."

"Sounds good."

"I'll be out of town next week. The realtor has a few properties to show us in New York City. I'll keep you posted if anything looks like it has potential, and we can run numbers on it," Fabienne says.

"You got it," I confirm. New York is where they want to open the next location. Fabienne spends a lot of time there as it is, making it an easy choice. The city also isn't as stingy when it comes to sex positive communities as some of the other places they have in mind.

"Also, we've updated the member list, a few memberships were revoked. Can you notify the next up on the waitlist?"

"Of course," I say, taking the updated list from Jasmine.

"Great. Last thing, our contractor will have painters here on Monday. I've already made Kevin aware of what needs to be cleared out beforehand. Since that's a day off for all of us, he'll handle it but wanted you to be aware." Kevin is our dungeon master, the last one out the door at the end of the night and the one who oversees all the floor staff. He's somewhat of an enigma, always there but rarely seen.

"What's being painted?" I ask.

"The white room."

"Oh. What made you decide that?" It hasn't been that long since the grand reopening, I thought their intention wasn't to make changes for the first year or so.

"We've had several requests. It's time."

"Okay.

"You'll be steering the ship mostly alone next week, with

Fabienne gone. I have a full schedule with meetings elsewhere."

"Shouldn't be a problem, but I'll call if anything comes up."

"We're not at all worried, darling," Fabienne says.

"I appreciate the faith." I smile at her, and she winks back.

"Are you walking down with us?" Jasmine asks.

"I have a few more things to wrap up, then I'm headed home."

"Okay, have a good evening."

"You too, boss ladies."

They leave, and I take a few minutes updating the cash flow spreadsheet, when my phone dings with a notification.

HATTIE

Mr. Blackwell is asking to come up.

Well, crap.

ME

Send him up.

No point pretending I'm not here. Other than his near daily text messages, I haven't seen or spoken to him. The messages he sends me are always short and never require any response. Some days it's a simple hope you have a good day, other days it comes at night with a hope your day went well. I never say anything back, because I'm not sure there is anything to say at this point.

Him telling me he was in love with me was like a dream. My initial instinct was to wrap myself around him and never let go. I can't be that woman though, the kind that caves at sweet words from a man when his actions don't back them up.

It wouldn't make me any different than my mother, and I never want to have similarities to her.

"Hey," Pope greets from my doorway. "You finishing up for the night?"

"Yes." I raise an eyebrow at him. "How can I help you?"

"Would you go to dinner with me?"

"What?"

"Dinner, Delilah," Pope says. "It's an evening meal, many consider it the main meal of the day. Will you go get it with me?"

"Hilarious, Mr. Blackwell," I deadpan. "Why?"

"It occurred to me that I've done everything wrong with you. I'd like to start over, if you're amenable."

"With a dinner date?" I ask, ignoring the flutters bursting to life in my stomach.

"Yes. I promise to be on my best behavior. I'll even try to be charming." Lack of charm has never been a problem; I've always found Pope interesting. "Please?"

"Where?" I ask, unsure. He said please though, that's a new character trait.

"I made a reservation at Cane and Table," he says sounding almost sheepish, something I've never seen before. "They have a rum cake that I thought we could try."

"Presumptuous."

"Oh, very." He smiles. "I fucked up, Delilah. But I'm not giving up."

"It's just dinner, Pope. And I'm only agreeing because I'm starving, and I want cake."

"I'll take it." He doesn't leave his post at my door until I've shut down my computer and grabbed my handbag, then he holds out his hand for me to take. Holding hands is a casual intimacy couples share. Since we are neither casual nor a couple, I shake my head and walk past him.

My heart can't be trusted in the presence of Pope Blackwell. My head will have to prevail.

It rained while I worked, and though we don't make conversation on the walk to the nearby restaurant, Pope guides me by the elbow so that I miss stepping in puddles. As soon as I clear one, his hand once again takes up residency in his pocket. He's dressed more casually today, too. Most times I've seen him, he's been in nothing less than dress pants and a button down. Or naked, but I won't dwell on a sight I miss so much.

Entering Cane and Table, he gives the host his name and we're led to a table in the corner, in front of an old fireplace draped in wax drippings. Whether or not Pope is charming tonight, he's picked a place that is drenched in it with white-washed exposed brick walls and painted black ceiling sparsely decorated with dim chandeliers.

Romantic, yet not intimate or quiet.

Our server is quick to come by for drink orders. Pope asks for one called Smooth Operator; I order the Devil in Disguise much to his amusement.

"How have you been?"

"Good. Busy, I'm at the club more than not, it seems."

"Fabienne says you're doing wonders for them."

"You speak to her about me?" I ask, playing my finger over the hem on my cloth napkin.

"We have some business together, you came up."

"Hmm. How have you been?"

"I've also been good and busy."

"That's nice for you," I say dismissively as the server drops our drinks. Quickly scanning the menu, I can't decide on what I want. "Oh, this all looks good. I've never had plantain. What would you suggest, sweet or tostones?"

"We'll get both," Pope interrupts.

"And a side salad, please."

"Great, and for you?" she asks Pope.

"The fish rundown. Also, add an order of the croquettes, please."

"You got it," she says, taking our menus and vanishing in the crowd of tables.

"You didn't have to do that."

"I do what I want. Currently, that is letting you try plantain two ways."

"Hmm."

"So, you are still mad at me," he says, setting his elbows on the table and his chin in his hands. It brings him to my level, eye to eye.

"I'm not mad."

"No lies, Delilah."

"No lies then, Pope," I throw back.

"I didn't fuck her, that wasn't a lie. I did… appease her in other ways."

"You don't need to tell me."

"I think I do. Tabitha's presence was unexpected, and I handled it the way I would have had she shown up before… you. It was a default reaction and incredibly stupid of me. I tried to keep her on a tight leash. But I did help her get off, your assumption was right there."

"It's not my business," I say with much effort to keep my voice even, now pinching my napkin tightly under the table. These aren't details I want knowledge of.

"That's bullshit, and we both know it. You're only saying that because of the parameters I put on our relationship. Those too were bullshit. Fuck, Delilah, they made me no better than your father in so many ways. Nobody could blame you if you never forgave me for that."

There are parallels between the type of lifestyle Pope leads and a life of a polygamist. The power dynamic all leaning toward the dominant male figure, being just one. However, here he's wrong. With my father, power wasn't handed freely over to him the way I had with Pope. My father, my uncle before him, took it. It was stolen from us and not an ounce was ever given back. There is a world of difference between that and playing submissive during sexy fun times with a man who respects you, or cares about you.

"I never compared you to my father, Pope. You are worlds apart."

"And yet not at all."

"Well, you are about the same age," I say, tucking my tongue into my cheek so I don't laugh.

"So, you can tell more than just bad dad jokes," he laughs, and for a moment I lose myself in it, forgetting the gravity of our situation. "Not that it changes anything, but it was a cold experience that only happened the one time while she was here. There was no kindness or intimacy involved."

I've laid awake wondering all the things they might have done together, images that played so clearly in my mind. Telling myself over and over that he wasn't mine to keep, and our relationship didn't bar him from other women took days to sink in.

"I didn't think it would hurt. When I agreed to your rules, it never occurred to me that I wouldn't be able to watch you with someone else. My childhood was surrounded by men with many wives who never showed jealousy of one another. I thought that attitude was ingrained. I certainly never thought it would make me feel insignificant and invisible."

"But I should have. The responsibility is on me to understand the situation and make sure you're safe in it. I failed there, but you were neither insignificant nor unseen to me, Delilah." Pope reaches his hand over the table, resting it palm up. "Give it here."

"What?"

"The hand you're worrying under the table. Give it to me." He's using his bossy tone that my body reacts to without hesitation. Before I realize what I'm doing, my hand settles on his and he soothes it with his thumb. "I'll do better from now on."

"This is just dinner, Pope."

"It's a start." His smile is different than any of the times I've seen him smile before. It's earnest.

"What do they mean?" I gesture with my head to the markings on the fingers entwined with mine. "You didn't have them when we first met."

"This is Algiz or Elk," he says, lifting his thumb. "It means protection, instinct, guardianship. My index finger is Ansuf or Message, which symbolizes the mouth, communication, or understanding. Middle finger is Nauthiz. It symbolizes restriction, conflict, willpower. They're Norse runes."

Studying them for a moment, I eventually start to laugh when the meaning takes shape.

"You shut me up with fingers marked with mouth and restriction. Asshole."

"Maybe it's more about communication and conflict."

"Doubtful."

"Doubtful," he agrees with a smirk. "I like it when you curse."

"Seems I only do it with you," I admit, feeling the heat on my face. It's still a rare thing for me to do.

"I like the things you only do with me, too."

The server brings our meal to the table. I'm happy for the break as it gives me a chance to steady myself under the confusion he showers down. His expectations of tonight are a mystery to me, my own are as well, if I'm honest about it.

I start with the tostone, groaning with pleasure at the first bite.

"Good?"

"Yes, so good," I say, finishing the bite and tasting the sweet plantain next. It's every bit as good, yet so completely different from the tostone. "How is that even the same food?"

He laughs, picking up a croquette and placing it on the plate with the sweet plantain for me to try.

"If you could pick one place to travel to, where would it be?" Pope asks, taking me completely off guard. He's never asked me casually random things.

"That's difficult to answer. I've been to so few places. Utah, Nevada, here. I went to Florida with Noah and Lorelai one year. But I've never seen the Pacific Ocean. Europe has so much history and architecture I'd love to explore. I'd also love to go someplace with huge forests of evergreens. Both Costa Rica and Santorini look gorgeous," I say, shrugging. There's way too much to list.

"Favorite music?"

"I'm obsessed with Sinead O'Connor right now."

"Really?"

"Yeah, why?"

"I guess I expected you to say someone more current."

"Cookie says I'm something like a petrified dinosaur that hatched hundreds of years past my time and am slowly catching up to this timeline. Maybe by the time I'm forty, I'll be listening to Cardi B and Billie Eilish." A weird look passes over him, but he blinks it away quickly.

"It's refreshing, if that helps. You aren't yet jaded by the world like most are. The way you're open to new experiences isn't normal for most people. Truthfully, it's probably not even normal for someone coming from a childhood like yours."

"I figure I should live every day like I don't have time on my side. It hasn't been easy, some days it's still not. I always feel behind somehow."

"You're not behind at all. In fact, I'd say you're light years ahead of a lot of people your age."

It's strange what his praise and confidence in me does to my dumb lady parts. I've resigned myself to the idea that I'm not capable of fitting into Pope's lifestyle, so this is all an exercise in self-control. My body isn't allowed to override what my head knows. It misses Pope. *I* miss Pope. But it's different with him than it is with Damian and Fig. Sharing him isn't an option. Either I have him all to myself, or not at all.

"What's the end game here, Pope?"

He drops his shoulders and sets down his fork, no distractions while he formulates his answer.

"I broke your trust," he says.

"You didn't," I interrupt.

"Stop talking," he says in *that* tone and doesn't continue until my mouth is sealed tightly shut. "I did. I'm going to win it back. After that, I'm going to spend as much time with you, and *in* you, as I can until you outgrow me."

"I haven't agreed to give you that chance."

"No, but I think you will," he says, once again picking up his fork.

"Why?"

"Because I'm letting you make the rules this time," he says, gesturing to me with his utensil. "Within reason, of course."

Of course.

CHAPTER TWENTY-FIVE

Dinner with Pope ended with him walking me home and bidding me to sleep well. Sans even a kiss on the cheek. Though he did ask me to keep my dinner plans clear for tonight as well. He's bringing food to my office so I can eat before my typical Saturday night below.

Even though I haven't played in weeks, I still at least make an appearance to chat with members and check in on the other employees. Pope wants to accompany me tonight, though I made it clear I don't plan to partake in anything more than perhaps a single glass of wine.

"I just want your company, Delilah," he'd said.

I still don't know what to think about this new, more reserved, Pope Blackwell. But I can't deny his intrigue.

"Pizza?" I ask as he walks into my office.

"Is that alright?"

"Sure, just unexpected."

"Why?"

"I don't know if you know this about yourself, but you don't come across as a pizza and beer kind of dude," I tell him.

"I'm not. I'm a pizza and wine kind of dude."

"Fair enough," I laugh.

"How was your day?"

"Good, I'm just finishing up all the quarterlies."

"You have Monday and Tuesday off still?" He opens the pizza box, and the smell permeates the room.

"Mmhmm," I answer distractedly, my focus on the cheesy goodness in front of me while I pull off a piece.

"I'd like to take you somewhere. It requires an overnight stay."

"Where?"

"That, my dear Delilah, is a surprise."

I neither refuse nor accept his offer while we eat, and he continues to pepper me with random questions.

"Favorite color?"

"Charcoal gray."

"Is that a color or a neutral?"

"Both," I answer, and he smiles around another bite of pizza.

"Favorite movie?"

"*Schindler's List.*"

"That's a morbid choice."

"I didn't know the holocaust happened until I was almost twenty. Cookie picked the movie one night and I spent the next two weeks reading everything I could on it and bawling my eyes out. I guess I like things that lead to knowledge and provoke thought."

"No need to guess, anyone who knows you would see that about you," he says. "You make it easy to forget how sheltered your life was as a child. Or even how young you still are."

"That's kind of my goal," I admit. "When I first arrived in Nevada, everything was so new. I'd never seen a television or heard music that was secular. I'd never even seen a building taller than two stories. I was the most naïve thing you could have imagined, and I hated the feeling. Worse, I hated that others looked at me and knew it. Being seen as weak or stupid isn't something I ever want again."

"You haven't been weak or stupid a single day in the time I've known you, Delilah. Quite the opposite, in fact."

"Except for maybe that night you threw me out of your house," I say, crinkling my nose in disgust.

"You weren't stupid then, either. Inquisitive and curious, sure. But who wouldn't have expected that of you?" he asks, opening a handy-wipe packet and cleaning his hands. "You know I didn't throw you out because I was mad you snuck in?"

"I certainly do not know that," I answer, surprised.

"I threw you out because the second I saw you, I came like a little virgin boy getting a blow job for the first time. You've always thoroughly undone me, Delilah. It pissed me off that a practical child had that sort of sway over me." He tosses the wipe into the trash and stands. "You still fucking do. Ready to go downstairs?"

Once in the salon, I greet a few members while Pope grabs us drinks from the bar. Damian and Fig are here somewhere, but I don't see them.

Halston is here, and though Pope made that off-handed comment about not wanting me on his radar, I approach to say hello.

"Hi, Halston. Are you having a good night?"

"It's only just getting started, but I suspect it's going to be good," he answers with his slight Southern drawl. "How are you doing this evening, Miss Delilah?"

"I'm good, thank you for asking."

"Do you want to sit and have a drink with me, or is that against Blackwell's rules?" Halston asks just as Pope steps up to hand me a glass of wine.

"I'm playing by the lady's rules now."

"Oh, how the mighty fall," Halston says with a smile that looks a lot like a sneer. It's obviously meant as an insult and my hackles instantly rise.

"My pussy brings men to their knees, it seems," I say, sending Halston a wink as I grab Pope's arm and lead him off. He chuckles lightly as he presses a sweet kiss to the crown of my head before we enter the rest of the club. But he doesn't say anything, seemingly happy to be nothing more than my shadow.

I check with Kevin to see if he needs anything from me, but as always, he's good.

Pope waits for me in front of the room called Moulin Rouge, intently watching the scene inside.

"Fig may be the most giving lover I've ever seen," he says softly, pulling me to stand in front of him. Pope rests his chin atop my head.

"Why do you say that?" I ask, taking in what's happening inside. Damian is lounging at the head of the bed, fully clothed, but that's not abnormal for him. He prefers to be uninvolved.

"Watch."

Fig is sprawled at the end of the bed, a naked Bree on top of him, her back to his chest. Shanna strips slowly out of her clothes.

"She's beautiful, isn't she?" Fig says in Bree's ear. Bree nods. "Do you want her to touch you? Tell her."

She stammers, "I want you to touch me."

"Here?" Fig asks, his fingers sliding through her folds and making her moan her answer.

"My pleasure," Shanna says, crawling on the bed. Licking her way up Bree's leg and making her tremble.

"I wouldn't be surprised if Fig doesn't fuck anyone tonight. This is for Bree and Damian," Pope says. "Is this her first time with a woman?"

"Yes. Other than the kiss with me."

"Was that for her or yourself?" he whispers in my ear.

"Her. Mostly."

"Are you curious about more? About that?" Pope asks as Shanna uses her mouth between Bree's thighs. Fig gently massages Bree's breast, talking her through the entire experience.

"Sometimes," I admit. "There's a lot I haven't tried, and I wonder if I'm missing out."

"Shanna knows what she's doing, Fig picked well for her. She's deliberate, doesn't make sloppy movements like so many inexperienced men. See how she's staring up at Bree's body, she's watching how Bree reacts. Studying her so she knows what she likes best. All while Fig focuses on Bree's needs, completely setting his own desires aside." Pope's palm comes to rest on my hip as he speaks. I've missed his touch more than I'd like to admit and I lean into it. "See that? Bree moves her hips up whenever Shanna sucks on her clit. It will be a good way to edge her closer, and when she's almost there, Shanna will back off, start using her tongue again."

Shanna pushes her hand up Bree's body, snaking her fingers through Fig's so they can work Bree's breast together.

"Oh, god," Bree cries. Shanna moves Bree's knee wider, opening her up and simultaneously giving us a better view. She thrusts her tongue in and Bree jerks, her back arching.

"She won't last much longer. Not surprising for her first time."

"She's earned this," I say.

"What have you earned?"

Love.

The kind that's real and lasting, is my first thought. Except I don't know what I've done to earn anything, really. All I've done is exist, surviving however I could. That used to mean hiding, staying quiet, *keeping sweet*. Now it means having tough enough skin to not be walked over, it's not being too foolish or rash.

But surviving doesn't entitle me to happiness, does it? If that were the case, then even the worst of mankind would have earned it, too. That just can't be right. There must be more to it, something profound that I need to do before true love comes my way.

"Where did you go, Layla?" Pope's voice breaks through my brain fog.

"What have I done to deserve anything?"

"Hey." Pope turns me in his arms, bringing my face to his by running his thumb up the column of my neck. "That's your old habits talking. There is no guilt in knowing you deserve happiness and pleasure. You're a good person, and that is enough."

"Is it?"

"Fuck yes. You don't have to be a saint and you don't have to repent for sins you never committed. You've done no harm ever. Why wouldn't you deserve good things?"

"It doesn't always feel like enough."

"It is, beautiful. It is."

I want to believe him. It's so easy for me to believe it in others, even as Bree screams through her orgasm behind me, I know she deserves it. She fought her way to happiness and brought her sister with her.

I haven't accomplished anything that worthy.

"Will you do something for me, Pope?"

"Anything," he says without hesitation.

"Take *his* money. Take all of it, and if there's a way, make sure he knows I'm behind it."

Agreeing to Pope's overnight date came easy by the end of Saturday night. He'd been perfectly gentlemanly, even respecting the boundaries I never put in place.

I didn't get a goodnight kiss that night, either. However, I'm packed up and ready for whatever he has in store for us today. He wouldn't give me details other than to dress and pack comfortably.

"Does my butt look too big in this?"

"Delilah, your ass looks big in everything, but it is never *too* big," Cookie says with an eyeroll. "Your bubble but, big tits, and barely there thigh gap is hot as shit, and you already know Pope likes it. Quit stressing yourself out over it."

"I can't help it! I'm nervous. I've never had been out of town with a guy before."

"Do you trust him?"

"Yes."

"Then what's to be nervous about?"

"You're right," I concede. "I'm being silly."

"Not silly, it's just not you. But new situation and all, it makes sense. You got this, though."

"That's probably him," I say when my phone beeps with a notification.

POPE

I'm downstairs.

ME

On my way down.

"Have fun!" Cookie emphasizes when I'm walking out the door.

Pope's waiting for me on the street, the trunk of his car open. He takes my overnight bag from me and drops it in before coming to the passenger side of the car to open the door.

"Good morning," he says, pressing a kiss to my temple.

"Hi."

"You look edible."

"Thank you," I say, dropping into the seat, some of my anxiousness instantly melting away. Pope is once again dressed down, jeans and a t-shirt, the most casual I've ever seen him, and I can't pull my gaze away as he walks around the car to the driver's side. "Are you going to tell me where we're going now?"

"Alabama. Have you ever been there?"

"A few times with Lorelai. She has friends there from when she lived in Mobile."

"Right. I sometimes forget she and Noah haven't been together forever. They're such a tight unit."

They are. There are still moments that I'm envious of it, when I want that same type of partnership that almost consuming. It takes a lot of reminding myself that I have that with family and friends, even if it never comes with a romantic partner. Even if it never happens with Pope.

If I'm nothing else in this life, I am a survivor, and I do have love in my life.

"Why Alabama?"

"You'll see."

"You're being awfully cryptic, Mr. Blackwell."

"It's about a two-and-a-half-hour drive. Then you'll know, Ms. Simms." I wrinkle my nose, and he catches it. "What was that look for?"

"People rarely say my last name. I still don't like it."

"Have you thought about changing it?" he asks, reaching over to take my left hand in his right.

"I have. It's a lot of effort, though. I want to be sure I'm changing it to something I'll keep forever."

"Makes sense."

"Can I ask you something?"

"You know you can," he answers. Pope has a lovely profile, straight nose, strong jawline that missed a shave this morning. Looking at him is no hardship.

"I know you don't believe in God. Do you believe anything in the Bible is real?"

"Nothing I say is an attempt to influence you, understand?" I nod, and he continues. "I think it makes logical sense that Jesus existed. But as a mortal man, not a divine being. We've seen plenty of religions formed in modern times based off the teachings of some guy, right? Mormons, Scientologists, any number of random cults. They all start with one person's beliefs that spread to others. Maybe Jesus was just a man, carpenter, purveyor of prostitutes, son to a woman who was likely raped by a man not a god. If someone went to the press today claiming to be a pregnant virgin, they'd laugh her off. They wouldn't build a religion around her. So, yes, I believe in the possibility of some. But very little."

"I've missed how honest you always are with me about this. There wasn't anyone I could talk to the same way as you during those years you stayed away."

"I'm sorry about that, Delilah," he says, and I hear in his voice how sincere he is as he brings my fingers to his mouth. "Do you want to talk more about it? We've got the time."

"There are people that pop up on my TikTok who've left Christianity. I follow a few because I find them interesting, and it sparks a lot of conversation with those who are still pious. The Christians often go back to the same arguments, and they make less and less sense to me the more I think it through. It's overwhelming sometimes."

"Like what?"

"Like how the Bible can't be false when there are prophecies in it that have come true?"

"Jules Verne predicted men on the moon some one hundred years before it happened. Does that make him a god, too?"

"No, not at all. If I can write some off as coincidence, or even causality, then maybe it all is."

"Maybe. Also, maybe you don't have to have all the answers, either. It's okay to find your own happy space, Delilah."

Find your own happy space.

What simple advice, yet exactly what I needed to hear. Maybe I'll never be done with my questions, or my quest, but that's okay. The answers don't have to fall in my lap all at once and I've learned I don't need a solid belief system to know that being a good person is right.

"Thank you, Pope."

I spend some time scanning through radio stations and trying to get Pope to sing along with me. He doesn't because he's still Mr. Grumpy Pants and it's okay because I like that about him, and the smile on his face as I belt out of tune song after song, tells me he likes this part of me, too.

CHAPTER TWENTY-SIX

POPE

She fell asleep, and while I could sit here and watch her for hours, peaceful as she is, we've arrived at our destination.

"Layla," I whisper her name, nuzzling her nape some. "Wake up, beautiful."

She hums sleepily.

"We're here."

"Oh." She pops open her eyes and blinks a few times at the scene in front of my car. "Oh!"

Her excited exclamation is exactly what I was hoping for.

"It's not Disney World, but they do have roller coasters," I say, and her eyes widen at the towering structures we can see from the parking lot.

"I'm so excited." Her voice is full of dazed awe; I'm not sure she's even aware she said anything.

"Well, let's go then." I laugh and stand so she can exit my car. She clings to me, bouncing with uncaged glee, as I purchase the admission tickets. As soon as we step inside the theme park, her head swivels from one thing to the next, unable to take it all in at once.

"Where do you want to start?" I ask, handing her the park

map. Unfolding it, she traces pathways with her finger for a few moments of contemplation.

"I'm not sure. Should I try something tame or dive right in?"

"It's your day, we'll do whatever you choose. If you want to start small, but not on an actual kiddie ride, I'd suggest the Mystic Mansion."

"Yeah?"

"Yes, it's slow but still fun. Plus, they give you these guns that look like boney cocks to shoot at stuff with." I wink as her cheeks redden.

"That sounds just crazy enough to be my first amusement park ride, let's go." Delilah's smile is wide and genuine and doesn't leave her face the remainder of the day.

She sits as close as possible to me on every attraction, opting to tangle her arm in mine whenever possible. Despite her fears and apprehensions about some of the wilder rides, she faces them like she does everything in life. Full on and strong backed. She laughs, she screams, she hides her eyes a time or two, yet nothing stops her from trying the next ride.

When she needs a break, we find a bench to sit on and eat shitty soft pretzels while she watches people. Then when she's ready, we hit all her favorite rides for a second time. Some even a third, she doesn't get enough until the park is nearly ready to close and she's too hungry to focus on much of anything but food.

"Let's pick up some moonshine here before we go to the hotel," I say, pointing to a distillery set up here in the park.

"Sure. Can we also go to the gift shop? I don't think today will be complete without a cheesy souvenir."

"Of course." She intentionally picks out the ugliest T-shirt the shop has to offer. Her follow-through only makes me fall in love with her more. Brave and self-assure, she's more confident than most women I know who are much older.

None of the hotels around the park are up to my, admittedly ridiculous, standards. We drive the twenty or so minutes to Gulf Shores instead. Not that the hotels here are that much better, but I like the idea that she'll wake up to a view of the ocean. It's not the Pacific, or the Caribbean, but it will do for now. If I believed we had a long future together, I'd plan to take her to all the places she dreams of going.

I don't believe that, though. So, I'll make the best of whatever time we do have and spoil her in as many small ways as I can.

Handing the front desk clerk my credit card and ID, Delilah drops her head on my shoulder. She claimed she wasn't sleepy but the activities of today have absolutely worn her out.

"Oh, happy birthday, Mr. Blackwell," the clerk says, handing me back my cards along with the room keycard. Delilah's head shoots up, and her mouth opens as if she's got something to say, but no words follow.

"Thank you." I pick up our bags and move to the elevators. Delilah presses the up button, all the while eyeing me curiously. "What?"

"Why didn't you tell me?"

"Because today was about you." Birthdays mean little to me. Truthfully, this one has greater meaning than most because turning forty feels like a milestone I don't want to reach. I never cared about it before I met Delilah, but now my age is like dragging around an anvil.

Entering the room, she goes straight to the large windows and watches the waves crash in the setting sun.

"Beautiful," I say, stepping up behind her.

"It is. I wish New Orleans had views like this."

It does, I think, but only because I was speaking about her and not the view.

"You're young, you could always move to another city. One on the ocean." Delilah looks up at me with a quizzical look.

"Do you ever think of moving away?"

"No. I love New Orleans; I think it's in my blood. Why do you do that?"

"Do what?" I ask.

"Say things as if there is no future for us." She turns to face me. "I mean, I know why I think there isn't, but what are your reasons?"

"You first," I counter her.

She paces away from me to the club chair in the corner facing the window. There she bends to remove her shoes and socks so she can pull her knees up. Curling like a cat getting cozy in its favorite spot to watch for prey on the other side of the glass. Only when settled does she speak.

"I would want monogamy with you. Or rather something close to that. Other people participating in ways to heighten both of our experiences is one thing, but I'd never be okay with sitting aside while I watched you have sex with another woman. And I'd never want that from another man." She curls her arms around her knees and rests her cheek atop them to watch me as I take in her words. "Now you."

Though I'm much too large to curl up the way she has, I sit in the chair next to hers, placing my head in my hands as I rest my elbows on my knees. Today has been great, I don't want to ruin that, so I try to pick my words carefully.

"There are a lot of things in life I can give you. I fear the list of things I can't is equally as long, or at least of equal weight. Children, a large family, a lengthy marriage that lasts until your old age hits, because mine would come far sooner. You deserve the world, and I don't want to be the cause you miss out on anything."

To my surprise, a soft smile touches her lips. The sadness in her eyes only a minute ago almost vanishes.

"Then I guess it's a good thing I don't want marriage and children."

"You can't know," I begin to say when Delilah jumps out of her chair to stand in front of me. When I open my mouth to finish, she thrust two fingers in my mouth.

"Don't you dare tell me what I know and don't know, Mr. Blackwell. If you think for even a second that I haven't weighed the future I want for myself time and time again, then you really don't know anything about me. I want a partnership, not ownership. While I adore children, there is not an ounce of blood in me that wants one for myself. My line is not one that needs to be continued by me. Eighteen years of rearing other people's children will last me a lifetime. Understand?"

Fucking hell.

Delilah has never been sexier. Her instinctual need to stand up to me has always turned me on, but this stunt has me hard as steel and I can already feel the precum at the tip of my cock. I nod and suck her fingers the way she always does mine, using the same movements as her.

"As for growing old. There is no guarantee I'll have that chance. I could die of anything at any time. Like I've said before, I live my life to the fullest with that knowledge in mind. The question isn't if you can fit into my life, Pope. You'd do that seamlessly, because there is nothing I need to give up to make that space for you. The question is how long are you willing to give up other women for me to be in yours."

She doesn't immediately remove her fingers; maybe she's building up defenses for whatever answer she thinks is coming. It's a tough reminder that even though she continually vocalizes her trust in me, I've yet to fully earn it. Delilah doesn't have faith in me to stick around, or to be the man she needs in the long term.

It's not true when she says she doesn't have something to give up to make room for me in her life. She does, she risks potential hurt and heartbreak because none of us truly know what the future holds. There are reasons I've lived my life the way I have, this is one of them. If I never trust a woman to stay, they can't ever leave me.

In that way, we both risk.

She told me once that she believes the rewards, however temporary they may be, are worth it. Any time spent with Delilah in my life is worth it. Something must change in my expression because her fingers retreat at the same time she takes a small step back.

"For this life and the next."

"What?" The word is more gasp than anything.

"In every soul. In every life." I stand to pull her close. *"As the woman is of the man, even so is the man also by the woman."*

"I don't think this is what the Bible meant by that," she says, but her smile has returned.

"I don't give a damn what it meant. I'm yours, Layla. You're mine. Partners, always." My thumb plays with her bottom lip as I wait for whatever reaction comes next from her. If she still has apprehension and doubts about me, I'll work until they're gone. I'm not living this life without her. Not for another...

"I love you."

...day.

"What?"

"I love you, Pope Blackwell."

The best five words in the history of man.

"Are you sure?" The tremble in my voice shocks us both. This woman has bewitched me wholly.

"This is going to sound cheesy, but I think you're the grate-est."

Blink.

"Even if there wasn't gravity on earth, I'd still fall for you."

The fuck.

"Do you believe in love at first sight, or should I walk past again?"

The best way to stop her onslaught of horrible jokes is to seal her mouth shut with mine, so I do. As soon as my tongue touches hers, she wraps her arms around my neck, letting me pick her up and carry her to the bathroom where I take my time stripping her down. We're a tangled mess. Eventually we make it under the warm spray of the water.

I wash the grime of the day spent at the amusement park off us. Neither of us speaks much, but our mouths stay plenty busy. Having just professed being together forever does nothing to diminish the idea that I will never have enough of her. By the way she matches my intensity, she feels the same.

Foregoing to towel us dry, I take her directly to the bed. Lying her down and sliding over her slippery skin, I pull our hands up above our heads.

"Are you absolutely positive about no children?"

"One thousand percent," she says with no trace of doubt.

"I had a vasectomy when I was twenty-eight."

"Then I can stop taking these horrible birth control pills and you can quit using condoms," she says, wiggling excitedly underneath me.

"I can't wait to fill you with my cum."

"What are you waiting for, Mr. Blackwell?" she asks, raising her legs against my hips until she can lock her ankles around my lower back.

"For you to say it again."

"I love you."

I push into her like the punctuation to her statement. She mewls long and loud at the new sensation for us both. I've never had sex without a condom. Not once in my forty years. It's better than I could have ever imagined, yet I know it's mostly because it's Delilah I'm in.

Sliding out a few inches, I immediately thrust back in. Pressing my lips to hers while I pick up a steady pace. Everything about us is different this time. *We're* different. I don't spank or pull. Instead, I fuck her like I should have that first time. There's time for all the rest. We have our whole lives for me to fuck my way inside of her with my hand on her throat or her chained to the wall.

Tonight, I can be sweeter, I can love her with my body the way I love her with my heart. Connect us together by flesh the way we're impossibly intertwined by spirit.

Romantic as it all sounds, the truth is she has me so fucking worked over I'm already fighting the need to explode inside her.

Quickly pulling out of her and reaching behind me to unhook

her legs, I push her thighs up to her chest. It brings her cunt close enough for me to bend and bury my face.

"Pope!"

Fuck, I love my name on her screams. She's so wet, so goddamned delicious I could spend hours here simply sustaining off her. I swirl my tongue around and back up, sucking gently on her swollen bundle of nerves. Delilah moans and pushes against me the best she can. Her hips trying to pick up a rhythm without the leverage of her feet. She's close, but I want her closer, so I don't stop fucking her with my tongue, or dragging the tip of my nose over her clit. Lapping her up until she's near convulsing with the need for orgasm.

Only then do I slam my cock back into her.

"Say it again, Layla."

"I love you, Pope."

"I love you, too, beautiful," I say as we fall over the cliff together as one.

CHAPTER TWENTY-SEVEN

"Thank you," I say as I snuggle deeper into his side, one of his arms under my head, the other thrown over his head as he catches his breath.

"You don't have to thank me for making you come."

"Not for that," I laugh. "For today. For giving me more firsts and for letting me spend your birthday with you."

"Best birthday ever," he sighs. "I want to be around for all the rest of your firsts, too."

"You mean it, don't you?" I tilt my gaze up to him and he must see that I'm asking about more than him being there the first time I see Europe or try some new adventure.

"I mean it, Layla. Only you from here on. I'm going to earn the faith you've always had in me."

"Thank you for that, too, then."

I draw my fingers over the broken cross tattoo on his chest and wonder how a man so fit, so confident in so many ways, was ever worried about keeping up with me in life. Not that it matters anymore, just further proof that we're more than what people often expect from us.

Looking at him, the way he carries himself, it's hard to believe he could ever have any sort of insecurity. But I guess that's not any different than how people expect me to have a basket full of them, when I have so few.

"Solomon."

"What about him?" I ask.

"Solomon David Blackwell, that was my name at birth."

"Eww." I crinkle my nose, and he laughs. "Pope suits you much better."

"Agreed."

"Does that mean I hold all the power over you now that I know your name?"

"You've held it since the day we met," he says before leaning down to kiss me. "Sleep now. I love you."

"I love you, too," I repeat before falling into the best sleep of my life.

We have breakfast at the deck restaurant that overlooks the ocean the following morning. The smell of the sea breeze and my plate of French toast and bacon just might be the best combination of scents ever. Or maybe I'm just feeling giddy and in love.

Either way, I'm enjoying it and the relaxed smile Pope has been wearing since I woke him up with my mouth on his dick.

His phone chimes. Setting down his coffee, he pulls it out of his pocket and checks it. The corners of his mouth turn down slightly.

"What's wrong?"

"It's done." He looks up at me. "The last of the money was all transferred this morning."

"Is that bad news?"

"No, it's good. I made Lorelai aware before I pulled the trigger on it, and she informed the FBI. It didn't take as long as I expected it to. I want you to be careful. Just in case, okay?"

"I will be," I reassure him. "But even if he does trace it back here, I don't know what it would accomplish for him to come after me for it."

"I hope you're right," he says, but there isn't much confidence behind his words. "Don't trust that though. It's more money than you and I will see in a lifetime, he's not going to take it lightly."

"Okay. Where does it all go?"

"To a new charity Fabienne founded in Nevada. She bought up a whole damn abandoned mining town."

"Seriously? What's she going to do with it?"

"House battered woman and cult escapees," he says with a raised brow. "You can ask her about the details, she'd love to finally share it with you."

"Why didn't she tell me before?"

"I don't think she wanted to put any pressure on you. There are already crews there getting it ready and she's working with Carlotta and that charity in Utah."

"Giving Hope?" I ask. They're the ones that housed me until I could get to Carlotta. Olivia stayed there too, until Lorelai was able to get the necessary custody and bring her home.

"That's the one," he says, picking his coffee back up. "She's ready to help support any member of your family that comes out of that ranch."

"I want to be Fabienne when I grow up," I say dreamily, making Pope laugh.

"You already are in some ways. The money is all being carefully funneled to this specific endeavor because of you."

"I know I've said it a lot these past twenty-four hours but thank you."

"You're welcome but quit thanking me now, you're going to give me a complex."

"Well, then quit doing such nice things for me," I argue, playfully.

"I do what I want, my dear Delilah," he says with a big toothy grin. "Eat up, let's get back on the road so I can fuck you again in my own bed.

Now that I won't argue with.

Not much changes over the next couple of weeks, other than the bulk of Pope sleeping beside me every night. He's expressed his displeasure with me not sleeping at his house every night, but I've put my foot down. I like living with Cookie and I'm not ready to give that up when we've not been doing it for very long. I have a lifetime with Pope ahead of me, Mr. Grumpy Pants can be patient.

Except, he's not. He just manages to find his way into my bed on the nights I don't stay over at his. Luckily, Cookie doesn't mind. She likes him more than she'll admit. They banter with each other every time he's around and while they try to sound serious about it, neither of them is. Plus, he watches movies with us. He found the way to her heart right away.

Pope still meets me at work on the nights I'm here. Some nights he takes me to dinner, others we go home. Occasionally we stay and like he's done before, he watches a scene with me and describes the things happening that I'm not always aware of. Or that I am, but he knows it turns me on when he narrates the dirtier bits in my ear.

We haven't taken it further than that at Lupus et Agnus. Pope has realized he finds the idea of even sharing the sight of me repulsive. It's silly, and I think he'll ease up after we've been together longer. But I don't hate that he's so possessive of me.

With everything in my life, we'll find what works for us as we go.

Fabienne returned from New York with a new building in her possession and a desire to tell me all the details of her tiny Nevada town. She bought it off a woman who'd been slowly fixing up all the old buildings over the last decade. There are fifteen different one-bedroom cottages, a larger building that houses a coffee bar and five hotel rooms upstairs, and several other communal buildings that can be used for any number of things.

I cried the first time we talked about it, and I've had to fight back tears every time since. Because I know she's doing this for me. Fabienne wants my input on what would best suit the woman who may walk out off the ranch for good. I'm not sure how I've become so lucky in life to have people like her in it, but I'm grateful for it every day.

Nothing has happened yet; we can only assume my father had cash hidden away that's keeping them going. For now.

Agent Daughtry hasn't said much, but did tell Lorelai it was close. I wake up every day and check for news. Jillian will be eighteen in a few weeks but she's getting nervous about moving out here, Hannah isn't doing well with the idea. She's only fifteen and we can't take custody of her without parental permission. Our only option is to keep her in Nevada with their loose runaway laws.

My spare time each day is focused on working with Fabienne to get her compound secure and ready in the hopes we can move them both there when the time comes that they need to leave Carlotta's. That takes more hiring staff, security, an on-site therapist. It's a lot to do, especially from across the country, but it's a group effort. Even Pope's assistant Lucinda is pitching in time and she's a force.

Whether one or two women escape, or we have a mass walk off when my father is eventually taken down, we'll be ready. Somehow.

POPE

I'm here.

The message pings at the same time my computer does, letting me know Pope has checked in.

ME

Be down in a minute.

I find him having a drink with Damian, a glass of wine waiting for me at the small table they sit at. Approaching, I smile at my friend and kneel at the feet of the man I'm so sickening in love with.

"What are you up to, Layla?" he asks, eyes widening in

surprise. He doesn't have these expectations of me here. The nights we spend at his house are different, he still very much likes his control. But here at the club, there are no expectations of me to be his pet. Pope says it's because he wants everyone to know I'm his partner first and foremost. It's a level of respect he never thought he'd care to give any woman, and it's one I never dreamed I'd have as a child. It's another thing I expect to calm down over time. Plenty of couples walk through these doors as Dom and Sub and have no small amount of respect for each other.

Not that we've ever had that sort of formality. We're taking baby steps with how we play in public. Pope doesn't want to ever make me feel like he did that last time. And I trust he won't.

"I do what I want, Mr. Blackwell."

"I've always said you were a brat," Damian says.

"You have no idea," Pope groans in agreement.

"Whatever, you both love me."

"Can't argue there, I'm going to miss you when I move west," Damian says.

"Maybe, Daddy Pope will let me visit you."

"You just said you do what you want." Pope laughs, though he narrows his eyes at my daddy jibe.

"So, you'll let her then?"

"I trust her. Even with you, March."

"Come with her, Blackwell. I fantasize about watching the two of you fuck, you could make my dreams come true."

"We'll see if we can work that out for you some time," Pope tells him, and I send my boyfriend a big grin before silently mouthing *I love you* to him. Pope and Damian have been getting along quite well, I often come down to find them in conversation about money matters. Pope still wears his air of grumpiness around my friends, but that's just who he is. I don't want him to change it.

Resting my cheek on Pope's thigh, I watch the other clients move through the room.

"Are you falling asleep on us, Delilah?" Damian asks.

"Mhm, too many nerves this week and I think my period is starting."

"Let's get you home, beautiful," Pope says.

"Okay."

"Is Cookie home tonight?" he asks, depositing me in his car.

"No, she's in Dallas for a few days with Logan. We can go to your house."

"Your place is closer, plus I like your smaller bed."

"Why?" I laugh. "You barely fit in it."

"Yeah, but that only means you stay wrapped around me all night."

"I think you're a closet romantic, Mr. Blackwell."

"I think I'm going to find a way to shut up that mouth of yours, Ms. Simms." I crinkle my nose as I always do at the sound of my last name.

"Please do," I say, laughing as I watch the pedestrians outside my window. It's a short drive from the club to my apartment.

Pope pulls into my designated parking spot that never gets used since I never bothered to learn how to drive. He says he'll teach me, someday I'll take him up on it, but my life lends to walking so it isn't a rush.

"I thought you said Cookie was gone," Pope says, low and quiet. He shoots his arm out in front of me to stop progress to my apartment door, because it sits ajar. The splintered frame shows forced entry. "Go back downstairs, call the police."

"No," I start to argue.

"Do not fucking argue with me right now," he says brutally. I hear how scared he is though, and I know it's for me. I silently plead through watery eyes for him to be safe. He nods at me and turns back to the door.

Rushing down the flight of stairs on trembling legs, I fumble with my handbag, trying to dig my cell phone out. It rings just as I get my fingers on it, making my panic worse. It's Lorelai but there isn't time for that! Ending her call, I type in 9-1-1. I'm shaking so badly while I try to tell the dispatcher what's happening and simultaneously listening for Pope's footsteps on the stairs.

Pope hasn't come down yet.

"Someone broke into my apartment," I tell the lady on the other end.

"What's your address, miss?" I rattle it off for her. "Do you know if they're still inside?"

"I don't know. My boyfriend went inside, and he hasn't come out."

"An officer is on the way," she says at the same time a lout gunshot rings out from upstairs. "No! Pope!"

I take the stairs as fast I can.

"Miss?"

"There was a gunshot," I say as another one cracks loudly. "Pope!"

An upstairs neighbor leans over the stairwell and tries to ask me what's happening but I don't spare them any time as I rush into my apartment. It's stupid, but all I can think about is Pope bleeding out and alone.

"Pope," I call again once inside.

"Hey," he calls to me, sounding more tired than I've ever heard him. He steps out of my bedroom just as I make it to the end of the hallway. Running toward him, I jump into his open arms and he hisses in pain.

"Are you shot?" I ask, my panic hitching even higher as I step back. Pope takes it from me and puts it against his own ear.

"Can you send an ambulance, too, please? Two, but one is dead."

Dead.

I blink past the word and take in Pope, and there's blood covering his left side. It's transferred on to the right of my white blouse.

"You were shot," I say, my voice shuddering as much as my hands as they lift his shirt to see the wound.

"I'm okay, Layla. I'm okay."

"You're not," I cry.

"Look at me," he barks, and my head bounces from his abdomen to his face. "I'm going to be fine. I need you to call Noah. Can you do that?"

"Y-yes," I hiccup, taking the phone he's trying to force back into my hands. Again, it starts ringing. "Lorelai."

"Delilah? What's wrong?"

"Pope's been shot. Someone broke into my apartment."

"Fuck. Fuck! We're on our way. Okay? We're on our way, sweet girl."

"Hurry, Lore. Please, hurry." I can already hear sirens getting closer. It should calm me down, but it doesn't.

The next few minutes are a rush of commotion. Pope won't let me go into my room or look at his wound, content to just wrap his arm around me while we wait for police and paramedics. I argue through every tear that falls out of my eyes, but he doesn't relent until the first EMT steps in my broken doorway right behind two police officers.

The female officer leads us to the kitchen table, having Pope sit down so the paramedic can assess his wound while she asks him questions, the other officer heads down the hall to my bedroom after Pope tells them the only other person here is dead.

A few moments later, the officer, I think he says his name is Brown, comes back.

"Do you know the man?" he asks Pope.

"No, sir."

"What about you, ma'am?"

"I don't know, I didn't go look."

"Can you do that with me now?" Officer Brown asks.

"Let me go with," Pope says.

"No, Pope. You need to go to the hospital."

"I'm not leaving you here alone," he says through gritted teeth. "He was looking for you."

"Did he tell you that?" the female officer asks.

"Yes," Pope says on a groan.

"Can this wait until he's at the fucking hospital, please?" I yell. Two more paramedics come in with a gurney, and Pope scowls at it. "Please, Pope. You go, I'll be right behind you with Lorelai and Noah. Officer Brown won't leave my side, okay?"

"Goddamnit," he yells, and I kiss his forehead before I slowly start to move down the hallway.

"Is there a reason someone would be trying to find you, Ms. Simms?" Officer Brown asks.

"Yes," I hedge, unsure how much to say. "My father. My family, they're part of a polygamist cult that the FBI is investigating." I'm at my bedroom door now but I pause to steady myself for what's inside. I've never seen a dead body.

"You ready?" he asks. I nod and step around the corner.

It's Paul. It's Paul, and I don't know if I want to cry, vomit, or rage for how tragic this all is.

"It's my brother." My voice sounds distant even in my own mind. "That's my older brother, Paul Simms."

"Why would he want to break into your apartment?"

"Because he's next in line," I answer the officer. The next words, I direct to my brother. "You stupid idiot."

"Next in line for what?"

"To be the Cleric. The man in charge, the one with power over the entire flock."

"And what does that have to do with you?"

"I'm one of the ones trying to stop them all," I say.

"Delilah," I hear Lorelai before I see her pushing her way past another officer who must have just arrived. "Oh my god, are you okay?"

She scans me up and down a dozen times before she accepts that I'm not hurt. Then I'm wrapped tightly in her arms as I quietly breakdown from the stress of the last however long it's been.

"I want Pope," I tell her as she leads me back into the living room and huddles with me on the couch.

"We'll go as soon as Noah talks to the officers. Martha called me today; it's why I was trying to call you. Your father ran."

"He ran?"

"Yes. Martha said he got wind of the upcoming charges and tried to flee."

"Does she know where?"

"Yes. Agent Daughtry knows where he is. He took two of his newest brides with him."

"Is this my fault?" I ask her.

"Of course not Delilah," she says sternly, tipping my chin to look at her. "This is on him. Not you, or me, or even Pope. *Him.*"

"My brother is dead on my bedroom floor, Lore." We weren't close. The sons and daughters never spent much time together. Boys were schooled separately, they had different goals. Provide, make money to bring back to the congregation, and learn how to keep your future wives in line. Besides Paul was one of the older siblings, some ten or twelve years older… I'm not even sure.

It's still upsetting that he came here, presumably at the direction of my father, and died for his efforts.

"I saw. I remember Paul. Martha told me once that he was at the top of list of names to marry Olivia when she was deemed ready."

"Then I'm glad he's dead." I sigh, collapsing in her arms.

CHAPTER TWENTY-EIGHT

Pope called before I was able to get to the hospital. We were only two blocks away, and he was still being stitched up, but I guess he threw such a fit they acquiesced and let him make the call. He kept me on the line until I was in the waiting room and told me I wasn't allowed to leave Noah's side.

I can't exactly blame him for being Mr. Grumpy Pants right now, though, he did take a bullet for me. A fact I can't quit freaking out about. I'm a stuttering mess trying to get any words out around the tears and panic that hasn't subsided in the least.

Between not having seen Pope yet and knowing that my father is out there with two young women as hostages or collateral, or whatever his plan with them is, I'm unable to control my emotions at all.

"Where are the kids?" I ask Lorelai.

"With the McKennas," Noah answers. "We thought it best they be with someone that isn't directly connected with you or Lorelai."

"Do you think he sent someone to your house, too?"

"It's possible, but the security system will let us know if that's the case," he answers.

"Is my father close by?"

"No, Delilah. He's in Utah, on the opposite side of the state from the ranch. Martha said his plan was eventually to get to the Idaho compound and then cross the border into Canada."

"I can't believe she called you," I say. "It's been so long."

"Yeah, but she's been working with an undercover agent. Daughtry wasn't allowed to tell us before, but they're moving in on the ranch now."

"Wow, Lore. That's big news."

When Martha got Olivia out, she got out too. But before too long, she went back. She didn't tell Lorelai she was going or why, but I've long suspected the reason was because she wanted to help others escape. Lorelai has been hesitant to believe that because she's felt abandoned by her mom her whole life. I can relate, even if I don't fully agree.

"Blackwell," a doctor calls, walking into the waiting area.

"Me! That's me," I say, jumping to my feet and rushing over to the man.

"Mr. Blackwell was very lucky tonight. The bullet entered and exited cleanly. No surgery needed, but plenty of stitches. He's banged up but refusing to stay overnight. It would be best for him to limit activities for the next several days, and we'll send you home with instructions on how to clean and dress the wound."

"Okay," I say, nodding my understanding. "I'll make sure he takes it easy."

"Good. It will be a little while before we can release him. I'll take you back to his room."

"We'll wait here for you," Lorelai says.

"Thanks, Lore."

Pope looks like a giant laying in the hospital bed, a frown on his face that only deepens when he sees me even though I see relief in his eyes.

"Layla," he says my name like its life itself, something I understand because he's mine too. "You look like a horror movie."

I haven't changed and his blood has dried to a black stain on my clothes. Lorelai offered to find me something else to wear, but I didn't want her to leave me, nor did I want her to go back to that room with Paul. The sobbing breakdown that takes over me surprises us both. My hands cover my face as I let all the tension of tonight, this week, my whole life release through my tears.

I could have lost him tonight.

Pope grunts loud enough to break through my current state. Removing my hands, I see him reaching out for me, but I'm a step too far away.

"I'm sorry, I'm sorry," I cry, rushing to his side. Placing my hands on his face, I hold it steady as I pepper tear-drenched kisses all over him. "I've never been so scared."

"I'm okay, Delilah." He tries to wrap his arm around me and groans again.

"You're not! You got shot."

"Barely. Look where it hit me so you can calm down." He throws back the sheet for me to see that the bandages are at the edge of his lower abdomen. It would be the fatty part if he had any fat. With tentative fingers, I trace the outline of both bandages, front and back. "See? It hit nothing but meat. Hurts like nothing I've ever felt, but I'm fine."

"Still, Pope. My brother shot you because of me."

"Is that who that was?"

"One of them, the oldest, Paul."

"I'd say he shot me because of me. I'm the one responsible for their dire financial state and I'm the asshole that didn't put adequate protection on you." He wipes the steady stream of water on my cheek. "And the one that startled him while he rummaged through your room. That's when he got the shot off. I'm not even sure he meant to do it. Lucky for me, he was easy enough to overtake."

"You're being far too calm about this, Pope," I argue.

"I'm not fucking calm at all, Delilah," he says, allowing his anger to bleed through. "What if I hadn't gone up with you? What if Cookie had been home? Every worst-case scenario keeps running through my head. It's going to be a long fucking time before you're allowed to leave my goddamned sight."

"Okay." I rest my forehead to his.

"Now who's being too calm?" he tries to tease. "Take that bloody shirt off and climb in here with me. I need to hold you."

I do as told, moving to the other side of the bed so I don't bump into his wound. I climb on the bed gingerly and let him pull me where he's most comfortable having me.

"Am I bad person for being glad he's dead?" I eventually ask.

"No more than I am for being happy I killed him. My only regret about that is that I wish it had been your father instead."

"Agent Daughtry is tracking down my father now. Paul was next in line. Between an arrest, a death, and a raid on the compound, they will be in disarray. It might be the best opportunity for Martha to get more people out. The ones who are willing, anyhow."

"Then no, neither of us is a bad person for being glad he's dead. Hopefully, it saves a lot more lives than just yours."

I send up a little prayer, just in case, a thankful one that Pope is alive, that Pope is in my life, and that it's me he loves. It's selfish, more selfish than I like to be. So, I send up a bigger prayer in hopes to save as many innocent souls trapped under my father's force as possible. As we wait for more news, and for Pope to be released, I keep my head resting on his heart, listening to the strong, steady beat, and for the first time I can fully accept that I'm not alone in this world.

***

News about my father doesn't come for several days. However, Giving Hope updates us on every newcomer that makes it to their doors. And it isn't only women and children. Surprisingly, a few of the younger men have left the congregation as well.

When the call finally came about the Cleric, it was to say he too had been shot in a standoff with federal agents. His two young brides were, thankfully, rescued unharmed.

Martha regularly calls Lorelai with updates on the progress. Many of the members refuse to leave, but Martha won't until she knows she's given her best effort to convince everyone. My mother, Beth, is one who refuses, though Martha has gotten her to agree to release those of my siblings that are eager to leave.

Pope has said we can move them all here if that's what I want. He doesn't quite understand that we don't have the same sort of sibling bonds that most families form. It's another thing the religion designs, they never let us girls develop meaningful relationships with anyone but our fathers and husbands. Not until we were wives, anyway. Then you were encouraged to befriend your fellow sister wives.

I will do whatever is necessary to care for my siblings, but I'm not certain I'm the right choice to provide that care directly. As much as I hate to admit that I want to be practical and do what's best for them.

Moving them to New Orleans to be looked after by a young woman that works at a sex community seems like a less than ideal choice. It's early days yet, we'll figure it all out in time and with the help of people much more qualified to help in making these decisions.

Reality hasn't sunk in yet. Every day is like a dream, something so close to my fingertips but just out of reach. That too is going to take time. But like Noah still reminds me, it's a journey and not a race.

Cookie has moved back to Jasmine's for the time being. At least until we come up with a solid plan. Noah moved all our things out and hired a cleaning crew, but neither of us want to go back there.

As for Pope, he is a horrible patient. Bossy, moody, and rarely follows directions. The first twenty-four hours were easier, as we were both too exhausted to do much of anything but lie in his bed. Even me running to the kitchen to get us food caused him to stress out and try to follow along. He's eased up since finding out my father is dead, but only just.

His mobility is better now that his wounds are beginning to heal. Moving to sitting is still a struggle, but once up, he's mostly pain free.

"Good morning," he says, voice still raspy with sleep as he sidles up behind me while I get the pot of coffee going.

"Morning." I turn in his arms, stretching mine up around his neck. "How do you feel?"

"Perfect," he says with a smile. I came down in only a t-shirt and panties, a fact he likes very much if the raging hard-on poking my belly has anything to say about it. Even if it didn't, the fingers that slide under the lace down through the slit of my ass do.

"Do you think you're up for whatever it is you're trying to start, Mr. Blackwell?"

"You can feel the answer, beautiful."

"Promise to slow down if it starts to get uncomfortable," I say, slowly lowering into a squat and taking his gym shorts with me.

"Mmm."

"Say the words, Mr. Blackwell."

"I promise, you fucking pixie."

I laugh at him before I suck his cock. This isn't his first erection in the days since the shooting, every other time I've told him no. His healing is more important than his desire to come. If I keep him upright, I think we'll be okay. Honestly though, I want this as much as he does. I've missed it, too.

"Fuck, your mouth is amazing."

Keeping a slow, steady speed, I suck as I pull back and curve my tongue to cup him as I push back forward, holding his hips as steady as I can keep him so that he doesn't strain to thrust his hips. He tries to push anyway, but I press my fingers into him harder each time.

"Let me move, Layla," he pleads.

I draw off him and stand, pulling my tee over my head and

tossing it aside. Then I pull off my panties and add them to the floor as well, before kneeling in front of him again.

"You get to come, Pope. You just have to take it easy." I nuzzle my nose along his wet cock and he fists his hand around it. "If you're good, as soon as you're fully healed, you can take my little, tight ass."

"Fuck," he moans, his hand working faster.

"Or we can use one of the bigger plugs, so you'll feel it more when you fuck my cunt," I purr, pushing my breasts up and fingering my nipples. I don't talk dirty too much, but I've noticed how he reacts when I do. It won't take him long to lose himself. "Even while I'm choking on that big dick you like to suction to the mirror. You can fill me up, Mr. Blackwell, and spill all over me."

"You'd like that, wouldn't you?" His hand grips my hair, tilting my head up as his other hand hastens.

"I can't fucking wait." I stick my tongue out, resting under the head of his cock just before he finds release. As he usually does, he calls my name.

"Layla! Fuck, fuck." He pants heavily while I swallow him down, all the while keeping an eye on his wound. "I'm okay, beautiful. I'm okay."

"Are you sure?" I ask, standing back up, wrapping my arms around his hips.

"I'm sure. In fact, I'm better than okay. I'm whole, because you're here in my life."

Whole.

I like that. I'm not the whore who betrayed him. Or the dark that blotted out his light. We're two equal halves making one world. Our own.

EPILOGUE

"It's so hot."

"Yes, but it's a dry heat," Pope says with an eyeroll.

"I don't know how that makes a difference." Frowning at the sun as if it's caused me personal offense, I close the door of the rental car and scan the horizon while I adjust to the lack of humidity.

Sage Springs, Fabienne's little dessert oasis, is abuzz with activity. I'm a bundle of apprehensive excitement.

It's our first trip to Nevada since Fabienne bought this place and my father's death. We waited only long enough for Pope to comfortably make the flight and for the police in New Orleans to close the case they had opened on the death of my brother. Pope was called in several times for questioning. Officer Brown had a hard time believing Paul's only motive was that I had given information to the FBI. Eventually, Agent Daughtry made some phone calls and the questioning stopped.

With that came a sigh of relief and immediate plans to get out here and see what my boss lady had accomplished.

The community of Sage Springs is a short drive into the hills from Elko, Nevada. Far enough away to be quiet, close enough to not feel completely cut off from society. It's a great location for my family members to transition into society at a slower pace.

Contractors quickly worked to make the village not only livable, but functional. A large barn is being built on the far side of the property that can house a few cows and goats for milk. The chicken coop was completed last week and already has inhabitants, and a greenhouse is next on the list. Fabienne's idea is that not only will it provide food for the residents here, but the excess can be sold at the farm stand she's having built at the front of the property. Another step at easing into the outside world.

Sage Springs isn't just a safe place, it's a therapy center, a half-way house of sorts, complete with a small schoolhouse.

"You ready?" Pope asks, coming around the car to wrap an arm around my shoulder.

"I am."

"Delilah!" As I turn to the sound of the voice, a crown of strawberry blonde hair perched over spindly legs comes running toward me.

"Jillian." I engulf her in my hug as she bounces against me in her rush. "You are a sight for sore eyes."

"You too," she says, her voice watered with emotion. I press a kiss to her forehead and take a step back so I can really look at her. She looks good; sun-kissed and rosy cheeked.

"This is my partner, Pope."

"It's great to finally meet you, Jillian."

"You too," she says, the blush deepening. I bet I looked at him the same way that first time. "Do you want a tour of the place? Hannah's around somewhere, too. She'll want to see you."

"Lead the way," I tell her. Both girls arrived here last week, just before a handful of the other congregation members who left the compound arrived. Jillian made the decision to come here instead of New Orleans. She wants to take on a leadership role here while she studies to be a social worker.

She shows us each of the communal buildings, and we meet with Brenda, a longtime friend of Fabienne's who eagerly agreed to move out here and spearhead the organization. She's well-qualified with a background in social work herself, and a decade of working at another non-profit that focused on victims of abuse. Jillian is like a starry-eyed child around her, obviously worshipping the woman.

When we get to the living quarters I'm surrounded by shy faces. Some I recognize, some not. Each one looks at me curiously when they realize who I am.

The girl who escaped.

Out of all my siblings that are older than me, of which there are countless, none left the ranch. Michael is the oldest one here, at nineteen. We share a father, but his mother is one of Beth's sister wives. He tells Pope and I that he knew early on he didn't want the life our father had. In fact, he was on the verge of being dis-communicated because he refused to take a bride as soon as he was of age.

Michael has taken up one of the cottages and is housing my father's other children that came with him. All teenagers, four girls and one other boy. My heart says it's not enough, but Pope reminds me it's a start.

A start at righting my father's and my uncle's wrongs. We still have a long road ahead of us, but by the end of the day, my anxiety has been replaced.

By hope. For the mothers that came here willingly, for the children that have a chance at real life, and for the team of staff that Fabienne and Brenda have assembled to help them all on their way.

This is what good people look like, these are the people that will find God's grace, if that's what they choose to believe. It's not the ones that lie, that manipulate the weak, or ignore those most in need. No, it's the ones that set aside time, effort, and wealth to help in any way they can.

The feeling of joyfulness still wraps me like a warm blanket as Pope and I sink into the bathtub before bed. It's become a habit of ours that I hope we don't ever lose.

"Thank you for coming here with me," I say, drawing invisible circles on his raised knee.

"Where you go, I go. No need to thank me, I want to help. And we'll continue to do just that." He works his hands through my wet strands, combing out the tangles. "I was thinking about selling the house. Maybe buying something bigger in case Cookie wants to move in and still have her own space."

I spin in the water to straddle him. "Before I agree to move in with you, I want to ask you something?"

"You know you can ask me anything."

"How would you feel if I changed my name to Delilah Layla Blackwell?"

"That's a mouthful," he says, but the corners of his mouth twitch at his attempt not to smile.

"No marriage, I am still adamantly against that. But family, partnership… I want that, Pope."

"You have that, Layla."

"Then I'll live with you," I say with a kiss.

"You already live with me," he laughs.

"Semantics."

"I love you, future Ms. Blackwell."

"I love you, too, Mr. Blackwell."

MORE FROM ALISON RHYMES

Subscribe to Alison's Newsletter for Early News and Bonus Scenes

Broken Play

They have ties that bind.

June grew up in the shadow of her brother and his best friend, Drew McKenna. She stood back while Drew dated his way through high school and college, watching and waiting. Waiting for him to realize he loved her as much as she loved him.

When he did, it was the happiest she'd ever been. Until she found him with another woman only five years after their marriage.

Leaving her husband was a simple decision, but there was no easy way to cut him out of her family.

When June receives a fresh start to her career, she also finds what could be a new lease on love. Reality hits Drew with a vengeance.

He wants her back.

She wants to make him suffer.

Brutal Play

Mistress.

Whore.

Lorelai has been called every name in the book. Except for the ones she's always dreamed of.

My love.

Mine.

Noah Anders is the only man to have ever owned her heart. But it's her soul he wants.

Theirs is a battle of wills, tempers, ego, friendship, and loyalty.

He wants retribution.

She just wants to survive.

Bitter Play

Reed Turner has loved his sister's best friend, Leighton, for damn near a decade. He's given her space to grow in her career and her life. Now he's ready to claim the woman he's always believed was his. It's too bad another man in her life keeps getting in the way.

Leighton Ward has never been in love. Now, just as so many things are changing in her life, she finds two men vying for her heart. Both hold strong ties to her future and making the wrong decision comes with heavy consequences.

He knows what he wants.

She's as confused as ever.